IGN
ESCAPING

SAGA

STACY McWILLIAMS

Enjoy the Story

Love

Stacy
McWilliams

DEDICATION

I would like to dedicate this book to my amazing sister Jennifer. Jen we have been best friends our whole lives. You were my maid of Honour and Corey's godmother and I couldn't ask for a better sister than you. You are always there when I need you and although at times you drive me demented, I love you more than you'll ever know. We are separated by two years, and it has made us so close.

I know Sharmaine and Morgan are gonna kick my ass if I don't at least mention them, but they know I love them too.

Love ya longtime

Stacy

CHAPTER 1
SHOULD I STAY, OR SHOULD I GO?

As my senses returned, I could feel Nathan kneeling beside me. His hair tickled my forehead as he whispered softly in my ear, "We can't be together. I love you, but I am so wrong for you. You deserve so much more than I can give you. I promise you this, though. I will help you. When the time comes, I will help you. I can't... I won't... I promise you will be safe from me, from us."

He moved his lips to my head and kissed me softly. As our lips met, he sighed and flames licked up my spine. We gripped each other, deepening the kiss. For a moment, he was mine and that was all I needed to know. I loved him and he loved me. His skin warmed under my fingers and I ran my hands up and down his arms as he moved us gently down onto the ground, kissing me so passionately that my head spun. I'd never felt this level of desire from him. In that moment, I would have given anything to him, been anything for him as I kissed him with a carnal need. He broke away, gasping for breath as he stuttered out, "I can't... we can't... We have to stop this...Jas, please?"

He shook his head and closed his eyes for a moment. I breathed heavily and I watched as his face scrunched up, as though he was in pain. My hand moved almost unconsciously and I touched his cheek. He leaned onto my hand and sat there for a moment, breathing quickly. His hands moved up as his head shook my hand away and it dropped to my lap. It hurt me that he didn't want my touch to comfort him and I watched as he rubbed his eyes before opening them. As he stared down at me, his willpower left him as he moved down towards me, pulling my head back to his, holding my neck and securing his face to mine. "Oh my God, I love you. Jas, I'm so sorry for how

I've been with you this week, but..."

He kissed me again, caressing my tongue with his own. My heart thundered in my ears as our hands began to wander. His arms snaked around my waist, touching the bare skin under my top. My hands rose up his back, gliding over rough skin. I paused as I ran my hands up and down his back. His breath came fast, and his face was drawn, in what looked to me like panic. "Nathan, what's this? What are these rough bits on your back?"

He closed his eyes and shook his head, whispering, "Never mind. They aren't important." His body tensed and he shook his head again, before touching his lips gently to my own once more. He said my name softly, leaned his head on my own, saved from saying anything else when a thundering crash sounded overhead and some pebbles rained down on us. He gasped and jerked away from me. "Jasmine, I have to end this. It's not safe." Safe for who I wondered as he touched my cheek gently with the tips of his fingers and gazed into my eyes, his green eyes flashing as I looked up at him, tears filling my eyes. I realised he was ending things with me. My heart splintered painfully and I swallowed the lump in my throat.

He moved slowly towards me before kissing me once more. As his tongue met mine, my body shook with renewed longing. I deepened the kiss and could tell by the ferocity of his kisses and the shuddering breaths that his willpower was crumbling when another crash made us both jump.

He pulled away from me and moved backwards, whispering, "I am weaker because of you. You are my weakness and if anyone ever found out about us, they would kill both of us..." His eyes filled with tears as he spoke hoarsely. "I'm not good enough for you. You need whole and mortal and I can't give you that. I have hit you and hurt you. Sometimes I have no control and I can't let you get hurt because of what I am. This, us is over."

"Nathan, please don't do this." I all but begged him, my voice cracking as I voiced my heartache. "I need you, I love you." He turned away from me and shook his head. "You deserve more, how can you love me when I'm a monster? How can you want me when all I want is to hurt you? That's not love, Jasmine, that's just pathetic and needy and I want no part of it, no part of you anymore." His voice was ice cold and his eyes when he turned back to face me were almost black and devoid of all emotion. His expression was as dark as his eyes and my head and heart were hurting at his callous words.

I gasped as he stood suddenly, gathered the picnic blanket, and walked away, leaving me sitting, panting for breath, and trying to figure how to survive without him. At the mouth of the cave, he turned back and stared at me coldly, "Don't bother fighting, you won't change my mind. I was right, I'm not capable of love and if I was it certainly wouldn't be some mortal I would love." He turned and stared out at the crashing water, as the tears began running down my face and I curled into a ball as wave after wave of heartbreak rolled over me. Thoughts crashed around my head, our first kiss, when he saved me, how I felt when he smiled at me and looked at me like I was the only person in the world. Could I let his darkness push out my light or would I just cause him more pain if I tried to make him see that he loved me as much as I loved him? Would my light be enough to save him or would his demons win in the end?

He turned back at the entrance and his cold voice caused my heart to break as he muttered, "Jasmine, don't fight for us. I don't want you to. We aren't good together. I'm a monster and you are in danger as long as we are together." He turned away from me as more tears strolled down my face and I could only watch as he moved away quickly.

I allowed myself a few moments to cry and to wallow in the devastation over Nathan ending things. I didn't trust easily, it was hard after all that I'd been through to know who to trust and who just wanted to use me, but I'd really trusted Nathan. I'd really believed he loved me, even after finding out about the demons and everything that we'd been through since I arrived here, creatures trying to kill me, James trying to kill me and Nathan turning on me again and again. I was stronger than this, stronger than them and I knew what I needed to do. If we couldn't be together and I was in really in danger, I had to leave. Leave him behind and move on. I had to run and never look back. I would need to close that box and lock it tight, but I could do it. I'd done it before when families had had enough of me.

I waited a while longer steeling myself before getting up and dusting myself off. My eyes were dry and I was determined to leave and put all of this behind me. I half-walked, half-crawled up the narrow ledge of the path, slipping, sliding, and gripping on for dear life. I finally reached the top and Nathan was thankfully nowhere to be seen. I began walking to their home, feeling the whole time the tingle on my neck as though someone was watching me. I reached a stone circle and as I walked into it, I felt a vibration almost like an earthquake underfoot, which caused me to fall over. I gasped in pain and looked around, in panic which turned quickly to terror as I spotted the reason for the vibration. James had returned and was glaring into the circle at me. He looked awful.

His face was all scratched and cut, one of his hands bent at a funny angle, and his leg twisted as he glared into the circle. He started towards me, grunting and dragging his leg along the ground. I wanted to scream, but some instinct told me not to, so instead I stumbled backwards. Roughness touched my back and I jumped in fright as a crash as loud as thunder sounded. I stared at him in absolute terror he hit the force field surrounding me repeatedly. A putrid smell emanated from him, like decomposing flesh and it almost made me vomit as it flowed around me and had me gasping for a breath of fresh air.

"Come on out, Jasmine," he bellowed, causing more of the stench to be released and the tree to shake with the quivering underfoot. Water drops and leaves fell around the circle as he tried again and again to get to me. I shook so hard because he looked terrifying and I just stood numbly watching him, not thinking or reacting, but worried about him finally catching up to me. My brain had shut down completely. The stench of him lingered on the trees, flowers, bushes, and grass. It flowed all around me, choking me, leaving me gasping for air as it drowned out the smell of the trees leaves and wet grass.

"I know why Nathan blamed me, I saw you two together today, all smiles and stolen glances. How could he betray us, his own kind, over one of your disgusting kind? I'll never understand but I will get to you, you filthy little parasite!"

I realised then that there was no getting out of this; this monster would try to kill me and I could die here, huddled up next to a tree, or I could fight him and never give up. I closed my eyes as I tried to make a decision through the numbness. I had to try and fight. I couldn't let him murder me. I needed to live; to survive somehow so I knew my decision to fight him was made. A stone whirled by my head missing it by a millimetre and I screamed in fright, because he had just figured out that while he couldn't get through the barrier, objects could. I had made a huge mistake screaming out loud. I'd just given him my location when I screamed and he might not have been able to see me, but he now knew roughly where I was.

"Jasmine, where are you?" Nathan's voice sounded in my head and I felt it spin from side to side as he tried to figure out where I was. I pushed him out, trying to block him so I could ready myself for the inevitable fight that was coming.

"Don't you dare fight him, stay there and I will find you."

I shook my head again to clear it when a large boulder flew through the air and smacked me right on the head. *Damn Nathan distracting me,* I thought as my head bounced back, hitting the tree. I slumped silently to the ground, feeling blood running down my face. I lay there for a few minutes fighting to stay awake but, blacked out as another boulder flew overhead.

Loud sounds woke me up, grunting and groaning and I kept my eyes closed, fighting nausea and dizziness. I opened my eyes slightly, watching a fight take place. Nathan danced around James, landing a few solid punches to his face and ribs. I was lulled back under again and when I came to, it was just in time to see Nathan twist James' head to the side, snapping his neck and causing a crack to sound like a gunshot in the silence. I watched as his body fell like a sack of potatoes to the floor. I stared at him, hearing voices calling out to me but not answering as I looked at the face of the demon that would have killed me without a second thought. All I could think about was how he had a mother somewhere who loved him and wanted him home.

My eyes began roaming around and I searched for Nathan. My heart thundered in my ears as I tried to push myself up from the ground. My eyes found Nathan and all pity for James went right out of my head. Nathan was hurt, badly by the looks of things as he stumbled repeatedly into the trees surrounding him, getting up and blindly walking around in a circle. "Jas," his voice was hoarse "where are you?" I made my way over to the edge of the circle, crawling over stones and leaves, to get to Nathan. I welcomed the sting as the stones cut into my knees because it gave me something to focus on, other than the pounding in my head and the dizziness that threatened to overwhelm me. Finally at the edge I moved a stone, and collapsed again onto the grass, smelling the wet grass and breathing deeply, trying to ignore the pain in my head. Nathan moved towards me, his eyes taking in the blood on my head and the tears in my eyes, as the pain reached a crescendo. He gasped as he stumbled, landing almost beside me. He looked up at me through puffy eyes and muttered, "I love you," before he blacked out.

I crawled over to him, ignoring the pounding of my head and the rolling of my stomach. I had to know if he was okay. I could feel stickiness on my head, telling me the blood was still flowing, but I ignored that completely as I made my way over to where Nathan had fallen. I touched my hand to his and felt nothing. I moved my hand to his wrist as footsteps sounded behind me. Crashing through the trees, as loud as thunder, I turned my head while finding a very weak pulse going in his wrist. Relief must have shown in my face because his father, had just arrived, growling and shouting at me. "Jasmine, what on Earth happened?" he glared at me as though I had done this damage to Nathan.

I shook, but answered as truthfully as I could, "James tried to kill me. Nathan pushed me in here and fought him, but he managed to get me with a boulder. I blacked out. I don't know what happened..." I felt myself slipping into darkness and when I awoke, I was in a strange room, surrounded by demons, all of whom hadn't noticed I was awake. I glanced about the room and saw the machines, and curtains. *Great I was in another bloody hospital, but where was Nathan.* As I looked about the demons I noticed that and their faces kept shifting from demon to mortal and back again.

My eyes closed and I tried to listen to what was being said, but I drifted off again, with random phrases repeating in my head. Nate's in resus. James almost killed them both and Nathan killed James. I heard these phrases over and over again as though they were shouting at me, echoing in my ears. My heart broke as I thought of Nathan, he had almost died protecting me and his last words before he blacked out were 'I love you." Was it worth sticking around? Could I change his mind about ending things with us? Would we survive if people found out that he loved me? I opened my eyes again much later and heard some random voices chatting as my eyes fought to open, "What happened, Nathan?" came a strange voice I didn't recognise.

"I saw him trying to hurt her and I knew there was a protected circle around. I pushed her in there to stop him from getting to her." Nathan answered gruffly.

"You should have let him kill her; she's not worth all the bother," his father's voice admonished.

"So you are saying that Nathan should have broken the edict you set and were adamant to remain intact?" his mother's voice inquired, sounding agitated.

"Yes, I am. Honestly this sacrifice is the worst we've ever had for invoking the demon in us and I wonder if we would be better just killing her and choosing another of the suitables to sacrifice."

"You can't dad, killing her would send a message that you allow sacrifices to be killed before the Hallowday and it could lead to others breaking the laws." Nathan's voice sounded tense and I peeked through my eye lids to see him sitting in a wheelchair, leaning forward, coiled as tight as a spring. I closed my eyes again and heard his mother speak.

"The boys right Mr Stevenson, killing her could cause so many more problems."

"It's settled then, but she better not cause any more trouble. Nathan, you must do a better job protecting her." With that they left and I listened to the squeak of the wheelchair and the door closing after them. My heart thundered as I thought about what had just been said. I lay there with my eyes closed, breathing in the smell of the hospital, wondering when to open my eyes and alert them all to the fact that I was awake. Lying there listening to them, I felt very far away from the afternoon, and from Nathan. My heart broke a little more as I remembered how he had ended things, but little did I know that he would push me away, harder than ever before. He would try and break me and I would be able to do nothing to stop him and nothing to fix us.

CHAPTER 2

FIGHT OR FLIGHT

Getting out of the hospital a few days later was great, but I hadn't had a moment alone with Nathan. I missed him so damn much it hurt. I wanted to chat about what had happened that day, but he never allowed himself to be alone with me. .

We were released on the same day and we had to wait for his parents in the discharge room, but he sat on the other side of the room, checking his emails. He spent his time ignoring me completely.

After two hours, I decided to go for a walk around the hospital to clear my head. He didn't look up as I walked out the green door and headed for the lift to take me from the third floor to the exit on the first. I walked along, thinking about anything but him, but I couldn't help it. He kept invading my thoughts and I spent the walk wondering where our relationship would go now. He was adamant he was so wrong for me, but all I could see was the sweet guy, who saved me time after time, but he didn't want an us anymore and I needed to find some way to live with that. I needed to find a way to get over him and stop myself missing him.

I walked around the garden for a bit; watching the birds and the trees swaying in the wind. I stood and stared into space, pushing all of my memories of Nathan into the recesses of my mind. I thought about the first time we kissed, how gentle he was and how conflicted he was. I thought about the first time he saved me and how he looked at me as though he wanted to run away from me. After a few more minutes I strolled back to the hospital, in no rush to be back with an indifferent Nathan. I wandered into the lift and my resolve weakened as the doors closed and Nathan caught my eye, standing at the exit, devastated. He had tears in his eyes, but he shook his head as my conflicted emotions began raging inside me. I didn't move, just let the doors close on him. I resolved that I wouldn't allow him to have any power over me, not anymore. No matter how much I loved him, I was strong enough to stay away from him.

Watching TV wasn't distracting me enough as I sat in the waiting room for Nathan to come back inside. I was bouncing on the edge of my chair when I felt a sharp pain, stabbing through my chest. I gasped and shot up too quickly. The room began spinning and I put my hand on the wall to steady myself. The pain worsened and I felt as though a steel band was tightening around my chest. Walking helped and I finally made it to the lift, punching the button angrily didn't make the lift come quickly enough so I stood on the balls of my feet, and as soon as the doors half opened I was inside, jabbing the button to close the doors.

I walked outside into the cold October wind and rain. The drops of the water on my face felt soothing and made me realise how much I had allowed myself to become a victim. I needed to stand on my own two feet and fight back without his help and as soon as this thought crossed my mind the pain in my chest eased. Thinking about doing this was hard, but knowing that it needed to happen gave me a feeling of power deep in my soul as I realised that, although I loved him more than anything ever, I was strong and capable of fighting any battles.

Standing in the rain with this new sense of power of my own, I glanced around the grounds and spotted Nathan sitting on a bench, staring dejectedly at his hands. I ached to go over to him, but I knew it wouldn't do any good. He had made it quite clear, we were over. Watching him scowl at the ground for a moment, my heart broke for the boy I loved, fighting against the man he could become and I knew a piece of me would always be lost to the boy who saved me over and over again. I turned away from him and walked over to the doors where a shelter stood and I slipped inside, plotting my escape from the family of demons who held me captive. I was thinking through my bank account and where I would run to, when a cold hand touched my arm, causing flames to run up and down. Nathan's broken gaze met my own and a piece of my resolve splintered, I didn't want to leave him, but he shook his head at me before staring away from me and muttering so quietly I didn't catch it.

"What?" I asked him in a quiet voice. He shook his head and spoke only a little louder this time. "My family's here," he said in a broken voice. "It's time we went home."

Looking at him, I fought the need to comfort him or hold him, even though he looked totally destroyed, I managed to hold firm and fisted my hands at my side. Walking away from him was one of the most difficult things I had ever done, but I managed and got to the car without looking back. As I climbed in, I saw him wipe his eyes on his hands and I realised that a part of my heart was broken. He had changed me so much in the short time I had loved him and he had returned the power I had let life take from me. How would I use it? This was what plagued me on the way home, sitting a few inches from the person who made my heart beat faster and made me stronger, but who wouldn't even look at me. How could I make sure our relationship had meant something? These questions would be answered over the next few weeks, scaring me more than ever.

Once we arrived back at the house, I tried to follow the family, but something held me back at the porch, as if I couldn't get through a charm. I fought it until Nathan's voice sounded in my head, "Jasmine, do not break this charm. If they know you have powers, they will kill you!"

I found it incredibly difficult to stop fighting, especially after my epiphany earlier, but I did. I knew Nathan loved me; some inner certainty told me he loved me more than his own life...

"I do, but we can't be together, especially now. They are starting to suspect something..." Nathan's voice warned in my mind. Closing my eyes, I could see him sitting on his bed, staring dejectedly at his phone. Tears clouded my eyes and one rolled down my cheek as I saw him in my minds' eye. I stood a moment and swallowed the lump in my throat as I thought about how hard it would be to forget and I knew I needed to forget he loved me, forget how his touch burned my soul and how his lips tasted. I had to keep him safe and become indifferent to him. I shook my head, trying to rid it of my melancholy thoughts and jumped as Mr Stevenson bellowed sharply, "Jasmine, follow me!"

As I turned to follow him, I saw Mrs Stevenson standing in the sitting room, watching through the window. Walking slowly because I still had my cast on, I followed him into the barn, which creeped me out, giving me chills. We walked into the externally decrepit barn. The tree in the middle drew my eyes as soon as we entered. I gravitated towards it, but I couldn't get close to it, a protective barrier surrounded it, like the house.

"This is where you'll be sleeping from now on," Mr Stevenson interrupted my thoughts, pointing into a horse stall, equipped with a tent and sleeping bag.

"What? Here? I don't understand." I answered snappily.

"Yes, here. You will be brought a laptop each day between half past three and five p.m. You will not come into the house. A bucket is there for you and you will have your meals in here. You will get into the house at half past seven each morning for a shower, but that is all." He walked away, but stopped at the door. Turning with the scariest look on his face, he said, "You will stay away from Nathan and Jenny. I want you nowhere near my children from now on. You will only see them when you walk to school. Do you understand me?"

Nodding seemed to be the best option since being spoken to like that strengthened my resolve to get the fuck off out of here. Could I really leave Nathan? I turned away from him and saw an oil lamp, a halogen heater, and some water bottles. I walked over to them, sitting down on a foldout chair. Putting my head into my hands, I thought about my options. I could run now and never see Nathan again. My heart throbbed painfully as I contemplated that option. Or I could stay, fight them, and fight for him. I knew option two could get me killed, but I couldn't leave without at least trying to fight for him.

I loved him and I was willing to risk my own life for him. I realised in that instant that without him, my life was meaningless. I had to fight, if I didn't fight for us then no one would. I needed him to know that, no matter what, I was strong enough to stand at his side and strong enough to bring him from the darkness into the light.

I awoke shivering in the middle of the night, with Nathan standing above me, looking down on me with a pained look on his face.

"I have to fix this," he muttered before fading away into the night, getting fainter and fainter. Just before he fully disappeared, he reached out and stroked my cheek, causing my arms to erupt in goose bumps. Rolling over on the straw, I snuggled deeper into my sleeping bag and awoke to a cold breakfast of sandwiches. No one was around so I sat stiffly, remembering the middle of the night. I glanced around to see nothing had changed, until I looked at the back of the tent where another thicker sleeping bag lay under a pile of my clothes.

Put this inside your sleeping bag and it will help you keep warm. I will try to fix this, but I need you to be patient with me, please? All my love Nate xxx

When I opened up the new sleeping bag, there was a large green thermos of hot chocolate in it with a smiley face sticker on it. Nathan was being sweet. I retreated inside my tent and zipped it up, changing into a warm, fleecy jumper and some jogging bottoms. The hot chocolate tasted good, but when I heard the creaking of the barn, I went out of the tent to see who had come in.

I stood at the exit to the horse stall, watching, waiting for whoever it was to come closer. It was Mr Stevenson, "We are going away for a few days as a family. My brother will be here watching the house. You may go in for your shower, but that is all."

He turned and walked away, but I saw Nathan standing at the barn door looking anywhere but at me. His father walked over to him, clapped him on the shoulder, and they turned and walked away. Pulling out the foldout chair, I sat and picked up my hot chocolate, wondering what the hell had happened while I was unconscious. Nathan wasn't speaking to me at all, his family were treating me like a leper and taking Nate away so I didn't corrupt him and I was sleeping in the fucking barn.

I sat and ruminated over the changes that had been forced on me for a while, until I heard their car pull away. As I finally moved the pain over loosing Nate hit me, and I crumpled on the floor in a heap. I pulled my knees up to my chest and allowed myself to cry over the loss of my first love. "I'm not lost," came his voice in my head. I shook my head and sat up on my heels.

"Please, Nate, don't do this. Stop talking to me in my head. I can't take it, it hurts too damn much." He didn't speak again and I splashed some water over my face to hide the tracks of my tears and ran outside, glad to see it was raining as I made my way over to the house to shower.

As I went into the house, all was quiet, too quiet and I had a hot shower, turning the water up scalding hot to distract me from the pain in my chest. I focused on each step of the shower, talking myself through things as I washed myself and since I was allowed to dry my hair before I was forced to leave I was completely focused until I completed that task.

As I left the shower no one was around, but I felt myself shunted out of the door. I would fight it, and was about to, until I remembered Nathan's message the previous day.

I sat in my stall all day, not seeing anyone, just staring into space. The more I stared the more worried I became about what would happen to me if I stayed here. I had to try to convince Nathan to run away with me; if we stayed here, I knew, without a shadow of a doubt, his parents would kill us both.

The mornings were getting colder as October chills set in. I had been sneezing constantly since the day before and my throat was scratchy. I shivered and burrowed deeper into my sleeping bags, trying to hide my face in the bag as I lay there. When I first woke up I thought that Nathan hadn't bothered to visit the night before, but I knew he had visited when I found some extra thick socks, a fleecy jumper, and some fleecy pyjama bottoms sitting in amongst my clothes. My eyes prickled at the thoughtfulness, and I had to swallow the lump from my throat.

I got up and made my way to the door of the barn, when I felt something holding me back. I couldn't put my finger on what it was, but I couldn't seem to make my legs want to move across the threshold. I struggled for a few minutes, and then gave in, returning to my stall and sitting on the floor. I could smell Nathan on my skin and I lifted my jumper to my nose and sniffed. His scent lingered there and my heart shuddered at how much I was missing him.

Spending the day huddled up in the tent seemed to suit me well. I was reading a book, one of my favourites when Nathan's uncle came into the barn. He walked around out of sight and seemed to be checking each stall out. He turned back towards the door of the barn before he reached my stall, not before I got a glimpse of short hair, stubble, and amazing eyes. He also had a well-defined back and sexy ass. I was taken aback by my thoughts, but this guy was as sexy as hell.

Watching him walk away, I almost breathed a sigh of relief. Just as I was about to breathe out in relief, he turned back and stalked towards me, with what looked like fire in his eyes. As he saw me sitting in the doorway of the tent, his mouth turned up maliciously into the creepiest smile I'd seen in my two months living with the Stevenson's.

"Well, well, little Jasmine..." he said, salaciously licking his lips as he got closer to me. I shivered and tried to back away, but only managed to back myself into a wall.

I jumped as he got closer, and prepared to fight him off, with whatever I could throw at him when Nathan's voice horrified sounded loudly in my head, "Don't fight him! Please, Jas, just don't fight him." I shook my head, trying to clear it as his hand fisted in my hair and I allowed myself to relax my hands. He pulled me out into the barn area and threw me onto the floor. Watching him, I noticed again that his face was absurdly handsome, even as it glared down at me twisted in disgust.

He stared at me, running his finger over his lips, muttering to himself,

"Oh, what to do with you little, Jasmine? What to do? Do I feast by myself, or do I want to wait for Halloween?" He licked his lips, leaned down and stroked a finger down my face. I scurried backwards and he grabbed my hair again. He pulled me up by the hair, and licked my lips.

My body shuddered as his tongue forced my mouth open and he bit down on my lip sucking some of the blood from my lip. He groaned and dropped me to the floor, rubbing his hands over his face and when he looked back at me, I could see the demon threatening to break through. He tapped his chin as I stared up at him in horror, "I'm not sure I can wait until Halloween." His voice was relaxed, but I could hear the strain under his words. Nathan didn't want me to fight him, but if I didn't he was going to kill me.

My insides were frozen in terror as his face lit up. Chiselled cheekbones, gorgeous smile, and sexy brown eyes looked down on me. As he moved towards me, I scurried backwards, cutting my hand open on a jagged stone and he froze in his approach.

"Run! Run now!" Nathan's voice came in my head as I scrambled backwards. "Hurry, Jasmine. I don't have the strength to hold him back for long. Go to our cave. Supplies will be waiting for you. I will make him forget he has seen you, but run now, PLEASE NOW!" I tried to stand up and he started in what looked like surprise,

"Oh, the little bitch has powers, does she? Well, we'll see about that..."

"JAS, NOW! FUCKING RUN! I can't hold him much longer."

Scrambling backwards, I ran for the door, but felt myself thrown against it as it slammed shut. It winded me, hurting my still sore arm and foot, but I stood and turned to see him standing there. Knowing that somehow he would try to kill me, I did the only thing I could think of. I pushed him back using the fire burning in my soul and I threw him as far away from me as possible without touching him. My arm tingled and I felt like a fire spread through my fingers.

The door flew open with a wave of my arms and I jumped in surprise. I took off running into the woods, manic laughter following me and Nathan's voice sounding in my head, "What did you do, Jas? What the fuck did you just do?" I ignored him and ran as fast as I could, stumbling over my own feet and hearing Nathan grimace and feeling him disappear. I ran as fast as I could not stopping until I got much further into the trees, I realised I was soaked and shivering. I questioned everything. Where did those powers come from? I needed answers. I allowed myself to relax and reach out with my mind, searching for Nathan, but something blocked me.

Taking off again hurt my ribs, but I could hear footsteps on the dead leaves, getting closer and closer to me. My heart thudded in my ears and along with the sound of maniacal laughter broke through the silence of the woods. I ran a little further, slamming into trees and shrubs, scratching my arms, slipping on the wet leaves, and stumbling over branches until I reached the cliff face. As I climbed down to our cave, I realised that I needed to take more care with my safety. I slowed my descent and slipped on a stone, almost screaming aloud. Suddenly the sound of a crash as loud as thunder sounded nearby and I jumped as I tried to climb down faster again, but the path was treacherous and my feet slipped on more than one occasion.

As I almost reached the cave, I slipped in some mud, sliding right off the cliff face. My scream caught in my throat and I scrabbled around for anything to hold onto, but I felt myself slipping right off the path. I glanced down, seeing the jagged rocks that I would hit at the bottom. I began falling when a hand grabbed me.

My eyes scrunched up of their own accord, but I heard a familiar voice speak to me in low tones, "Jas, it's okay. I've got you. Help me though please, grip my hand." Nathan's voice startled me enough to make me look up and I stared at him in shock, seeing him standing there, holding onto me as though his life depended on getting me back up safely. I shook my head and he glared at me, "Jas, please, don't do this. I can't lose you. You mean too much to me." I shook my head again and he pleaded with me, "Jas, come on please, I can't do this without you. I love you." I nodded once and wrapped my hands around his, letting him pull me up.

He slipped with me into the cave and he held me while I shivered and sobbed on his shirt. "It's okay, it's okay. You're safe. I've got you," he murmured repeatedly until my breathing settled. He leaned down, and looked into my eyes, kissed me gently, "you will not do that to me again. I love you so fucking much that I risked everything to get here and you tried to let go. How could you do that to me Jas?" He lead me to the back of the cave sat me down on a large boulder that was nestled against the cave wall.

My whole body shook as I answered him, "Nate, I don't know. I just for a second thought how much easier your life would be without me in it. I'm just a complication for you."

The look he gave me when I spoke almost broke me in half, "is that really what you think of me, of us? That I wouldn't give up everything I have, everything I am up to save you? Have you no idea how fucking much I love you? I risked my life to come to you and you want to..." His voice broke off and he swallowed, rolling his eyes as I stood and watched him.

"Nate," I moved towards him, but he stepped back, shaking his head at me and I dropped my hand to my lap, looking down as my own tears began again. His breathing became heavier and he paced around for a few minutes, but I didn't look at him. I couldn't, I had no answer for him. After a few more minutes he came back over and sat down on the floor at my feet, putting his head on my lap.

"That was the scariest few minutes of my life Jas. You can't do shit like that to me. I don't know what would happen to me if you died." His voice broke and I ran my fingers through his hair. He sat for a few more minutes and I continued to run my fingers through his hair. His fingers reached up and laced through mine, as he pulled my fingers to his mouth and kissed them one by one. He sat up and I could see the fear and doubt in his eyes, so I did the only thing I could think of to make the feelings change.

I leaned over and kissed him hard on the mouth. At first he didn't respond, so I slipped forward and sat on his thighs, kissing hard and I pulled my hands from his, wrapping them around his neck, and kissing harder. He pulled back and pushed at my arms, but after a groan he relented and he kissed me until we were both panting, breathless.

"Jas, baby, I have to get back. I brought you some clothes, a sleeping bag, and some food. Stay here tonight and I'll fix his memories. He won't come after you again, I promise." He smiled reassuringly at me, but my face fell at the thought of spending the night in the cave without him anywhere near me. As I looked down, he lifted my chin with his finger. "I love you, Jas. God, I fucking love you so much. Please believe me, but I have to go, right now!" He leaned in, kissed me gently, and I watched as he faded away again, becoming nothing more than a shadow.

While I sat there, shivering with cold and with longing for Nate, his voice sounded in my head, "Jas, make a protection line. Do it now." I moved to the door to make the protection line, but I froze looking around at the stones. I hadn't ever done it before, but somehow I knew what to do and I knew Nathan was feeding me the information. I blessed the larger stones and lay them in a line, feeling like something took over my body. I went with it because I was sore, cold, and extremely freaked out.

I found out a little later that the line worked and it helped to settle me down. I felt more lost and confused, and I couldn't reach out to Nathan, no matter how hard I tried. After a while, I fell asleep with one ear open. I heard a sinister voice carrying on the wind, calling out, looking for me. "Where are you, Jasmine? Come out, come out wherever you are!"

I huddled at the back of the cave, but I could still hear the sound of someone crashing about overhead as stones began falling around me. I could feel myself being pulled back into the cave wall. I wanted to run, but I was being held back, something was keeping me in the cave and since I was sure it was Nathan I tried to force myself to relax. I rested my head back, and could hear the sound of his heart beating and smell the familiar scent of his skin, musky aftershave, and the feel of his warm arms around me. He held me wordlessly for a few moments and then turned me around. "James is headed home. As soon as he's asleep, I'm going to place an enchantment on him to make him forget about today. Go back at first light and slip into the barn. I'll meet you there."

I nodded into his chest, as he pulled me in for a hug. "I almost lost you today. You can't leave me. Without your love, I'd be a monster like them. I need you to know you have saved not only my heart, but my life and my soul." Gently, he kissed my forehead and faded away.

"Wait. How are you here? What's with the fading away?" I asked him, but got no answer.

I snuggled down into the sleeping bag, comforted by the smell of his aftershave and fell into a deep sleep, waking in the early morning light, freezing cold. A loud sound made me jump but listening intently, all I could hear was the sound of the waves hitting the cliffs and the birds flying and cawing.

CHAPTER 3
SAFE HAVEN

Leaving the sanctuary of the cave was hard but necessary if we wanted to keep my growing powers a secret. Being more careful on the way up the cliff, I came upon a scene of complete devastation. Trees were ripped up from the roots, leaves floated everywhere, and the ground had been ripped up. Something about this mess scared me. I walked through, creating a path out of the destruction, and made it back to the barn. At the door of the barn, there was a welcome sight. Nathan stood just inside the double doors, smiling. He looked exhausted, but relieved.

I walked at his side into the barn and he sat on the chair, leaving me to sit on the floor. He looked at me; his eyes drooped but he fought it.

"Nathan, what's wrong?" I asked him worriedly. He yawned and stretched, causing his brown shirt to rise slightly, distracting me by the sight of his sculpted stomach. He smiled as my gaze reached his face, but it didn't quite reach his eyes.

"I'm exhausted. I haven't been sleeping very well these last few days." He nodded towards me. "I have been busy protecting you from my fucking family and it hasn't been fucking easy, in fact it's been an absolute fucking nightmare." I sat staring at him expectantly, waiting for some answers, but he shook his head at me. "I need to get some sleep. I'm meeting my family in three hours. I will explain everything to you to—" His words cut off, as a sound came from the barn door. It slammed open, clattering off the wall. Nathan faded away, shaking his head and leaning over to give me a whispering kiss on my forehead.

I sat watching the door, but no one came in and the door fluttered open in the breeze, as I sat there watching it blow about in the wind. I thought about Nathan and how tired he was and tried to send him some energy. I wasn't sure how the thing with him worked, but I was worried about him and I didn't want him put in danger. Eventually, I got up and made my way over to the door to close it over. I was surprised to see a vivid red hand print on the door and when I thought about how I would let Nathan know about it, his voice sounded tiredly in my head, "it's ok, I see it." As he spoke to me his voice broke and he closed our connection.

The rest of the day passed without further incident, but I was on high alert for James. I hadn't seen him at all, all day, which meant I was cold, hungry, and irritable by the time Nathan showed up that night and I took my foul mood out on him.

"Are you okay?" he asked as he appeared beside me after two a.m. He had just awakened me and I was cold, hungry, and very tired.

"No, I'm bloody not," I snapped at him, furious with him and his stupid family for making me sleep in a stupid barn with no stupid heating or fucking food.

"What's wrong?" he pushed sounding concerned. "Did my uncle try to hurt you again?"

"No, it's not that. I'm cold, I'm hungry, and I'm tired. I haven't eaten all day and you've just appeared and woke me up." I knew I was whining, so I stopped and turned away. After a few seconds, I glanced back at him and he was gone, no goodbye or nothing. Feeling even more pissed off, I snuggled down into my sleeping bags and tried unsuccessfully to find sleep. I shivered, and my teeth chattered so hard as strong wind and rain battered the barn. The wind seeped through the cracks in the wood and the barn was freezing as the rain pelted down. I was studiously trying to ignore the sounds of the wind and rain when a warm hand touched my cheek. I jumped away so fast that he almost dropped the things he carried.

"Whoa, Jas, it's just me, sorry, I didn't mean to scare you."

Looking over at Nathan from the other side of the barn, I was comforted by his smile and what he held in his hand — a bag full of sandwiches, crisps, biscuits, a tray of cakes, and a flask full of what smelled like hot chocolate.

"I really love you just now," I said without thinking and his head snapped up towards mine. The look on his face scared me into silence.

"No, Jas, you can't. We have to stop this, you need to stop." His eyes dropped to the floor as he spoke and his voice went hoarse as he continued, "We can't, not anymore... I mean, I can't... " his beautiful eyes filled with tears as he ran his hand through his hair, messing it up. Moving towards him slowly, I put my hand on his knee and he looked up at me with tears on his cheeks. "I have to go. I'm sorry," he whispered before fading away. I sat there confused and hurt. He gave me so many mixed signals and I couldn't figure out why he wanted to stop, unless his family really suspected something about us, was that what he meant about us stopping?. I sat there for a while, picking at a sandwich, my appetite all but gone, and had a small cup of hot chocolate before falling asleep again.

I awoke a few hours later and Nathan sat beside me, watching me sleep with a small smile playing around his lips and his eyes. "Sorry about last night," he said sullenly. "I guess I better explain what's going on, huh?"

I nodded in agreement, and sat up a little. He walked away from me and placed a line of stones with scribbles on them across the entrance to the barn. "Just in case anyone comes into the barn, they'll see you but not me." I nodded at him again and he continued to place the stones in every corner. "These will also help protect you, when I'm not around. You have a penchant for attracting trouble and every time I'm away from you, you need to be rescued." I was about to say something when Nathan stepped back towards me and the look on his face stopped me, "You know it's true, but never mind that. I have some explaining to do. When we were unconscious, a gypsy came to visit my father. This man has been a friend of my father for many years now and he trusts him above all other consultants. This man, Geordan, told my father that the tides were shifting and that someone close to him was turning away from our values..."

"What? How could he possibly know that?" I asked, feeling more than a little curious.

"He has the gifts of his forebears, meaning he can see future events. He can also sense great changes in the balances of power; if the pendulum swings from evil to good or back again, then Geordan knows about it, and warns my father. Anyway, he," Nathan smiled, shaking his head at me, as I opened my mouth to speak, and placing a finger on my lips, as he continued to speak uninterrupted, "warned my father that the tides were turning, that the evil under my father's rule, was being corroded by love and that someone in his close circle would betray him by falling in love with a mortal and not just any mortal. The Destined."

"What's a Destined?" I asked and my tone showed that I was more confused than ever.

Nathan reached over and turned my face to his. "You are," he answered simply. "You are the Destined, the one who has the power to ensure that our race, the race of demons, stay in control of the powers and that no one can ever or will ever take that power away."

"What does that mean for us then, Nathan?" I asked him, my voice cracking, feeling my heart splinter as tears fill my eyes.

He looked at me full of concern and with tears in his own eyes before answering, "Jas, by falling in love with you, I may well have signed both of our death warrants. I can't be with you, but I can't be without you. I don't know what to do..." The tears in my eyes spilled over, one rolling down my cheek as I watched the pain cross his features. His voice trailed off as he looked at me in the soft light of the lantern. "Move over. I can't sit over there and know that I might never get the chance to hold you again."

He crawled over to my sleeping bag, and squeezed in, holding me tighter than I'd ever been held before. His arm snaked around my waist holding me as though he was worried I would slip away, without him. I turned my head and kissed him softly on the neck and he shivered, kissing me softly on the head. I turned back and faced away from him, relaxing into his embrace and trying to memorise the feeling of him holding me, because I knew that it would be a while before he held me like this again. His gentle voice, brushed over the back of my neck, making me shudder as he spoke.

"I'm getting interviewed tomorrow by him and I have to convince him there is nothing going on between us. Things just got a whole load more difficult, but for the moment, I just want to hold you and stay with you."

His lips pressed onto the skin at the back of my neck. His lips linger there for a moment and then he sighed and moved them away. I tried to turn to give him a kiss and could feel him tightening his hold, shaking, "No, don't turn around. I can't kiss you on the lips. It will break me apart and I need tonight to be perfect..."

"What do you want, Nathan?" I asked him quietly.

"You, just like this, Jas. I want you, but I need to protect you. I had no soul until you came into my life, no heart until you touched it, and no awareness until you awakened it in me. I have never loved like this before. I know I will never feel like this again. You mean everything to me and I will love you with everything I am, all the days of my lives..."

"Well, isn't this cosy?" a voice from outside the barn sounded and looking into the middle of the barn, all we could see was Jack standing there, glaring at us. "Nathan, I never expected you to betray your father, but here is the proof."

I could feel Nathan shaking behind me and it galvanised me into action.

"No, Jas," Nathan warned, but I didn't listen. I walked over to the edge of the stones and felt power coming from the ground. Power flowed through me from the stones, the tree that grew through the barn, but mostly from inside of me and I could feel the zip and zing of it through me. I thrust my arms out from my sides and whoosh! Jack went flying through the air, cracking his head on a branch from the tree. There was such immense power radiating through me, but it wasn't until Nathan touched my arms, I felt how powerful I was. My skin thrummed with electricity.

I walked over to Jack and touched his chest, murmuring as I did, "You saw nothing. You came out here and checked on me, but you saw nothing and you heard nothing. I was sleeping alone!!!" His body tensed as shockwaves rolled down my arms and I used the power again bringing my hands them together with a crash of light. Jack was back in his bed and I turned towards Nathan. "Wow, what a rush," I said, smiling at him.

"Stop now, Jasmine. He's gone. It's just me..." His voice was high and terrified, and his eyes widened with each step I took towards him. He had to know I would never hurt him. He was the other half of me and I loved him with every fibre of my being. I kept moving, watching in dismay as Nathan backed away from me. "Nate, what is it?" I asked as I reached him, and touched his face gently with my fingers.

More electricity flowed through me and he shuddered and disappeared, fading away into nothingness, which brought me down, crashing to the ground, feeling more drained and exhausted than ever. I crawled into my sleeping bag and was asleep within seconds, not caring about why Nate disappeared. I dreamed about Nathan calling me for help, but when I woke and heard activity outside of the barn, I didn't immediately associate that with my actions from the previous night. It wasn't until I tiptoed over to the slightly open door that I realised the Stevenson's were all back from their holiday with a gruff-looking man, with long shaggy hair and an overgrown beard. He wore clothes that were all patched and frayed. I realised things had taken a turn for the worse.

CHAPTER 4
THE VISITOR

I stood at the barn door and watched as Geordan arrived which was worrying because of everything that Nathan had said, but seeing Nathan carried out of the car by his parents was far worse. A pit opened up on my stomach and something squirmed uncomfortably. He seemed to be unconscious and I had no clue what was wrong with him or why he was asleep during the day, unable to walk.

I walked back into my barn, the small area becoming like a sanctuary for me. I spent the rest of the day thinking about Nathan, wondering where he was and what was going on. In the early afternoon, it started raining heavily again. I was lying on my back listening to the sounds of the pounding rain on the wood, hearing the drip of continual water falling and feeling the soft whisper of a breeze on my face, I wasn't paying much attention to anything near the door. A shadow caught my eye and my eyes darted over to see Nathan standing in front of me. His appearance made me jump, because it was so quiet and was he blurred around the edges. I could see he said something, but I couldn't make out what.

Suddenly his voice sounded clearly in my head and I jumped again as he said, "Jasmine... block...help me, please..." before his voice faded away to nothing. The cold air around me swirled as I thought for a few minutes, but I couldn't figure out what he meant by block. What was he talking about? What was I to block?

The answer became clear a few moments later as the barn door opened and Geordan, Mr, and Mrs Stevenson all walked into the barn.

"Well, let's see her then. Perhaps we can figure out if she has something to do with Nathan being unable to awaken," a raspy, wheezing voice said, making my skin crawl and shivers break out.

Again, Nathan's voice made me jump, "Block now, Jasmine..."

Focusing all my energy on blocking him from reading me, I watched as they walked slowly towards me, listening intently.

"So is this where you keep all the sacrifices?" Geordan asked Mr Stevenson.

"Yeah, we enchant them and put three in each stall." Mr Stevenson answered, sounding a little uncomfortable.

"I would keep them away from her." Geordan said quietly as they finally reached the door of my barn. Redoubling my efforts to block him, I glanced up as the barn door swung open revealing the odd trio. Mr Stevenson glared down at me. Mrs Stevenson looked anywhere but at me, but Geordan looked at me curiously, as though he would like nothing better than to dissect me, making me feel exceptionally uncomfortable.

"Hello, Jasmine. My name is Geordan. I'm a friend of Mr and Mrs Stevenson and we are here to speak to you about Nathan." As he spoke, he moved closer to me, making me feel more uncomfortable and his eyes roamed all over me, making me feel as though he was violating me. He reached out and took my hand, saying gently, "Something is wrong with Nathan and we think you can help us figure out what."

The moment he touched me, I felt an odd sort of pulling, as though he was stretching the muscles in my head, but I had already decided to block and focused all of my powers on making sure those muscles snapped back into place. As they did, his head snapped back.

"I can't get a read on her. Something is blocking me. This is very unusual." He looked at me and his dark eyes gleamed malevolently. He snatched my hand again and this time, white-hot knives darted up and down my body, stabbing me in places. I screamed aloud, only just managing to hold the block in place. He smirked down at me and looked over at the Stevenson's standing at the door of the barn.

"Whatever is blocking her is strong, but I have weakened it. We can try again later and hopefully this time, I'll manage to break through the defences."

"Can't you do it now?" Mrs Stevenson asked sternly, "I want my son back as soon as possible!"

He shook his head and turned back towards me, looking at me questioningly. He pushed up with sudden agility and walked away, shaking his head at Mr Stevenson. Mrs Stevenson however lunged at me, shoving me backwards.

"No, Emma," Mr Stevenson shouted, grabbing at his wife, but she shook him off. She grabbed my hair, dragging me backwards further into the barn.

"What have you done to my son?" she screamed in my face, spit flying.

"I've done nothing; I don't know what you're talking about!"My body shook in fear as I shouted at her and I tried to calm my voice down as I asked her, "What's wrong with him?" She glared at me and began to growl at me and smack my head on the stone floor, until my vision blurred.

"I will kill you unless you bring him back to me," she shouted, hitting my head again and again until Mr Stevenson and Geordan pulled her off. Stars popped in front of my eyes and, I lay there, curled up in the foetal position on the floor, jumping as I felt rough hands probing my head.

"She's okay. She'll live," a voice above my head said. "Let's go."

My head swam and drifted off, curled up in the middle of in the barn. I floated away and awoke in a shadowy place. The smell was vile and it made my stomach churn. I swallowed hard and my head hurt and as I stared around. All I could see in my field of vision was various shades of grey, some almost black, and some almost silver. There were trees in shades forming from dust before my eyes, but terror overwhelmed me and I stood there shaking and shivering as I glanced around. The rank smell was stronger in the slight breeze, blowing dust particles swirling around my face. It smelled like rotten foods and excrement, making me my stomach roll and retch.

A hand touched me and I spun around to face whoever it was, after jumping away from the unknown party. My heart rate sped as I saw Nate standing there, smiling at me, but looking him up and down, I noticed that his legs were shaded grey, almost black.

"How did you get here? I mean I'm glad you're here, but how did you get here?" he asked, smiling wider at me. I reached out and touched his face, noticing him shuddering as I did so. He tried to step towards me and I noticed he seemed to struggle, as though he was glued to the floor. He grimaced in pain as he tried to move towards me. I looked down and noticed the darkness crawling over my feet and felt as though my feet were being sucked into the floor. I looked at Nathan in terror and he smiled though his eyes told another story.

"We need to move now, Jasmine," he said in a soft voice, glancing down as he spoke. I nodded in agreement and we moved. As he lifted his legs, his face was strained, with sweat pouring down his face as he bit his lip. I pulled my legs one at a time and felt as though they were sticking to the ground. As we walked on, I could smell a sickly sweet scent with each footstep. "Don't breathe in the fumes; it wants to consume you." Nathan's voice sounded farther away as I fell forwards. His hands snaked around my waist and he pulled me back upright and dragged me a few steps. We moved uphill and he held onto me as though I was his lifeline.

As we finally reached the top of a hill, the blackness swirled about the bottom of the hill and the top was in lighter shades, almost leading to silver. We sat at the top of the hill and I glanced down at Nathan's legs. They were covered in bright red blisters with black stuff oozing out of them. Looking down at my own ankles, I discovered the same stuff was on them, oozing out and trickling down the hill. Upon reaching down to touch the stuff, Nathan pulled my hand away, hissing, "Don't touch them. It's poison."

As I turned around to face him, I noticed greyness overhead and the sour, rotting smell getting stronger, "Come with me now, Jasmine. Hurry!" Nathan stiffly stood and ran without even looking to see if I followed. I ran as fast as I could, but fell into a patch of darkness and awoke freezing cold, soaking wet, and shivering in the barn. I opened my eyes and it was pitch black. Looking around, trying to get my bearings, revealed Geordan watching me from the door of the barn.

"Lost something, have we?" he snarled, glaring at me. I was about to shake my head when two pairs of hands grabbed me and dragged me out into the main barn area. They placed me onto a chair and tied me up. My sight was hindered by the ringing in my ears and I shook worse than ever. I managed to make out Nick, Nathan's older brother, watching with a look of sick fascination on his face. Looking away from him, I met the eyes of Jack who looked at me as if I was something edible, which turned my stomach more.

"Leave now, both of you!" Geordan's voice ordered from the shadows.

"But what if she gives you trouble?" Nick's voice asked to the left of me.

"How much trouble can she possibly give me tied to a chair?" Geordan asked with what sounded like disdain in his voice. "Just leave and I will find out why I was blocked earlier." He looked at both men who nodded and walked towards the door. I sat there in complete silence, which was difficult, but something, some instinct told me to keep quiet and sit still until they were gone.

"I can see that you don't trust me, but you have to let me help you. I've been working on defeating demons for twenty years, but never in all my years have I felt a shift in the balance of power like this. You are incredibly special and you and Nathan together are more powerful than anyone could have imagined or predicted."

I watched him speak, though there was still something I didn't trust. Why was I tied to a chair? Why hadn't he reached out to me before? I asked myself these questions, all the while eyeing him warily as he watched me curiously.

"Why now?" my voice cracking as I spoke.

"I haven't had a chance before now. You have been exceptionally well hidden. You must know that, Jasmine. Plus, if I had acted before now, Mr Stevenson would have had me killed, but believe me I can be a useful ally."

I shook my head trying to clear it, since I was still confused, dizzy, and sore from the earlier exploits. He reached under my chair and pulled out some hot food in a clear container — pasta. I hadn't had a hot meal in what felt like forever.

"Here. Eat this. It will help build your strength. It's going to be a long night, but we need you to tap into all your latent powers..."

"How do you know I have any powers?" I asked sullenly, remembering he was the reason Nathan and I couldn't be together. He had reported us and had made my already difficult life even more so. As all these thoughts went through my head, he just stood there stiffly. Without warning, he spun on his heal, leaving me still tied up with the pasta on my lap, burning through my grey jeans and warming my legs.

He was gone a few seconds before coming back with a folding chair, "I think we'll both be more comfortable if I sit down. Now you have been thinking about why I informed the Stevenson's about you and Nathan..." he broke off, looking at me and finally noticed that I hadn't touched my pasta, "Oh dear, why didn't you say something?" He reached behind me and untied my hands. "Dig in."

Not realising how hungry I was, I took a bite then stuffed my mouth full of food. It was exceptionally good with a cheese sauce. He watched me for a few minutes, looking slightly revolted before speaking again. "You eat and I'll talk. Okay??"

Nodding since my mouth was too full of food, I didn't want to disgust him anymore than I already had, especially if what he was saying was true about Nathan.

"So, Jasmine, where were we?" he paused for a moment as I swallowed.

"Why did you tell the Stevenson's about my powers?"

"Oh yes, you are wondering why I told them of you and Nathan's dalliances. Well, my dear girl, I had to. Don't you see that if I hadn't and you and Nathan had escaped, and then questions would have been asked. I checked and I am sure it won't hamper your destiny."

I had been continually eating while he spoke, although I was beginning to feel sick. It was too good to stop, but I forced myself to put the fork on the plate and moved it towards the floor.

"Why are you telling me this? Would you even be here if Nathan was okay?"

"Well, I'm telling you because you need to know and no, I wouldn't be here if you hadn't banished Nathan. Where you banished his soul to, I cannot say, but I believe you have seen him there."

I nodded in answer, and I held my hands on my lap trying to show that I was willing to listen.

"Jasmine, he is your better half. With him, your powers multiply and there will come a time that they even may scare you. Now you have to use them to track him down and bring him back. I have until morning to convince you; otherwise, they are going to kill you..."

Gasping as he said this, I realised it didn't matter if I trusted him. I needed his guidance to bring back Nathan or it didn't matter. We would both be dead.

"Okay, I'm on board. What do we have to do?"

"You aren't going to like this. You have to drop your block completely, otherwise this won't work. We have to open your mind and roam out to find Nathan. He could be in a number of different realms or worlds, and we need to find him quickly. We can't do that if you are blocking me."

Something he said made me instinctively back away. I decided to remove part of the block I had placed up, but not all of it. I knew he didn't need to know all the powers I had, and I still had trouble trusting him.

"Okay, sit back now, Jasmine. Close your eyes and reach out with your mind until you feel the walls. When you feel them, move around them until you reach the edges. Take a grip of the edges and pull them down." I decided to pull them back slightly, knocking a few bricks from the top, but leaving three quarters of them still standing. "Now, focus on Nathan. Think of how you feel when you're with him. Can you do that?"

IGNITION

I nodded and closed my eyes, deciding to at least try and trust Geordan to do what he was asked, help me to rescue Nathan.

CHAPTER 5
RESCUE FROM THE SHADOWLANDS

As I began wadding through what felt like water, I focused on him, but just as I began to zero in on his location, the barn door slammed open and I jumped, my walls snapping back in place.

"Jack, what are you doing here?" Geordan's' voice asked waspishly. "We were making progress there and you ruined it."

Jack completely ignored Geordan and stormed over to me, "What the fuck did you do to me?" he growled at me before slapping me in the face. My full cheek felt like it was on fire and the chair went flying backwards with the force of it. I landed on the tree. Both Jack and Geordan froze.

"You better get your brother. We are going to need him to get her out of there."

I sat there, wondering why they hadn't moved me, when I felt immense power flowing through me, I was floating. I gazed down on them, with such immense power flowing through me, and it was one of the scariest moments I had ever had. Jack turned and bolted out the door, looking like a horse sprinting from the barn. I let out a chuckle and the whole barn shook with the force of it. I had more power in me than ever and it scared me almost out of my mind. Geordan looked up at me in dismay as Jack returned with Mr Stevenson at his heels.

"What is she doing?" he snarled. "Get her down now!" he commanded, but they couldn't reach me. I just smiled and watched as it enraged them all further. "We can't touch her while she's on the tree. How did she get there?"

Geordan just looked at Jack and he snapped, "It was me. I wanted to know what she did to me!"

"For fuck's sake, I told you to leave her alone. We need her to get my son back! Did you forget about that, you selfish prick? My son's soul is out there in the ether because of someone, and she is the only one with the power to get him back. I told you I will strip her powers when she has brought my son back to me."

I continued to gaze down at them, as Jack turned to leave. Mr Stevenson said into his ear, "One year, brother, and you can do the honours. Now go please while we work out how to get her down from there." He turned his green eyes around and glared up at me. "Well, Jasmine, you have caused quite a conundrum. We need to get you down from there or you'll collapse into a coma, which at the moment wouldn't be advisable," he said with a horrible grin at the end.

I allowed my mind to roam out, after closing my eyes and blocking them out, until I reached Nathan, but he was weak. Going to him was the easiest decision I ever made, but I could hear them shouting at me, screaming at me to stay awake.

"What are you doing, Jasmine?" Mr Stevenson's voice hollered, making my ears ring with the power behind his words. "You must not use the power of the tree. Stop now."

"Jasmine, not this way," came Geordan's voice. "Come back."

Feeling reckless, I didn't listen, but pulled myself to Nathan. I glanced around, looking for Nathan, and he was almost in complete shadow. It had covered him right up to his neck. He gasped in pain, grimacing with tears streaming down his face as the shadows moved further up. Arms of shadow reached up and almost tickled his chin.

Reaching down, I pulled him up the hill towards the silver lights and could see the shadows reaching out repeatedly, trying to grab hold of him and pull him back down. One of them caught hold of his ankle and he yelped in pain, his face going paler and his head falling. Giving one almighty tug, I managed to break its hold and saw a little colour returning to his cheeks.

As we reached the top of the hill, I sat and looked out while he panted for breath. We sat like that for a few moments before he reached out and slid his hand into my own. His hand was icy cold.

"Oh my God, Jas, you feel like you're on fire, baby. What happened? How did you get back here?"

He sat up, but started shivering worse. I pulled him into my arms and wrapped my arms around him. "Your uncle slapped me into the tree in the barn," I said simply, pausing as he sucked in a breath. "Geordan tried to help me find you, but your uncle interrupted. Where are we, by the way? What is this place?"

"This is the Shadowlands," he whispered so quietly I could barely hear him so I sat back to watch him as he spoke, his voice getting stronger with each sentence. "Demons and monsters come here to die. It's kind of like what mortals would call Purgatory. I almost died, but I knew you'd save me. I realised you were tough enough not to give up on us, or me. Somehow, you'd save me." He smiled over at me and I moved towards him, slipping my hand around his waist as I lay me head on his chest and listening to his voice as he continued speaking, "You didn't show Geordan all of your powers, did you? I don't trust him. He's been working for my dad forever and my dad trusts him implicitly, which means we absolutely shouldn't."

Shaking my head, I answered him, "No, but we need to find a way to get us home and to remove all traces of this from everyone's minds. If they remember, they'll kill us both."

"How do you know that? I would suggest the same thing, but how are we going to work it? We might need to bottle some of the shadow as a sleeping agent and send them all to sleep. However, it will be a while before I'm strong enough to collect any. Can you do it? I have an idea how we can get home." Nathan twisted in my arms and kissed me full on the lips, leaning into me until we both lay on the ground as he ran his tongue over my lips.

"I missed you, Jasmine," he kissed me slowly, slipping his tongue into my mouth. He groaned softly, and then muttered, "God, I missed you, but we need to be careful..." he broke off, kissed my head, and sat up abruptly, leaning forwards and resting his chin on his knees. The sour smell was back, and it was as if the walls were closing in around us. Everywhere I looked now, the shadows became thicker, denser, and the areas of silver decreased.

"The Shadows are angry. We better hurry. Can you collect some shadows and place them in this?" he asked. "I'm going to collect some of those silver fruits ahead and some of the berries in the bushes, along with some silver leaves."

I looked at my hands and nodded. He'd pressed into my hand the hot chocolate container from the previous day. I sprinted down the hill even though I could barely see where I was going, but I judged by my nose. I got closer to the sickening fumes and I started to retch, I reached down and licks of fire started to spread up my arms and cold reached into my heart, freezing me in place. Thinking of Nathan, I shook it off and pulled some shadow away. It was tough like pulling apart magnets, only stronger. It kept trying to go back, and it made this sickening, crunching sound, like bones being snapped.

Eventually I had three handfuls, which seemed like enough. I headed back up to Nathan. I watched him for a few minutes and my heart beat a little faster. His hair was mussed up and his face still pale, but his green eyes searched me out. A smile played on his lips as I made my way up the hill.

"Like something you see?" he asked me playfully.

"You know it," I answered him with a smile and walked up to him, placing a kiss on his lips. We both knew as soon as we got back that we would have to stay away from each other, or risk discovery. I knew I was going to miss him, and that it was going to hurt like hell, but it had to be done. I leaned towards him again, wrapping my arms around his neck and bringing my lips to his, wanting to make the moment last, I slipped my tongue into his mouth and he groaned, drinking me in. He eyes opened and he gazed into my eyes as we kissed. He pulled back after a moment, panting hard and leaned down to put his hands on his knees.

"Nate, are you okay?" I asked him worriedly, while he stared at the ground. I glanced around and the shadows reared up, looking like a slow moving six foot tsunami coming towards us and I looked at Nathan in alarm. He straightened up and glanced over it me, nodding at me as he moved to my side again.

"Ready?" he asked me, taking my hand.

"As I'll ever be, I suppose." I replied, looking at him, my long dark hair swishing behind me. He leaned over and kissed me, pulling me around until I was in front of him. He held me tightly. "I love you, you know that. Right?"

I glanced up at him once and nodded, tears stinging my eyes at the realisation that he would never be mine. He shook his head, "I'm yours, baby. I chose you and I will choose you, even when you think I haven't. You make my world sparkle and shimmer, and I adore you. We do need to go back though, but never, ever doubt that I love you more than my own life." He kissed me gently and then moved to my side, taking my hand and squeezing my fingers with his own, before he sighed and said, "Open a portal, Jas."

"No, I don't want to. Can't we just stay here and hide out?"

He smiled at me and kissed me softly on my head, "no, baby, I'm sorry, we can't. We have to go back and face reality." I shook my head sullenly and wouldn't look at him, "you aren't gonna touch me at all when we get back are you?"

"Jas, I can't. If they catch us they'll kill us. They'd make me watch them cut your throat. Don't ask me to watch that, we aren't worth that. You are worth so much more than that."

"But I can't lose you Nate, you mean everything to me." I knew I sounded like a whiny brat, but I couldn't help it. Nate kissed me once more on the lips, drawing my bottom lip into his mouth and sucking on it, before murmuring against my mouth "Jas, come on. I can't lose you. Please, let's just go back." He glanced about as I opened my mouth to protest and gasped.

"Jas, we need to leave now. Turn around and look about."

He watched me as I turned slowly around, taking in the dense dark grey fog that rolled towards us on the right side and the tsunami of grey waves approaching from the left The tension between us rose as I reached out, felt about for a fissure, letting my fingers roam through the air, until heat or a cold breeze hit me. Finally finding one, I gripped it, ripping it apart. It tried to push back together, but I stretched my arms out and forced the fissure further apart until my arms were stretched as far as they could go. Once it was far enough apart, it stopped and just sat there, vibrating with a slight humming noise. A sweet smell floated through and there was a light shimmering through it, as though the sun was hitting the mirror and we were looking at our reflections.

Nathan took one final look at me, kissed me on the lips with so much passion my knees buckled slightly. He kissed me on the forehead and stepped backwards through the gap, eyes on me as he left me standing there. I looked around once more and followed after, seeing dark grey hands trying to get through the gap to us as the fog closed in and the wave lapped an inch to my left. By the looks of things we'd just made it.

"Can you hurry and close that up, Jasmine? We can't let any more of that to come through here. It's dangerous. We need the portal shut so we can work on the enchantment."

Opening up my mind and stretching my arms until I found the edges, I closed the space up until only a small fissure remained.

"Close your eyes," he whispered and I obeyed, but didn't expect to feel my skin burning as he turned on the lantern. After a few minutes, the burning reduced to a dull ache. I opened my eyes and took in our surroundings. I'd brought us to the little rock crevice. Looking down at Nathan, I could see things weren't good. Where my burning had only lasted a few moments, he looked as though he was on fire. His face was red and blistered, sweat poured his face, and he grimaced in pain. I reached over to touch him and felt him shudder before he hissed out, "Don't touch me. This is your fault. Just don't fucking touch me. Okay?"

My hand snapped back and I crawled away from him, moving closer to the mouth of the crevice and looking out at the ocean. Tears dripped softly down my face, but I stayed looking out, feeling more betrayed and hurt than ever. I couldn't believe that he'd been so nasty to me when I'd just brought him back. I watched the water lapping against the rocks, the waves rolling about and smelling the salt of the sea with the wind blowing my hair gently around my face. After a while, I turned back to check on Nathan and he was curled into a ball, sleeping. Thinking about him sleeping made me tired, but I knew we had to work on that through the night. I stayed awake, sitting at the edge of the crevice, thinking.

I must have nodded off because I was dreaming about my parents, something I hadn't done in the longest time. My dad had me in his arms, running around our backyard. I was laughing, as was my mum watched with an amazing look on her face. She was larger than I remember, but the love I felt from them was unlike anything I had experienced since, until I met Nathan.

Rough hands shook me awake, "Jasmine, wake up. We have to cast this enchantment. Come on." His voice sounded off to me, high and cold and I shivered. I glared up at him sleepily as I forced my eyes to open and muttered under my breath. I closed my eyes over and tried to find a comfy position to fall asleep in but he leaned down in front of me, shook me until I looked at him.

"Come on. If we don't fix this, they will kill you and possibly me. We can't live with that threat hanging over us..." He broke off, grabbing my hands roughly and pulling me to my feet. I slipped a little and he caught me in his arms, backing away quickly after he had steadied me. We began the slow walk up the cliff face and through the woods. Stopping just beside his house, he whispered, "Give me the flask and hold my hand. Don't let go for any reason."

I watched as he placed the ingredients, along with some others he must have collected at home, into the flask and shook them together. He handed the flask to me and I again felt fire spreading down my arms, into my fingers, leaving them tingling, as he whispered in my ear, "you must use the words omit and tell the concoction what you want remembered otherwise it will leave the memories that you are trying to erase. Also, Jasmine, make sure you say omit three times otherwise the enchantment won't take." His eyes moved up my face, lingering on my lips before he reached my eyes, "Got it?" I nodded slowly at him and watched as his face transformed from the boy I loved, to the demon I hated. I turned away from him, whispering the words, as a single tear rolled down my cheek.

"Omit, omit, omit... You will omit these past two days from memory. You will only remember Nathan catching the flu and coming back early because of it. You will remember asking Geordan to come to help prepare you for the feasts, and that is all!"

Feeling my fingers itch, I watched as the top of the flask opened and the contents swirled up, changing the scenery. I saw Nathan disappear and felt myself shunted into the barn. Geordan, Jack, Mr Stevenson, and Nick all moved from the barn into the house. Everything went eerily quiet and I knew the spell had worked, but what I didn't count on was Geordan changing everything.

CHAPTER 6
CHARMS AND COMPLIANCE

The next morning, I lay in my barn, under the sleeping bags trying to get back to sleep, ignoring the sounds of the pounding wind and rain. I felt a pair of hands grab me and drag me out of the sleeping bag. Looking up through bloodshot eyes, since I hadn't had any sleep, I saw Geordan standing there. He looked at me in awe, but wasn't speaking. I shook my head and looked around for my hair tie, so I could tie my hair up, since it annoyed me if it was hanging loose and it needed washed. Eventually, I found it amongst my clothes from the day before. Noticing that they were singed around the edges, I grabbed them and stuffed them into the tent.

"Come with me, Jasmine," Geordan's rough voice commanded.

Shaking my head, I looked around for my clothes. He grabbed my arm, hissing in my ear, "It's not a request. Move now."

I had no choice but to comply with his wishes, since he was much bigger and stronger than me and I didn't want Nathan's family to remember what had happened the previous day. I was curious to see where this was going. I grabbed my done-in Nike trainers and my favourite jumper from a local coffee house. They were giving them out when I lived with the Greene family. The jumper said, Coffeelattetea and was an incredible café that I used to visit with my friends. Reminiscing as I moved around slowly, Geordan tugged on my arm impatiently.

"Hurry up, Jasmine."

We walked in complete silence into the woods, in the cold predawn darkness, heading for one of the protected circles that I had been in recently.

I knew this for some unknown reason, and I kept pace with him, wondering why he wanted to get me alone and so far from their home. The beginnings of nerves started to play on my mind when we reached the circle. He stepped in before me. I watched in awe, completely frozen as he transformed into one of the most beautiful creatures I had ever seen Gone was the shaggy brown hair and beard. Gone were the bloodshot eyes. Gone were the saggy, frayed clothes. He now stood before me, bathed in the glow of the sun, looking like an angel, with clear blue eyes, chubby cheeks, and a smile that would melt hearts.

He stood a few moments smiling at me, waiting for me to find my voice, but the difference in him was incredible. He wore a crisp blue suit, with a creamy-coloured shirt and a blue and cream tie. His hair was brown and his face was breathtakingly beautiful. I opened and closed my mouth several times before the words finally came out, "Wh- what... erm, what are you?" I stuttered, cursing myself for failing to get the full sentence out without looking like a complete idiot.

"I am a Nephilim and my name is Joaquin. My father was the archangel Gabriel and my mother was a human woman named Madelena. Nephilim are half-angels and one of our powers is that of illusion. I have been Geordan for a time out of mind, but I can see the power in you. Even when you tried to hide it, I could tell that you were important. I will not be back here so I must now part some valuable information onto you. When you are running, head for the coast, and cross the water. Use your common sense in choosing where to go and trust only Nathan, and those you travel with."

Nodding in agreement, his voice was buttery soft, sliding into my mind, working its way into my subconscious, which was what he wished. I was sure of it.

"I have something for you, but you must never, ever take it off, as it will protect you from evil. Any enchantments they try to place on you will not work as they should while you wear this. It will enhance your powers when you are ready, but will also help you control them in the meantime."

He handed me a beautiful charms for bracelet, three silver charms. The charms felt warm to the touch as I examined the charms. One was a feather, one was an angel, kneeling and praying with its eyes closed, and the other was a horseshoe.

"Each of the charms has a special significance. The feather will keep you safe from the enchantments. The horseshoe will aid you in your escape. The angel will keep your mind focused, help to develop your powers, and strengthen your mind. Wear them well and they will keep you safe, but you must not ever take it off. It is invisible to demons, but will be visible to mortals. Keep it hidden at all times; you do not want questions asked about these charms on your bracelet."

We stood in silence for a few minutes as I clasped the charms onto my bracelet on my wrist, feeling my arm shiver as the bracelet touched it with its new charms.

"We better head back. I'm leaving this morning and I won't see you again for quite some time. Be careful and remember that Nathan is going to do everything he can to keep you safe. Promise me that you will not judge him for what he has to do."

"Why would I judge him?" I asked, just as we reached the edge of the circle.

Joaquin touched my arm and said, "Just promise me." I nodded and we walked back through the woods, coming out right next to the barn. "Good luck, Jasmine. Until we meet again."

"Thank you," I said in a whisper before walking back into the barn and climbing under my covers. I was asleep within seconds, finally feeling secure enough to sleep.

The next few days passed without incident and without Nathan. He would avoid me in the house when I showered, and never brought me food to the barn. He never visited me at night and I missed him so much, but I let him be, since I knew that he was trying to protect me. Finally, Sunday night came and I lay on the floor of the tent on my mats, trying to do some schoolwork. I hated math, but this was a new level of torture. I looked up to see Nathan standing there watching me with the pained look he used to wear on his face.

"What's wrong?" I asked him in his head, but he just shook his head and placed the food down on the floor before turning to walk away. "Nathan, speak to me please."

"NO!!!" he answered forcefully in my mind, making my head ring like a bell, before walking to the door of the barn. As he reached the door, I heard a noise, a voice that I knew and hated; it was Lisa, his ex-girlfriend. "Current girlfriend," his voice corrected in my head.

"Come on, Nathan," she called in her babyish voice, turning my stomach. "Are we going out or what?"

I could feel my face burning and tears forming in my eyes. Looking down, I felt the tears running down my face and could feel my breath coming in short sharp gasps. This hurt on a whole new level.

"Wait, I forgot to give her this."

"Oh, but Nathan, she doesn't need it. Come on," she said, whining at him like a petulant child.

"I'll just be a second," he answered and I heard his footsteps coming towards the barn again.

Keeping my head down, I tried to focus on what I was doing, but I felt him pause as he looked at me. "Sorry," he murmured almost under his breath and I made the mistake of looking up. Catching his eye, all I could see in his green depths was pain and a tear running down his cheek, which he swiped away angrily.

"Nathan, come on. What are you doing?" Her voice rose again breaking the moment between Nathan and myself. He shook his head, not looking at me, and my heart shattered as he turned away from me. A gasp escaped me, having never felt a pain like that before in my life.

The rest of the night was spent lying in the tent with it zipped up, trying and failing to get a hold of my emotions. Eventually, at around three a.m., my eyes were puffy and red from crying, my chest hurt, and I had a sore throat. I finally managed to drift off to sleep, stirring as a hand stroked my hair.

Turning away, I shook my head and burrowed deeper into my sleeping bag.

The next day at school passed in a blur and walking to and from school, I walked a little behind Nathan and Jenny. Nothing stood out, but that night, I felt again like someone was there. I lay in my sleeping bag, trying to will myself to sleep, but my mind ran constantly over the past few months. I couldn't switch off. I felt a hand stroking my hair again, but when I opened my eyes and glanced around, no one was there and eventually I was tired enough to drift off to sleep.

The following day I awoke feeling groggy and out of sorts. It was Wednesday, the day of all my favourite classes. Going into the house for a shower was awkward as I walked with my head down and Nathan walked right into me, bumping me down three steps. He didn't apologise as he stepped over me, but he caught my eye, giving me butterflies even though I tried to quell them. The butterflies turned to wasps though, as Lisa walked down the stairs and stepped onto my hand.

Marching upstairs, I went into the shower and scrubbed myself red raw, trying to focus on anything other than the dead feeling building in my chest. Looking in the mirror after my shower, I gave myself a stern talk. *He's not worth it. He's hurt me time and again. Perhaps it's time for me to leave.* Nathan's voice again sounded in my head, making me jump, "NO!!!!" he screamed. After a few seconds, the bathroom door opened with a bang. I glanced at him in the mirror and could see the fury on his face, though he tried hard to hide it. He watched my eyes appraise him and scowled at me for a moment before speaking.

"Are you ready?" he snapped at me, sounding furious.

I shrugged and walked towards him, ignoring him. As I went past him, he pushed me into the bathroom and shut the door behind us both, locking us in. He moved towards me and I backed up onto the wall as his glorious face, leaned closer to me, "Do not even think about leaving. You can't, okay? I forbid it!"

Glaring at him, I slapped him hard across the face, spitting out, "Don't you fucking dare. You have hurt me over and over. Why should I stay here, to be killed or hurt? I'd rather die than feel like this. I'm leaving today." Snatching my arm back, I reached for the handle, turning away from him again for what I hoped was the last time.

"Please don't leave me," he whispered, his voice crackling and shaking.

"I'm not leaving you. You've already left me."

Storming out of the bathroom, I ran downstairs and over to the barn. I grabbed my out of charge mobile phone, laptop, purse, and threw some clothes into my school bag. Nathan stood at the barn, waiting for me with his sister and Lisa. We all left for school together. He kept glancing back at me as I walked behind them. I decided to go to school and figure out what I would do from there. All the way to school, I could feel him fizzing, but I didn't give him the opportunity to speak to me. I walked in with Danni and Katie, both of whom had apologised profusely for what happened, claiming that they didn't know what was going on until it was too late.

Going to classes, I just got on with my work but also worked on blocking Nathan's access to my thoughts. Realising at lunchtime I had succeeded, he walked into the dining hall, apprehensively sweeping around and a smile lighting up his face as his eyes landed on my face. The relief was palpable. He got his lunch and walked back to his table. He didn't look up as I walked out of the dining hall, but caught up with me as I walked out of the school doors.

"Come with me please." he asked solemnly.

Shaking my head as I headed in the other direction, I looked back and he had tears running down his face. "Jas, I'm sorry... but please... I... I need you... I can't do this without you..." he broke off as I turned away and walked into the shaded trees, by the side of the school. He followed me, catching my arm as I walked away from him and I spun towards him, "No, Nathan. You do not get to do this to me again. You can't keep swinging backwards and forwards from me to her, have her stay, and expect me to say everything is fine. I can't do it and I won't. If you really love me, let me go."

I stormed away from him into the woods, but could hear from the snapping of twigs and leaves that he followed behind me. I could see a circle of stones up ahead and stomped towards them, but heard an odd sound in the bushes behind me. Nathan's footsteps had stopped and I heard an odd gurgling sound. Turning back and unable to see him scared me.

"Nathan, where are you? This isn't funny!" I called out, scanning around the different trees with my eyes. Walking backwards, I could just make out an odd shuffling sound and a dragging sound. After walking along for another few moments in the gloom with only the sounds of the dripping raindrops for company and heavy breathing somewhere close by, it felt much longer. Stumbling over a branch, I scrambled but kept my balance then slipped in a pool of what looked like blood. I couldn't see very clearly, but I reached down and touched it. It felt like blood. Suddenly, something solid hit me on the back of the head and I was knocked to the floor, seeing stars. My head ached, but I felt myself dragged deeper into the woods.

Eventually after a few minutes, we reached a small clearing and I could see a circle of stones, but my head was foggy with a sick dizziness upon me. I turned my head slightly to the left and could see Nathan lying on the ground, holding his stomach. Beyond him, I could see these odd-looking half-bird men, where the faces were covered in feathers and mouths in the shape of beaks. Their eyes were a deep yellow, almost gold. I gathered all this in a few seconds as my hands were tied behind my back.

Looking back at Nathan, I tried to figure a way out of this. I willed the ropes to loosen and could feel them oblige. I focused on this as Nathan spoke in a raspy, gurgling voice. "Let us go now..." he said before dissolving into a coughing fit. Blood and saliva flew out of his mouth. It made me stop what I was doing. I could see he didn't have much time left, judging by his colour and how his eyes rolled in his head, but he continued regardless, "Do you know who I am?"

One of the birdmen answered, "We do not care, human boy. We shall feast here today and move on before anyone misses you." The voice made the hairs on my arms rise; it was high pitched and squeaky, but cold as ice. My heart pounded as the rope binding my wrists fell away, but I lay with my arms in that position as the birdmen all convened around Nathan, shielding him from view.

I slowly sat up, trying not to disturb the foliage. My head was dizzy but I managed to find my feet. As the first birdman bent towards Nathan, I threw my arms out and tried to push him away as fast as I could, feeling the heat travel not just down my arms but from the very tips of my toes up into my head and out of my fingers. My eyes were closed, but I could hear rustling wings beating and footsteps coming closer to me again. I focused every fibre of my being on forcing these things away from us and when I opened my eyes, I could sense them circling above us like vultures.

"Hurry," Nathan whispered. "They'll be back."

"Can you walk?" I asked him.

"Not really, but you can help me..."

He broke off as I moved towards him. There was a huge puddle of blood beneath him and as I pulled him upright, he sagged into me.

"Get... us i-in...to..." he broke off as we heard wings coming closer, followed by the sound of leaves rustling and twigs breaking. He slipped lower and I pulled him closer to the circle as the birdmen walked back into the clearing, smirking in the beak mouths. All I could see were teeth, razor sharp and grass green in colour.

"Well, well, what do we have here?" one asked.

"Not sure, but I bet it's tasty!" a voice came from my left.

"Dibs," another voice came from behind me, to the right.

Nathan slipped and hit the ground at my feet. "FIGHT," his voice commanded faintly in my head. Closing my eyes, I could sense the creatures moving towards me. With all the rage about Nathan and his family, his constant mood swings, and all these creatures that kept trying to kill me, I felt this almighty fire spread down my arms. I spun around, hearing these squeals of pain and smelling singed hair.

Looking down, I could see Nathan's eyes rolling around. Looking up, I could see the birdmen flying overhead, circling again like vultures. The rain came down heavier. I reached down, grabbed hold of Nathan, and dragged him a few feet further into the circle, placing the stones around us, just as the birdmen landed again.

"Where did they go?" I heard one ask.

"They are still here. Can't you smell the blood?" said another viciously. "Find them. She will pay for hurting us. The silly girl has no idea what we are capable off. Now all of you fly and bring her to me, I will break her bones one by one."

Focusing on Nathan, I touched his injury and he shook. Drawing my hand across it, I could feel some tingling in my fingers, followed by some burning and then numbness. I hadn't been looking at the cut, but could feel the blood slowing. His breathing eased and he relaxed. The sounds of the birdmen faded into the background, as they shrieked and flapped around, trying to find us. Watching the colour come back into Nathan's face was like nothing I had ever experienced before, or since. It was the first time I knew that I could save him as much as he could save me.

Sitting there for a few hours, covered from the rain by a canopy of trees, with the occasional shrieks from the birdmen, Nathan slept and I kept watch. After the few hours passed, there was activity in the woods, as Jenny, Lisa, and some of the boys from both of our years called his name. They walked right by us, pausing at the puddle of blood.

"This is Nathan's blood." Jenny told the others. "We need to find him now. If she has hurt my brother, I will end her." Jenny sounded vindictive, but Lisa had noticed the feathers dotted around.

"Oh my God, Jenny. There are Kinnaras here. Your dad must be told. Oh my God, if they have Nathan..." she choked out, with tears running down her face. Jenny walked over and slapped her.

"Nathan is too smart to walk into a trap set by them. There is no human blood here. We need to move on, but stick together. Kinnaras hate demons and will kill us to get back at my father." They walked through the woods to our left and I watched them go, feeling a little apprehensive as I thought about how we would explain this one. Nathan squeezed my hand and I started. Looking down, he smiled up at me, looking a little perplexed.

"Hey," he managed, his voice sounding crackly.

"Hey, yourself. How are you feeling?"

"Okay, I guess, considering I was nearly eaten by a Kinnara. How did you save me?"

"Honestly, I don't know. I couldn't lose you, but I don't know how I managed it."

He smiled up at me again and sat up slowly, using my arms to help himself up before leaning into me and kissing me. He groaned as his lips met mine. We were both wet from the drips of rainwater from the canopy of trees. He kissed me harder, one of his hands snaking behind my neck and the other pulling my back closer to him. He kissed me so passionately and with such fire, my breath came out in pants. Stopping suddenly, he looked at me, his face flushed. "We have to go now!"

I just looked at him, trying to get my breathing under control. He stood, held his hand out to me, and pulled me to my feet. I stumbled and fell into his arms. He just steadied me, and then moved me away from him. Turning away from me, he walked to the edge of the circle. "Come on. We can't stay here. Hurry."

He walked away quickly and I followed, wondering what had caused his sudden change in behaviour. I thought about it as we walked back home. He stayed a little ahead of me the whole time and when we arrived, he walked into the house without once looking back. Watching him walk into that house was difficult, but not as hard as going into the barn. I walked in, changed, and pushed my already packed bag into a plastic bag, and then into the sleeping bag. Having just finished that, my head was yanked backwards and I was dragged into the barn area.

"What happened to you today? Why were you off school this afternoon?" Mr Stevenson asked me, his hand still snaked in my hair. When he had finished, he pulled and I yelped. "Well?" he asked again.

"I felt sick so I came back." I answered quickly, gasping in pain as he pulled again.

"Was Nathan with you?"

"Nathan? Your son?" I asked, terrified about Nathan.

"No, I bloody wasn't," Nathan's voice came from the barn door. He looked at me in disgust. "Why would I spend my time with a mortal?" His tone suggested complete contempt.

Mr Stevenson threw me across the barn and I smacked my head in the exact same spot that I had been hit earlier. "Don't leave school again without permission. Nathan, what do you want?"

"Mother asked me to find you. You have a phone call." They walked out together and I retched. My head spun, but clarity had formed. Oh my God, Nathan had kissed me like that to make sure I stayed. He couldn't have me leave because his family would know he helped me.

"Yes." His voice said sadly in my head.

"I really hate you now. You used my feelings for you against me."

Crawling into bed shivering, I closed myself off to him. I didn't want to speak to him, or hear him. He was just using me. I was numb and I fell asleep with this numbness inside me. I awoke freezing at four a.m. Looking around, I caught something moving from the corner of my eye, but before I could make it out, my eyes closed and I drifted back to sleep.

I awoke the next day, Thursday, not realising the date until I went to school. I was numb and wasn't paying attention to anything. School passed in a blur of numbness and hurt. As I left school, I saw Nathan and Lisa sneaking off into the woods, laughing. It was like a knife in my gut. When I got home, I changed my soaking wet clothes into some dry jogging bottoms, a thick fleecy jumper, and fleecy socks, and climbed into my sleeping bag. I found a wrapped present and a small note.

I opened the gift — a small rose pendant for my charm bracelet. I attached it straight away then opened the note.

You have my heart. It belongs to you more than it belongs to me. I am so sorry I am hurting you, but it's the only way I can keep you safe. All my love, always and forever Nate xxx

CHAPTER 7
HEAT AND HEARTACHE

The next few days passed without Nathan speaking to me, or even acknowledging me. By Saturday night, he hadn't spoken to me at all since Wednesday. I spent most of the morning in the barn, doing homework and messing around with some Sudoku quizzes.

Around lunchtime, the barn door opened and I heard footsteps. I didn't bother to look around, thinking it was just them brining food. The footsteps got closer and I flinched, until I smelled a familiar scent of vanilla from his aftershave. It wrapped around me and I turned to look at him. He smiled down at me. "What are you doing?" he asked with a glint in his eyes.

"Playing Sudoku. What do you want?" I asked, turning away with difficulty.

"I miss you. I'm bored and I wondered if you wanted to come in the house and watch a movie with me. I have popcorn, chocolate, and marshmallows."

"No, we can't. I'm not allowed," I answered sadly, not bothered one way or the other though.

"They aren't in and will be out the rest of the day. Come on, baby. I miss you."

"Are you still with Lisa?" I asked snappily.

"Well yes, but you know why I have to be with her. Come on, Jas. I wanna spend some time with you please."

Opening my mouth to say no, I made the mistake of looking at him and said something completely different.

"Okay then, but I get to pick the movie, and you have to break up with

Lisa."

He looked sadly at me, "I can't do that."

"Then I'm fine, thanks. Enjoy your movie."

Turning back to my Sudoku, I ignored him and he left after a few moments, staring at me morosely. I didn't flinch, but as soon as the barn door closed, I let out the sob building up in my throat. I fidgeted with my pendant and the tears flowed. The barn door opened and he stood there looking torn.

"I did it, just texted her. I can't hurt you like this. If I could do it over, I wouldn't get back with her, but I need you safe." He pulled me into his arms and his familiar scent enveloped me. He cried as well and eventually he said, "Come on. We have a movie to watch."

Walking into the house, he held my hand as we settled down to watch *The Fast and the Furious*. His choice, but I wasn't really watching. I couldn't relax and after twenty minutes, I walked back to the barn. Twenty seconds later, there were sounds of a car and his sister's voice yelling about how she had forgotten something.

The barn door opened and there were footsteps. I didn't glance up and the footsteps went right back out the door, closing it softly. I knew that it was Mr Stevenson checking that I was where I was supposed to be, but I didn't know why he was checking. He supposedly trusted Nathan.

Fifteen minutes later, Nathan walked back into the barn, sporting a bloody nose and two black eyes. I hadn't looked around on his arrival, but as he walked into the barn and kicked away the camping chair, I jumped up.

"What happened?" I asked, walking over to him with my hand outstretched. He slapped my hand away, fuming,

"Oh, don't fucking ask!" he snapped at me. "This is all your fault. Break up with Lisa, Nathan. I love you, Nathan. Yeah, you love to see me hurting, don't you?"

Looking at him, I stepped back. "Get out. Just go away, Nathan!"

He turned around and stormed out, slamming the barn door so hard it bounced back and hit me full on the head. I yelped, but he didn't even turn round, which made me angrier. Putting my hand up to my head, I could feel blood tricking down. My head throbbed but I was too angry to heal myself. I got an old t-shirt and pressed that to my head for a few minutes until the blood stopped.

I sat, but I was too angry to settle to anything. I got up and walked to the door of the barn, but just as I reached it, Nathan walked in, holding a bag of goodies and a laptop.

Stepping away from him before I hit him, he just looked at me. "I'm sorry, Jasmine. I don't know where that came from. Please forgive me."

"That's all you say? Sorry and I love you? I'm sick of it. I want a normal relationship. I have to leave here."

"You can't leave here; they will kill you. We will leave soon, but for now, you have to be patient. Come on, let's watch a movie." He moved towards me, smiling, but looking wary, "Oh my God, what happened to your head?"

"Some asshole hit it with a door..." I answered him waspishly.

"Oh, I'm so sorry. I didn't realise. Baby, I'm so sorry. Please forgive me."

"I don't know if I can. What's real, Nathan? Are we real? Do you really love me or are you just trying to keep me here for your father? I can't figure us out. I want to believe that you love me, but I can't. I don't know what to trust anymore and all these games tear me up and make me question everything." My voice cracked and he reached out to touch my cheek, but I stepped back. He looked at me longingly and dropped his hand to his side as he spoke quietly to me.

"Jas, I love you with every fibre of my being, so much so that it terrifies me. You are the only thing with any power over me. My whole life I've had any girl I wanted and because of who I am, they have wanted me too. But with you, I never wanted to feel like this. I feel like every move I make hurts you. I want you to see how incredible you are and to feel how deeply I love you, to the very depths of my soul." He shuddered and reached out again to touch me, running his finger down my cheek before I stepped back, moving away from him and shaking my head to try and block out his words.

He continued speaking, but his voice was hoarse and pain rose like a tsunami in my chest. "Before you, Jas, I didn't have a heart. Then you appeared like a lightning bolt and now my heart beats just for you. Your smiles make it all worthwhile. I'm scared, more scared than I've ever been. Not only could I lose you, but I could lose us. We mean more to me than anything, ever has or ever will. Every time I touch you, kiss you, feel you, I feel my soul light up. It's all because of you. I can't let you leave. I love you more than my own life, and when the time comes, we will leave here and make a life together. You're the other half of me."

Hearing him affirm how he felt about me made my knees weak and I buckled, landing on the sandy ground. He sat beside me, and reached over to touch my hand. His fingers stroked my hands as he continued, "Please believe me. I love every single little thing and I'll do whatever I can to protect you, to save you. You have to believe me, I won't let anyone hurt you and even if it seems like I'm hurting you, I'm just trying to shield you from them." He pulled me into his arms and held onto me as though I was a wisp of smoke. He held on to me so tight it was as though he was trying to keep me from vanishing. I went to pull away, he shook and I could feel the tears dripping down my own face; seeing him lose it made my heart ache badly. We sat like that for a while, at the door, with the wind and rain battering us. Eventually though, we got too cold.

Moving was hard; he was still upset and I was more than confused. I loved him with everything, but I couldn't say it to him. He had just poured his heart out to me and I said nothing to him. Moving away from him, I walked over to my stall, and changed out of my wet clothes.

He still sat in the doorway as I fought with my jumper. It stuck to me and I shivered with the cold. Suddenly, I could feel his hands helping me. He turned me towards him and looked at me with a hunger I had never seen in his eyes before. He pulled me towards him, running his hands up and down my arms, and reached down to kiss me. The rainwater ran from his hair, raising goose bumps on my arms. Shivering again, he pulled me in tighter and his top soaked right through my own. My white top had become see-through because of the water, making me very self-conscious.

He looked down and smiled, running his hands up my chest. My breath sped up and he kissed down my neck, the water from his hair still running as he moved his head. He kissed back up to my lips and pulled me down to the floor, his hands wandering with one hand around my waist, holding me in position; the other rubbed circles on my breast.

All of a sudden, the front door of the barn banged open and crashed off the wall, making us jump, breaking our moment. Both our hearts raced, but the spell of lust was broken.

"I should get back." He stood up slowly and moved away from me.

"Nathan..." I said, unsure of how to continue.

"Jasmine?" he asked as he turned his whole body towards me, half-smiling at me. I just looked at him, feeling dumbstruck. His face was flushed and his eyes were on fire. His lips were red and the way he looked at me gave me butterflies.

The barn door flew open and we both looked around in shock to see Lisa standing there. She glared at me.

"Lisa, what the hell are you doing here?" he asked venomously.

"I knew it. I fucking knew it. You two are together. I told Jenny and she said there was no chance, but I knew it!"

Abruptly, she turned and flew towards me, screaming obscenities. Nathan caught her before she hit me, spitting out, "What are you talking about? Of course, we aren't together. She's nothing but a fucking mortal. Are you insane?"

"What are you doing in here then?" she asked, sounding petulant.

"I'm helping her with her homework! She struggles with math and I was helping her. Her failing reflects badly on my father, but enough about the mortal. What are you doing here?" he commanded in a voice that caused the barn to rattle.

Avoiding looking at them, I turned around and pretended to be concentrating on my textbook, which had suddenly appeared at my feet.

"I wanted to talk to you. You dumped me by text. Who does that?"

I smiled a small smile as I flipped open the pages of my maths text book. I had turned my back to them and I felt Nathan stir.

"Come on, we are not talking about this here. I never texted you. I don't know what you are talking about."

My breath caught, but I didn't look around.

"Go over to the house. I'll be there in a second. I need to grab my phone and some of the stuff I brought over earlier."

I heard her walk away, muttering to herself. Nathan stood there for a few seconds, "Do you understand now? Does it make sense?"

"Perfectly," I said in a low voice, with tears in my eyes.

"Fine. See you Monday." He walked away without turning back. I was exhausted and I didn't want to give him the satisfaction of crying. I changed again out of my wet clothes, curled up in my sleeping bags, and fell asleep within a few moments.

I awoke a few hours later to the sound of paper crinkling.

> *I'm so sorry, baby. I couldn't think of what else to do. If she had reported us, we both would have been dead. I love you and I will make this up to you, but for the moment, I have to pretend to be with her. P.S. Here's a cupcake for your birthday. It's at the back of the tent.*

I read the note, but didn't bother looking for the cupcake. I was too mad at him and too hurt. I turned around in the tent, turned on the lantern, and almost knocked the tent over as I jumped. Nathan sat at the bottom of the tent watching me.

"What are you doing here?" I hissed at him.

"I needed to see you."

"Why? I'm just a fucking mortal after all."

"Shut up, you know why I said that."

He crawled up the tent, freezing as a voice sounded outside the tent.

"Jasmine, are you in there?" Mrs Stevenson's voice called. He looked at me with pure terror in his expression and I got up and flew out of the tent.

"Yes, sorry. What's wrong?"

"Have you seen Nathan? He was supposed to be home by now, but we haven't seen him yet."

"No, sorry. I don't know where he is."

"Okay, if you see him, tell him to come straight home please."

Nodding at her, my heart raced at having to lie, but there was no way I could tell her Nathan was currently in my tent. I climbed back into my tent and Nathan was as white as a ghost. Opening my mouth, I was about to ask him what was wrong but he put his finger over my lips and shook his head.

I listened and could hear breathing outside the tent, followed by quiet footsteps and the barn door closing softly. I went out of the tent again on the pretext of getting another jumper from my bag and noticed Mrs Stevenson standing in the shadows of the door. As soon as she saw me looking curiously at her, she turned and walked out the door.

Nathan came out when the door was closed, but stayed crouched down so he was hidden from all other stalls. I looked around and saw Jenny and Lisa sitting in a stall across from us, staring right at me.

"What's going on, girls?" I asked, sounding braver than I felt.

"Nathan is missing and we figured he might be in here with you?" Lisa's voice suggested waspishly, stinging through the air. I could almost feel the hatred rolling off her in waves.

"Why would Nathan be here? He hates me. Remember?"

They just shrugged and sat there staring at me. I shook my head in mock exasperation and climbed back into the tent, followed by Nathan. Picking up a pencil and some paper, I motioned to Nathan to read my note.

> *I have to get you out of here.*
>
> *Yeah, but how?*
>
> *A portal?*
>
> *Sure, go for it.*

Closing my eyes, I focused all my energy on finding the cliff face, the cave where we felt safe. I found a portal after a few seconds, but it was struggle to open it in the right location. I opened it up and Nathan kissed me quickly on the cheek, before jumping through. He had been going for my lips, but I turned away from him and he caught my cheek. Seeing him in the cave, I quickly closed over the portal, picked up my notepad, and put that piece of paper down my top.

Seconds later, my tent opened and Jenny dragged me out by the hair, snarling at me. "Where is my brother?"

I shook my head, "I don't know." I gasped out in pain as she dragged me across the barn to the opposite side. Lisa opened up the tent and looked around, but came out looking disappointed, "She's telling the truth. Nathan's not here."

"Lucky that you are," Jenny hissed in my ear, throwing me down to the ground and kicking me in the ribs viciously. Feeling all the air escape from my lungs and the burning in my sore ribs, I rolled over onto my stomach, as the barn door closed and the two of them walked away, leaving me gasping for breath.

The next few hours passed slowly, but eventually Nathan appeared in the barn, holding Lisa's hand. Sitting in the doorway of the tent wrapped in my sleeping bag, I saw them coming as I read a book by the light of the lantern. Lisa smiled vindictively and Nathan looked very uncomfortable. When Lisa looked at him though, he possessed a nasty glint in his eye.

"Here is your food." His voice was loud and sounded as though he was smiling, but I stared away from them. He spoke again, this time directly into my, his voice disgusted as he muttered, "Don't eat it. It's made of mud and other disgusting things."

They turned and walked away, but not before she spun towards him, face turned up, looking for a kiss. I grimaced and Nathan glanced quickly back at me before complying and kissing her deeply, though not with as much passion as he kissed me.

My eyes burned and a lump rose in my throat, I turned my eyes back to my book and fixed my face into a mask of feigned indifference. I didn't look up as he apologised in my head, or as the barn door slammed shut.

Getting up, I needed to move, needed to get out of the barn as that image burned into my vision. "Don't. It's a test. They are watching you to see how you react."

Pacing up and down for a while, I realised I wanted to go for a run but I knew that they were watching me. I changed into my PJs, emptied the food out at the back of my barn, in a hole covered by a large boulder and I went to bed, trying my hardest not to think about him kissing her. Failing, I could see a small spark there and it hurt like hell.

Eventually I fell asleep reading my book and I awoke the next morning feeling determined that I would break away from Nathan. I felt like that for a while until I opened my book and found a note tucked up inside it.

They are testing you. I am so sorry, but it feels like it's all I can say at the moment. Just know it's you I love and I won't give up on us. Please don't give up on us. We have an amazing future together and we will be amazing when we get away from them.
All my love, N xxxx

The next few days passed without incident but at night, Nathan visited me, trying to get me to speak to him. I ignored him until Tuesday night. I hadn't acknowledged him at all, ignored him on our walk to and from school, and at night. One of the boys in school bumped into me on the stairs that day and knocked me down three stairs, right into Nathan. Electricity flowed down my arms as I steadied myself on his arm.

Looking up at him, about to apologise, I was dragged away from him and shoved towards the stairs. Lisa was there and I was so consumed by Nathan that I didn't notice. Stumbling again, Lisa chose that moment to say, "Oh, for fuck's sake, will you move?" She shoved me and I just lost it. I hated everything and everyone in that moment and I went for her. I slammed her face into the wall and felt numerous hands trying to grab me, but I wriggled out of them and clawed at her face.

"Jasmine, stop right now. What do you think you are doing to my girlfriend?" Nathan asked, sounding disgusted. He grabbed me and threw me against the wall. "Leave now, everyone. Leave now..." he broke off, looking angrier than I had ever seen him. Lisa went for me again and he stepped in front of me. "LEAVE..." he bellowed.

He turned back to me and I shrank away from his furious glare. After a couple of moments, the staircase emptied but his gaze didn't soften. "What the fuck are you doing? I'm trying to protect you and this is how you behave. Are you completely insane? Do you want them to kill you?"

All the rage left me and I started shaking.

"Don't start with the water works. I'm not interested. How could you do that, Jasmine?" I looked anywhere but at him, fighting against the lump in my throat. I couldn't speak. I knew opening my mouth would mean I would break. Nathan reached out to touch me but the door at the stairwell opened, "LEAVE NOW..." he bellowed and whoever it was moved backwards and closed the door.

He pushed me against the wall, growling at me, "I can't protect you from your own stupidity, so I'm done trying. Whatever this was, it's over now. You're on your own. I'm done."

He turned and stormed up the stairs, leaving me feeling broken. He actually broke me apart. I couldn't believe I trusted him. Turning, I ran downstairs to the lockers and got my bag. I knew what I was doing was dangerous, but I couldn't stay anymore. I left the school, sneaking out the door near the trash bins.

The tears flowed freely and I ran into the woods and beyond. Once I was in town, I went to the bank and withdrew some of my savings. I knew where I was going — Glasgow. I had a friend from my days in the home there. I walked over to the bus stop to wait for the bus.

My head swam and I could feel Nathan trying to get in so he could figure out where I was. "GET OUT!" I shouted at him and felt him wince at the power. He didn't try to get back in again and I sat there for thirty minutes waiting on the bus. As it arrived, ten minutes late, so did the cavalry. Nathan appeared at the bus stop. He didn't say a word, but grabbed my arm as I walked towards the bus. He held on so tight he hurt me. I tried to fight him off and as the bus drove away, leaving me behind, I was more than furious. He held on tighter as I turned on him. "You are an absolute fucking bastard! What did you do that for? You said you were done. I NEED TO LEAVE HERE..." I all but screamed at him.

He pulled me towards the trees, deeper and deeper into the woods, not saying anything at all. Once we were in the woods, he continued pulling me along, not stopping as I tripped over branches and slipped on the wet leaves. Eventually, we reached the path to the cave and he was forced to let me go, but he pushed me ahead of him down the path, still not saying anything.

Going into the cave, I was stunned. There were roses and chocolates, candles and a note to Lisa. I turned on him, trying to leave, but he blocked the cave mouth.

"Let me go..." I hissed at him.

"No, listen to me."

"Why did you bring me here? Do you like hurting me, Nathan? Does it... does it give you some sick twisted pleasure to say that I have your heart... then to bring me here when you have done all this for her..." I broke off, the lump in my throat closing off my words.

"Yes, that's why I did this. Jasmine, look at me," he sounded desperate, but I couldn't. I hurt more than ever.

"Why... why couldn't you just let me leave? I hate you for this. I will never forgive you for this."

He stepped aside, his face showing indifference, but his eyes glossed over as he spoke, "Then go. Just leave. We're over anyway." He closed his eyes and turned away from me as his voice came out in barely more than a whisper, "If you really believe I did this for her, then go."

Walking away from him in that cave was one of the most difficult things

I had ever done, but I knew he wanted me to leave. I walked back through the woods and straight into the barn. I went straight to bed, but within twenty minutes, Mr Stevenson dragged me out of the tent by my hair and he punched me a few times in the stomach. After a few minutes, he left and I just lay there, curled into a ball, wondering how I would escape from this nightmare.

Nodding off, I awoke shivering and in pain. Nathan watched in tears. He walked towards me and I flinched, pulling back from him. "Just leave please. I can't take anymore today."

He paused then walked over to me, lifted me up and carried me into the tent. Placing me in my sleeping bag, he leaned down and kissed me on my forehead, whispering, "I'm so sorry. I'll fix this. Please let me fix this?" His tears dripped onto my forehead as he held his lips there and I drew in a fortifying breath before speaking to him.

"I can't, Nathan. It's over. We're done."

"I will fucking fix this, Jas. Just fucking watch me. Please don't give up on us. You have to know I'm trying to save you."

I shook my head and he leaned down and kissed me again on the lips this time, then he vanished. I fell into a sleep where I dreamed that we were through all of this and we had three beautiful children running around playing. When I awoke, I was sore, tired, and hurting more so because of the dream. We had been so happy, and now I was back in the present where I couldn't trust him not to fuck with me. My head and heart pounded as I decided that no matter what, I couldn't let him hurt me again.

CHAPTER 8
HELL AT THE DISCO

The next few days were hell, even by my standards. No one at school spoke to me until Thursday. Nathan blanked me out during the day, but visited at night, trying to convince me that he loved me. I didn't believe him. I couldn't.

Danni spoke to me at school that day, asking if I was going to the Halloween disco the next night.

"Sure, if you girls are going, I will come along." Anything for a distraction would do. I was wallowing and needed to cheer up.

"Yeah, we are all going. Do you want to come to my house and get ready? All the other girls are."

"That sounds great. I can't wait." I tried to muster some enthusiasm, but I couldn't seem to find the energy to care.

Nathan approached me later that day in the dining hall. "I need to tell you that we're all going to the Halloween disco tomorrow. You're going too." He spat the words at me, not looking at me, and walked away before I could say anything. I watched him walk out the door, past Lisa who glared at him, and then turned. I looked away and started talking to Katie.

"Lisa is drawing daggers at you." Katie supplied.

"That's not really a surprise, is it though?" I asked her. "She hates me. I mean she has tried to kill me this year."

"Yeah, and she is convinced something is going on with you and Nathan, especially since he dumped her again at break." It sounded like Katie was fishing, but I didn't rise.

"They'll be back together tomorrow, anyway. What are you dressing up as? I saw a cool costume from *Alice in Wonderland*. I'm going to try to get that after school."

"Dressing up? No, we don't do that here. That is so uncool. Girls, Jas just asked if we were dressing up."

All the girls laughed and I breathed a sigh of relief at the subject change. The topic of dressing up carried us through lunchtime and into our next classes. I dreaded this class — English. Nathan was not only in this class, but he sat beside me.

He studiously ignored me as I arrived, but as I sat, he took my hand under the table, giving it a little squeeze. It made my heart gallop. I snatched my hand away and put it on the table, focusing on the teacher. Today's subject was hyperbole and it was really interesting. I soon became engrossed and Nathan nudged me after a few moments when I ignored him. I shifted in my seat, placing my hand on my lap. He placed a piece of paper in my open palm.

Did you hear I dumped Lisa?

I nodded my head, but didn't reply. He took the paper back and wrote more.

Tomorrow will be fun. I'm going to get you alone so we can talk.

Shaking my head, I wondered why he wasn't speaking to me. Why was he resorting to notes? When the teacher asked me a question, I was stumped, but Nathan passed me a piece of paper, with the answer written on it.

Hyperbole is a type of exaggerated statement and shouldn't be taken literally. An example of hyperbole is in Dulcet et Decorum est. when Yeats describes the solders as drunk with fatigue, deaf even to the hoots, of gas shells dropping softly behind which shows that they are exhausted and almost blinded by how tired they felt to dangers of the shells dropping nearby,

I answered and the teacher glared at us, but continued to question the rest of the class and I concentrated on the poem in front of me, examining it for more metaphors, alliteration and examples of hyperbole. I studiously ignored Nathan and although he would occasionally squeeze my thigh, he ignored me too, focusing on his work.

He didn't pass any further notes, bar one, which he slipped into my textbook before he left. I didn't find it until that night when I was about to start my homework.

> *You were wondering why I didn't just speak to you. You've blocked me. I can hear you, but can't answer. Please let me back in. I love you. I miss your smile, laugh, and I will never forgive myself for making you hate me. Please Jas, just try let me back in. My world isn't the same without you. I miss you. N xxx*

I shook my head, but could feel my resolve wavering. I felt him sigh as the walls tumbled down, even though I tried my hardest to build them back up.

Much later in the night he appeared in the barn. "We have to talk," he whispered, pulling me upright. I groaned as he pulled me into his arms, kissing my head, but I was stiff and cold so I didn't respond.

I glanced down at his watch and pulled it up close to me so I could see it. "Nate, for fucksake, it's two in the morning. Couldn't this have waited."

His chest shook with laughter and I wanted to punch him. "No babe, I'm sorry, it couldn't." He kissed the top of my head and the tip of my nose, tilting my chin up so he could capture my lips in a soul shattering kiss. "I've missed you," he breathed against my lips before he sighed and started speaking quickly. He sounded nervous as he spoke.

"Tomorrow is the eve of Halloween. We will be at the disco from half past six until half past nine. We don't dress up in costumes since that would be ridiculous, but you have to make an effort. My mum has bought you a dress and tomorrow night, you will be allowed into the house to get ready."

Nodding sleepily, I didn't say anything, but tried to go back into my sleeping bag to get some sleep. He sat beside me in the tent and turned on the lantern to the lowest setting. After a few moments of silence he squeezed my hand and I closed my eyes as he laced his fingers with my own.

I started to shiver with the cold and he let go of me. I moved into the sleeping bag and he followed, snuggling down beside me and laying his head beside mine. "I love you. You know that. Right?" He pulled my head onto his chest as I nodded at him and he leaned down, kissing the top of my head. "Whatever happens in the next few days, remember that I love you and you are the only person who has the power to make me better..."

He broke off and I fell asleep in his arms, wondering what he was talking about, but too tired to dwell on it for long.

The next day passed quickly and everyone was consumed with the disco that night; even I'd started to get a little excited. Getting home from school, Nathan's mum approached me in the barn and told me she had set up my room for me to get ready, but after the disco, I was to come back to the barn. Walking with her into the house felt odd, but not as much as walking into the room and seeing a few of my belongings still scattered about.

"You can collect the rest of your stuff another day. You have to get dressed now. You have one hour."

As she walked away, I went straight in for a shower and scrubbed until my body felt red raw. Getting out of the shower, I walked into the room and saw a gorgeous emerald green dress sitting on the bed. The dress was long and had waves at the front, with a silver hoop belt. Silver shoes and a silver clutch sat on the bed with an assortment of makeup.

I dried my hair, curling it down the side so it hung over my left shoulder and I accessorised with a silver necklace that had a teardrop on it and earrings to match. I put on a minimal amount of makeup, just eye shadow, eyeliner, and mascara with a little lip-gloss, I was ready to go.

Walking into the hall, I saw Nathan at his room door, looking very dapper in a grey shirt, striped black and grey tie, and dark jeans. As he turned towards me, I saw him groan, and his gaze heated up. He walked towards me, looked like he was about to compliment me, but I then heard his sister's door open and he barged past me, growling, "Watch where you're going, mortal."

He walked down the stairs, saying sweetly in my head, "I'm sorry, baby. You look stunning."

As I turned and walked towards the stairs, his sister glared at me but didn't say a word to me, which made me very uncomfortable. As we reached the bottom step, I could make out a conversation between Nathan and his father, "Remind them that if they touch her, I will end them," his father said, sounding exceptionally angry.

"I will, Father, but are you sure you want them to be tempted by her?" Nathan asked, sounding worried.

"They will not betray me. They know better!" With that, his father walked into sight as he stood at the bottom of the staircase, smiling at Jenny. "Daughter, you look wonderful."

He said nothing to me, didn't even look in my direction as he motioned to the door, saying, "The car is waiting. Come on. Let's go." As I reached the door, he grabbed my arm, hissing into my ear, "Stay with Nathan and Jenny. Do not leave until I come to get you. Do you understand?"

"Yes, sir." I nodded solemnly, noticing that Nathan was in the front seat of the car and Jenny was in the back, the car had seven seats.

As I climbed in, Jenny said, "Sit in the back. We have a few pickups to make."

Driving into town was fine, but as we started picking up more people, I noticed that they all ignored me, with the exception of Lisa who sat directly in front of me. She kept glancing back and glaring at me, her long blond hair swishing as the turned. If looks could kill, I would have been dead and buried.

Finally, we arrived at the school and I met Danni, Kate, and Lisa Q walking into the hall. I didn't see Nathan for a while, and then noticed him with his friends, all of whom kept looking at me, making me very uncomfortable.

Lisa felt it too and said, "Are you feeling like the last piece of candy in a sweet shop?"

"Yes, thank God you're feeling it too. Let's go and get a drink?"

"Yeah, sure. We can stop looking like a deer in headlights."

We walked away together and chatted about books when Nathan and a few of his friends materialised at our sides — Joe and two others, named Jackson and Liam. Jackson and Liam stared at us almost hungrily, but both Nathan and Joe looked uncomfortable.

"Well, girls, don't we look delish tonight," Jackson snidely commented, reaching out to touch my arm. His touch made my skin cold and I ice shot up my arm from his gentle fingers, but it was the look in his eyes that churned my stomach. He watched me hungrily and licked his lips as he stared down at me. I couldn't move and I began to shiver as the ice flooded down towards my heart. Nathan cleared his throat once and he ice feeling left me. As I chanced a glanced at Nathan, who just stood there, he asked, "Can't we just have a bite?"

"No, my father's edict is still in place. Now let her go. Go back to the dance, you two. Now." He wasn't asking and his tone had scared me, so we did as he ordered. We walked away, but Jackson wasn't about to let Nathan ruin his fun. He reached out, grabbed me by the throat, and pulled me towards him. He twisted my arm up my back and pulled it tighter and tighter. Nathan looked furious as he dragged me across the corridor and into a vacant classroom.

"Come on, Nathan. Just a taste. Here, I'll start." He cut my wrist so a little blood dripped out, but before he could bring it to his lips, Nathan had thrown us clean across the classroom.

"DON'T YOU DARE BREAK THE SANCTITY OF AN EDICT..." he bellowed at him while he held me. I could feel myself getting breathless and my face grew redder. "NOW LET HER GO, OR I WILL FUCKING END YOU."

Jackson's hand loosened on my neck and Nathan walked over, helped me to my feet, and said, "Go clean yourself up and tell no one of what happened in here."

I nodded and walked out of the classroom, heading towards the bathrooms. As soon as I was inside the bathroom, the tears threatened, but I swallowed the lump in my throat. As I stood cleaning the blood on my arm, I decided to thank Nathan for rescuing me, knowing that it couldn't have been easy for him to curb his friends or make them let me go.

My body moved almost of its own volition back towards the classroom and as I walked I thought about what I was going to say to Nathan. When I reached the room the first thing I noticed was that the door was ajar and that a funny smell came from inside, kind of like cooking meat. Walking closer, I could see through the window panel on the door that a boy around my age was being stripped of his flesh by a crowd of demons, all gathered around him.

I stared blankly into the room, unable to move and I could see sinew, muscle, and blood dripping onto the floor. The boy seemed completely unaware, but turned his gaze towards me. In his eyes, I could see only pain and terror. Gasping aloud, I shoved my fist into my mouth and bit down hard as the flesh in their hands sizzled and turned browner, and the aroma of cooking beef became stronger. The smell then turned sour and the smell made my eyes water. My voice caught in my throat and made me gag.

I felt my stomach turn, but it soon dropped right through the soles of my feet as one of the demons turned towards me. I recognised him. Nathan stood there with muscle, blood, and flesh, in his hands as he froze, taking me in, before he shoved everything in his hands into his mouth.

Revolted I spun on my heel and flew back down the corridor, trying not to throw up. Hearing footsteps, I moved faster as one of them chased after me. "Wait, Jasmine. Please wait," Nathan called after me. I ran around the corner and saw the same thing happening in a number of different classrooms. Feeling sicker than ever, I stopped, and leaning against the wall, I placed my head down to my knees.

Nathan touched me and I flinched, jumping away from him, "Don't touch me." I hissed out the words between my teeth, trying to stop myself from being sick.

"Move then; I can't be seen standing here beside you." His tone was ice cold and my whole body shivered at it.

I bit out, "I'm not going anywhere with you." I stayed with my head between my legs, wanting to lash out at him and feeling a tingling in my fingers. I worked to control it and breathed quickly in and out as I fought to control my emotions.

"Jasmine, come on. Please, just come with me." He grabbed my arm and I felt my stomach roll again, as an image of flesh in his arms threatened to overwhelm me. He pulled me along and shoved me into the medical room, locking the door before handing me a sick bowl.

"Look at me please," he begged, kneeling on the floor at my feet.

"I can't..." I answered, breaking off and swallowing hard.

"You were never meant to see that." His voice sounded distant, as a ringing sound took place in my ears. His hands made a circular motion on my back and I shivered at his touch, feeling revolted.

" Jas," he whispered, "I'm so sorry..."

I cut him off, unable to listen to him anymore. I couldn't stand it. "So that makes it okay? What happens at a Halloween disco? Is it just a... a ... well a fucking feeding fest for demons? And you are okay with that? Why...?" I broke off again, feeling sick at the thought.

He swallowed loudly and sighed before he spoke again, "Yeah, that's pretty much what happens and I'm sorry you had to see that. It's all I have ever known. I have to get back. Stay in here. Lock the door and I'll collect you later."

He leaned down, ignoring my flinch and softly grazed his lips on my forehead. He stood there for a moment, breathing me in and then turned to walk out the door, closing it behind him. As soon as he was gone, I locked the door, opening it a few moments later for Lisa, who looked faint.

She sat on the bench beside me and laid her head on my shoulder in an oddly comforting move. We sat like that for three quarters of an hour before Nathan came back, and knocked on the door. "It's time to go, ladies. Lisa, you are staying at our house tonight."

Lisa blanched at this and looked extremely apprehensive, which made me wonder what would happen next. Little did I know it would be worse than I ever imagined and would almost break Nathan and me apart for good.

As we arrived back at the Stevenson's there were more cars than ever, and the barn was lit up like a Christmas tree. Lisa and I were shown into the barn by Jenny and I noticed that Lisa suddenly had a sort of deadened look in her eyes. My breath caught in my chest as we walked further into the barn. There were a number of people, both old and young in age, with a few children, some as young as two or three, all sat with the same dead look on their faces.

I went into my stall, changed, and climbed into bed, wondering at the silence from Nathan and trying to get the image of him feeding on that person out of my head.

CHAPTER 9
A REAL TASTE OF HELL

The whole night I spent tossing and turning until the next morning. I saw the light rise through the window. Later that day, Nathan's mum came to the barn.

"Jasmine, wear this today," she said as she handed me a blood red dress, with a straight collar across the neck and a hem dropping down to the knees. She handed one to Lisa and the younger children, helping them into their dresses. Others wore robes of white with red roses on them and no one spoke, not even the youngest of the children.

Something struck me as ominous and as that thought entered so did Nathan's voice, "Behave please, Jas. This is important."

"What is, Nate?"

I could feel his smile at me using his nickname, but he didn't answer and didn't speak to me again for the remainder of the morning or afternoon.

Eventually, at around three p.m., Nate came into the barn with some food for me. He told me to hide the bowl of pasta and bread and not tell anyone he had fed me. He would get into a huge amount of trouble. He never said anything else to me and never answered any of the pleading questions I kept asking him.

At five minutes to six, his parents, brother, and sister, aunts, uncles, and cousins all came into the barn. They ordered everyone to stand at the tree and blindfolded all of the mortals. We were all led out of the stables, into woods and walked through the trees. I felt my clothes tugged at and asked Nate again, what was going on.

"Please just be quiet or you'll be killed."

The blindfold was then taken off for a short time and when I looked down, I was in some sort of blood-red cloak over my dress. I had no other choice than to follow the 'party' deeper into the woods where more and more voices gathered, each voice sounding louder and more rambunctious.

The atmosphere became quite jolly within the 'party', with members joking around with one another and laughing. I kept looking at Nate, but he kept his eyes straight ahead, moving swiftly through the trees. I then heard his dad and uncle talking about what I thought was me. I was in the lead, you see, the only one not bewitched and the only one alert enough to feel some fear about what would happen. I had concluded that everyone else was under some sort of enchantment as we were blindfolded; they all held still, but I glanced around before Nathan re-blindfolded me.

I almost cried aloud, but a word from Nathan made me stay quiet. "Don't make a sound, Jasmine!" he commanded.

I hated this and I wanted out of here. I could hear excerpts of their conversations, which scared me more than anything else that had happened that night. The people nearest me, the ones whose conversations were clear, were Mr Stevenson and one of his cousins. I had only met Jack, Nathans uncle, but this relative was even scarier. Nathan whispered, "Jas, don't even look at him, he's vicious."

"I have a blindfold on," I countered and Nate groaned, "Jas, for fucksake, just walk straight ahead and shut up."

A voice carried over the wind and I stiffened, only Nate's hand on my arm kept me moving forward as I took in what they were talking about. "Have you seen her luminosity? It's so bright." It was Brian, Lewis's best friend. Nate's voice travelled into my mind, telling me I needed to be very wary of him. Brian was deadly and he was almost one hundred so he could sense things that others missed. Nathan stopped there and I focused again on the conversation ahead of me.

As Mr Stevenson answered, "Yet, there is some force protecting it." I found it hard to keep walking and stumbled as Brian asked, with an odd tone, "But you will break that down surely?"

"Jas, please, focus. You are going to get us both killed here. Just walk okay? Just walk" I moved one foot in front of the other as I listened to their whispered conversation, trying to control how badly I was shaking.

Nate's dad answered, "Oh, yes. Of course, we shall, but we need to wait another year or so. She will not be ours until after she is eighteen. The laws of mortals, ridiculous huh?"

They then laughed and walked farther ahead. My head swam with this information and I could feel how uncomfortable and upset Nathan was. I felt completely alone and wondered how long it would take them to break me. I wondered what this meant.

All Nate said at that point was, "You'll see, but please don't dwell on it today. Just keep walking please." I tripped over a tree root, banging my head on the ground as my hands were tied. Not making a sound though, I was roughly picked up and pushed forwards. The whole time all I wanted to do was to ask Nate more questions. Where were we going? What was going on? Why I was blindfolded? Something made me keep my mouth shut.

My head bled a little as someone walked over to me and muttered something over my head. The blindfold was then taken off and I was able to scan my surroundings, but I heard a warning in my head from Nate and had to stop looking around. I wasn't responding to the incantation that had been placed on me in the proper manner. I was worried, tired, and more than a little hungry.

Mr Stevenson walked away to join the party and I was left standing with the other humans, none of whom looked scared or bothered by being in the woods, tied, and blindfolded. We were also on a path lit by low-hanging lanterns and extremely old trees. Looking around again in the lantern light as we started walking, my foot caught on a root again.

The night around me seemed filled with a tangible malice I could almost taste and one that I had never felt before. Since I was busy thinking about that and looking around at the trees lining our path, Nathan caught me before I could fall again. "Will you fucking watch where you're walking, you stupid little mortal bitch?"

It would have hurt less if he had slapped me. When I looked up, he wasn't looking at me but at his sister standing a foot away. She turned back to walk and he squeezed my hand gently before letting go. I heard his apology in my head and watched him walk back to his place in the procession.

What was going on here? I couldn't figure out what we were doing in the middle of the woods, why we had to come here, or what kind of people celebrate in the woods. I knew I had to stop thinking about these questions, which had no answers, and concentrate on where I was walking. I had a feeling that if I fell over again, that would be bad. Very bad indeed!

Eventually, after a little over an hour of walking, the pace quickened. We entered a clearing full of people I knew and others I had never seen. The women wore beautiful blood-red silk dresses and the men wore black shirts and trousers with red ties. The young were dressed in colours not as deep a blood red as the adults. Our party led us to the corner and sealed us in a space with other such mortals. Blood red ropes went around the circle and I sat there trying not to shake as I took in the scene around me.

The trees were basked in the glow of the lanterns, and although the clearing was large, it could barely fit the number of people in it. Every face out-with the ropes looked excited and expectant and within the ropes most of the people looked dazed, unable to focus and some had expressions as though they were completely out of it.

Most of them were older, over thirty. Two other young people had the same wide-eyed expression that I felt on my face. I tried to see if I could find Nate through the crowd, but it was too thick. I tried to reach out with my mind, but I couldn't get my mind to stretch as it normally would. I tried to untie the ropes at the edge of the circle and when that didn't work, I tried those on my hands, but I had no joy. It made me tense up to be sitting without being able to use my powers and I began freaking out as a group of around sixty and more came through the trees. Some of these people looked bewitched to me; it was just something about their deadened eyes that bewildered me.

I watched as those with the dead eyes were lead into another penned in area across the clearing from us. Some wore the same blood red clothing as me and others the white with red roses. My stomach began churning and nausea rose in my throat as I tried to figure out what was going on.

Another girl of around my age, and a boy not much younger than us showed some awareness as they came in with the next group, filling the clearing to a bursting point. Time went on; it was almost eight p.m. and the noise was all consuming. It seemed to be coming from everywhere when suddenly everything stopped. The music, the voices, and the chatter instantly died as if someone pressed the mute button.

Nate's dad then stood as everyone else sat as one, with no sound at all. The only thing I could hear for a moment in the dead silence was my heart thudding in my ears. I closed my eyes and felt four different pairs of hands on me. I tried to scream but no sound came out.

I was lead backwards and placed by a tree, held there by some invisible force as Nate's dad started speaking, "My dear brothers and sisters, nieces and nephews, we, family and friends, come together tonight October thirty-first to celebrate our birth from the blackness of the world. Our real faces shall be seen from this point forth until six a.m. tomorrow. No demon shall cover their true identity. It is now time for our first course. We have the blood of newborn lambs for your drinking pleasure and music from the harpies. Let's drink, dance, and be merry."

The faces all around turned into the hideously evil things that I'd seen a few times around school and although I knew what they looked like the sight of them creeped me out. They had skin like the bark of a tree, eyes as pitiless and black as the night, and mouths with teeth as sharp as sharks. Their hands curved into claws and the fingers joined to make two pointed fingers with a thumb behind them. These were the only visible changes and I wondered for a second what other changes would be taking place. I was terrified and looked down, but some unseen force turned my head towards them to watch them drinking and dancing around.

The music started and it sounded like breaking bones, cracking wood and nails on a blackboard. As it started a huge roar went up from the party goers and my blood ran cold as I caught a glimpse of Nathan. I could tell him, even with his demon face and he was standing with a demon with flowing blonde locks. Before he was swept up again in the crowd I saw him lean down and watched as his lips met hers.

I stared away and saw the harpies dancing around and laughing. They had flowing brown hair, pointed ears and wings that protruded from their simple brown dresses. They each had some sort of instrument and when one danced closer to me I could see pale coloured string, like a harp but made with bone and skin. My whole body revolted as she came closer to me, her brown eyes boring into my own.

"Well," she whispered, in a high pitched, breathless voice, "you're a special one aren't you?" I wanted to shake my head when she walked closer to me, but someone caught her arm. I didn't need to look to see it was Nathan, but hearing the coldness in his voice was painful, "what are you doing Entralla? You are supposed to be supplying our music. She is of no consequence to you, so stay away from her."

She nodded at him and backed away, as Nathan sank into the crowd again. I closed my eyes trying to block out the awful sounds that had started, it sounded like screeching, high pitched and so loud my ears rang. Everyone around danced to this, with the exception of those of us who were penned in like cattle.

After the harpy coming close to me not one of them looked at us and since they had only five of us lucid enough to feel fear and disgust, it didn't seem like they cared. I had no idea what would happen. Nate wouldn't answer me and I knew without knowing how or why, that I was all alone now in this nightmare. He had turned back into a monster and wasn't coming back for me.

CHAPTER 10
HELL ON HALLOWEEN

Eventually, the 'music' and dancing stopped after around three hours and my ears rang in the silence. I could barely hear as Nate's dad again stood. I gave myself a good shake as his mum stood. Together they spoke, "As it approaches the magical hour, we invite you all to bring out your offerings and enjoy. It's now dinner time!"

A loud cheer went up, breaking the sudden silence around the group gathered in the clearing, with the exception of the bewitched mortals who as time had gone on looked even more bewitched than before. I counted thirty-two of them, but there could have been many more, bewitched and unaware of what was going on. They were gathered and led into the centre of the group by numerous pairs of hands. Those who remained were left to watch, attached to the trees surrounding the clearing.

Placed in a loose circle around each family member, they were all naked, except for a sheet covering their modesty. Those in the middle of the group of demons didn't show any sign of fear. It seemed as though they were resigned to their fate, but I wasn't sure what this fate was. I had the sickest feeling in the pit of my stomach and I could barely watch what was going on.

Nate's parents then cleared their throats and spoke into the expectant silence "Let us consume our offerings now!" I already had an idea of what was coming, because of the disco. I knew it would be awful as each family member surrounded an offering. I became more than petrified and I tried to close my eyes, as the scene grew more horrifying. Because I was still attached to the tree, I was unable to run away, or fight.

I stared transfixed in horror as they sucked the various body parts around their victims, and although I was not able to see what they were getting from it, I could only imagine from the conversations I'd heard earlier in the evening.

Attempting not to look was difficult, as one by one, each victim fell to the ground, cut open with a sacrificial knife, or so Nate said in his mind, forgetting I could hear him. This was done, I assumed, by the head of each group, since Nathan's father opened three different offerings. Each member was given a different organ to eat with Nate's father eating the heart of the victim, his mum the brain, Jenny the kidneys, Nick the liver, and Nate got the lungs.

I watched in terror and tried to close my eyes, but they kept opening and I realised that Nate had placed some sort of enchantment on me so I had to watch. My heart throbbed as I thought of the boy and I loved and the monster who he had become. I tried again to close my eyes, using my powers, but it wouldn't work no matter how much I wanted it to. I wanted to un-see this, to go back to my innocent lives where demons were in stories and monsters didn't kill innocent people for whatever the hell this was.

As the crowd moved I saw a little one fall to the floor and a rage unlike any I had ever known rose up in me. My ties loosened and I was about to stand, with no thought in my head, but avenging the baby that had just been devoured. Tears stung my eyes and my feet dug into the earth.

Joaquin's voice sounded in my ear, "do not move precious. You will be killed and consumed this night if you move." As he spoke the ropes retied themselves onto my wrists and I sat staring at the ground until the blood reached my feet. I tried to scramble back in disgust, but I couldn't move without great effort. I offered a silent thank you to Joaquin, as I sat there plotting revenge against these monsters for the deaths of the innocents I had, had to sit and watch.

After a while those gathered had devoured each of their offerings and the ground was saturated with blood. The remains of the bodies lay facing a stone altar covered in blood, making it look like a sick clock made up of uneaten body parts.

The bodies then disappeared and the party continued, much as it had before. There was singing in some foreign language I didn't understand, dancing and kissing. I finally caught another glimpse of Nathan standing with his arm around Lisa and as I watched, he leaned to her with a passion usually reserved for me. I sat watching as he worked on destroying my feelings for him completely. The kiss seemed to go on forever and I felt like this night of horrors would never end, watching him practically grope her. I managed to turn my head away, as his voice sounded, loud and clear in my thoughts, "Look at me, Jasmine. I never wanted you. I was just using you to make sure you were here. I have never loved you."

Constantly seeing and feeling the death strokes of our relationship, I felt so sick. All I wanted to do was lie down. My head swam and my insides wobbled like jelly. I wasn't sure I could stay standing, tied to this stupid tree. All I wanted was my mind to shut down and to not think ever again, of what I had seen. Realising at that moment that these faces would haunt my nightmares for months, possibly years, I would never, ever get over seeing so many helpless victims devoured by a crowd of monsters.

Jasmine, you must be dreaming. Monsters don't exist, not in real life. Jasmine, what are you thinking? You must have a sick mind if this is what you dream about.

Eventually, the crowd thinned and the remainder of the partygoers left around six a.m. Nathans family left last started the walk through the woods, after blindfolding me in the clearing. Nathans gentled hands tied the blindfold, but he was quick and touched me as little as possible and I wondered if his words were true.

Had he just used me? Was I just a game to him? Was I really only something to toy with until after Halloween?

Jagged pains rocked across my chest and my brain hurt from all the things that rocked through it. I had to stop with the thinking and after a few moments, we started moving. I had someone on each side, holding on to me in case I what, I wondered, decided to run?

As much as I was going to run, and after what Nate had said, I was completely certain I would run. As that thought crossed my mind, hands tightened on my arm, but I ignored it and focused on the colour black, trying to shut my mind down.

. The atmosphere was still like a family party as Nate and Jenny pulled me through the woods. I was pulled as if I was a marionette who had strings attached to my arms, torso, and legs. This, and only this, led me forwards.

My stomach twisted and rolled, nauseous the whole way back to the barn. My mind was finally fully numb. I never even looked around as we made our way back through the trees and it wasn't until much later that I realised I was no longer blindfolded. I couldn't tell if Nate was talking to me, if anyone was talking to me. Knowing no one else could hear our thoughts, as a part of the charm of our relationship, I still couldn't figure out what had changed this weekend to take him from me. At that point, I didn't feel particularly bothered, but seeing him beside me holding hands with Lisa was like a knife in the stomach.

We eventually got back to the house and Jenny led me into the barn. I was told to lie down and go straight to sleep. Nodding in agreement, I lay down, closing my eyes and fighting back tears. I lay there trying to force the images of the last few days out of my mind, but they played on a loop — Nathan in the school eating parts of that boy... walking in the woods... at the clearing... seeing Nathan kiss Lisa... seeing Nathan eat someone's lungs...

Eventually I nodded off, straight into dreams about it, only this time I was a victim and Nathan was the one who stabbed me. His knife sliced into me as though I was butter and the pain in my chest increased. I awoke cold, shivering and screaming into my pillow. Lying there, I tried to control my breathing but I couldn't stop the sobs and the tears. Pulling out my favourite book, I lay trying to read, but couldn't focus on the words. My eyes blurred and tears kept falling. Eventually I gave it up as a bad job and closed my eyes, this time falling into a dreamless sleep.

A while later, it could have been minutes, hours, or days, I heard voices in the barn but I couldn't lift my head enough to see who it was. I eventually fell asleep again and had the most horrific dreams. I dreamed again about Nathan as a demon, killing me, but this time stabbing me with a burning machete. The pain was incredible and I awoke groaning, but I safe in the knowledge that they were just dreams now, although I had no idea when they would again turn into reality for me. That thought was truly sickening.

The next few days passed in a haze and I tried not to think or look at anyone. I knew seeing their faces would remind me of the awful events of Halloween. Lisa Q had disappeared by Sunday afternoon, leaving only myself in the barn, but the house was still very busy, with what looked like gifts lay on a table. There were a number of pumpkins on the table and at each pumpkin, small cups of blood sat around them. Having noticed this as I went into the house to shower on the Monday, I wondered what the gifts meant.

Monday evening constituted a family feast and Juliette, Nathan's aunt, came over and asked me to help. Although she asked, I didn't feel like I had any choice. I was still numb from Saturday night so seeing Nathan with Lisa sitting on his lap didn't bother me in the slightest. When she turned and kissed him, I noticed that their hands were in places they shouldn't be. Reacting in shock, one of the glasses I carried slipped out of my hands and smashed all over the floor.

"Oh, for fuck sake, can't you do anything right, mortal?" Nathan asked. Sickened, I quickly placed the remaining glasses on the table and picked up the larger pieces of glass, cutting my finger as I did so. I wasn't bothered about the cut, I'd been through much worse pain that a stupid cut finger. I glanced at it as Lisa walked out through the other set of doors into the living room. I tidied up, ignoring Nathan completely and turned away from him.

"You're hurt?" he asked with a question in his voice. He walked over to me and reached for my hand. Just looking at him made my stomach churn, especially with what I had just walked in on. My head spun and I turned away, not answering him.

"Oh my God, you saw that?" he said in a low voice, obviously listening to my thoughts.

I refused to answer and walked towards the door with as much composure as I could muster, I muttered, "I hope you're happy." Instead of sounding unconcerned, my voice cracked and I walked out, fighting the lump in my throat again.

Before the door closed, I thought I heard him whisper, "Not at all."

The rest of the evening passed in a blur with me ignoring everyone, serving them food and drinks, and clearing up. The numbness was back in full force and eventually I was dismissed at nine. I couldn't stomach being in the same room as Nathan and Lisa. They hadn't touched, that I had noticed. Nathan, when I glanced at him as I was leaving, looked troubled, but he didn't look up. In fact, he stared morosely into his glass of whatever he was drinking, sitting in the far corner of the dining room.

On Tuesday, we returned to school and for the remainder of the week, even in class, he ignored me completely. Going back to school was a relief; I was sure the work and daily routine would provide a welcome distraction from the horrors going on still in my head. I also wondered why I still had thoughts about Nathan. Although my head was still full of the images from Halloween, I sometimes wondered if there was any way we could survive this.

He had shaken my faith in him before, but I was completely disgusted in him and had blocked him completely from speaking to me. I walked with him to and from school, but spent my days in the school library, reading, doing my homework, or doing extra credit work for my teachers. Unable to bear being in the same room as him, I avoided the dining hall like the plague and only saw him in classes.

Thursday afternoon, walking home from school, was the first time since Monday that he had spoken to me. "You are to attend the bonfire tonight." That night, his family had a huge bonfire in their front yard with a number of fireworks, sparklers, and food.

Not answering was difficult, but I kept my eyes straight ahead and I could see him shaking his head in dismay. "Jasmine, did you hear me? You have to attend and at least look like you're having fun."

Fun he wanted? How dare he?

I couldn't even speak, I was so angry. I walked quicker so I could get away from him, but he matched my pace. Walking into the woods, trying to get away from him, I soon slipped on the dead leaves that lined my path. All I could think about was getting away from him.

"Will you just speak to me, please?" He reached out to me with the hand that had been touching Lisa and my face screwed up in disgust. "I'm so sorry about all that. I wish I could explain it to you, but I can't." He held onto my wrist and pulled me closer to him, but I just looked at the ground. As he touched my chin, I snapped my head back away from him.

Shaking my head, tears filled my eyes as I pulled away from him, turning and running away. I didn't care where I ended up as long as he wasn't near me. Finally slowing and relaxing a little because he wasn't anywhere near me, I sat underneath a tree stump. The ground was damp from the rain, a little muddy, but it was mostly sheltered and it was all I needed at that moment.

I finally let my guard fall and allowed myself to feel all the emotions I had been bottling up. I sobbed until I felt like there was nothing more inside me. I didn't care how much of a mess I looked as snot and tears streamed down my face. I wish I could have said I was an attractive crier, but my eyes went all red and puffy. My face reddened and my throat hurt. Sitting there staring out at the trees, watching them swaying in the breeze, a light rain began to fall. I ignored it, enjoying the peace and tranquillity of this part of the woods.

Nathan appeared and looked down at me, pulling me out into his arms, but I backed off again and watched him breaking down, "I-I am s-s-s-ssorry about all this. I really do want to... to explain," he said between sobs, but he then properly broke down crying and I just sat there looking at him, not saying a word. "I-I love... I love you... I know it's a poor excuse for everything I have put you through, but it's all I have..." My heart thundered and I didn't know what to believe. His pain looked real, but I didn't trust him enough to even try to forgive him. "Jas, please, try to understand my family..." He broke off again drawing in a deep breath and shuddering as he glanced at me through his tears and seeing the cold expression on my face.

He shook his head, looked at his watch, and turned back to me. "We have to get going. Come on!"

Processing his words, I let him pull me up, but when he reached out to touch my face, I slapped his hand away. He looked at me with tears in his eyes. "Oh God, I've really fucked up this time, haven't I? Just tell me what I can do. I will do anything..." He dropped to his knees, his brown wavy hair falling down as his head dropped. "I'm begging you. Please, Jas. Please forgive me. I love you, more than my own life, but I had to act like that. Please just, just say you'll give me, us another chance..."

I shook my head, watching as tears fell from him eyes, feeling tears streaming down my face as I looked at him. I couldn't forgive him. I didn't know how to.

He stood, dusted himself down, and leaned into me, kissing my hair, forehead, and nose. "I will make it up to you. I promise, somehow I will make you forgive me." He kissed my head one last time and looked at me in the eyes, the kind of look that scorched my soul. I began to waver until he hissed, "Quick, hide..."

He shoved me back into the roots of the trees and pushed the roots down, hiding me from view as Lisa walked into the clearing, "Where have you been, baby?" she asked in a voice sounding ridiculously babyish.

"Just walking and thinking," he answered, with an edge to his voice.

"Are we still on for tonight?" Her high voice, sounded babyish as she spoke to him and she leaned over to him, giving him a quick kiss as I sat under the root watching their display.

"Yes, of course," he answered her, sounding nervous.

"Are we still going to, you know?" she asked nervously. I could see her through a gap in the roots and she was twirling her long blond hair around her finger and licking her lips. Stuffing my fist in my mouth, I bit down so I wouldn't make a sound.

Nathan shuffled his feet and cleared his throat. "I dunno; we'll need to see if we can get away without being noticed..."

"Are you seriously doing this to me again, Nathan Stevenson? When we got back together on Saturday, you said you were serious, and that to prove it, I would be your first. Clearly, you don't want me. It is so over. Don't bother calling me or trying to get back with me again. We are fucking done and that little whore Jasmine is welcome to you and your fucked up ideas on relationships."

With that, she turned on her heel and walked away. Nathan called out after her, "Wait, Lisa. I didn't..."

"No, I'm done waiting on you."

She didn't even turn back as she answered. After a few minutes, when he was sure she was gone, Nathan pulled the tree stump up and looked at me apprehensively. I didn't say a word to him, nor him to me, all the way back to his house.

As we reached the driveway, I skirted around the trees and was in my barn, changed into my fleecy jogging bottoms and my warmest jumper when Jenny flew into the barn as I brushed my hair, shouting at me, "Have you got something to do with my brother and Lisa breaking up?"

Looking up at her, I made my face look perplexed as Nathan came running into the barn. "Oh, for God's sake, Jen, I told you no. She just went skitso at me and began shouting at me about her. There is nothing going on with us, is there?" he sounded pleading and for the first time all week, I spoke in front of him.

"Definitely not. Your brother is not my type at all!"

I couldn't look at Nathan, but when I did, he looked sadder and more defeated than ever. Then, as I surreptitiously glanced at him, he shook his head and half-smiled at me. Jenny turned around, missing the look by a moment, and they marched out of the barn together.

Nathan came back a little later, speaking quickly over my shoulder before he walked away. "You have been ordered to come out to the fireworks show..."

Walking out of that barn was difficult, but not as difficult as facing those I now knew were demons, like my social worker. I had seen her in the woods on Halloween, but it took me a few days to look at the faces in depth and strip away the demon on them. Seeing teachers from my current school, two of my previous doctors, teachers from primary school, social workers, and some of the women who took care of my while I was in the home.

All of them were at the bonfire, celebrating, but I just stood in the background, glad that I had figured out my way out and that no one, not Nathan or his family, were going to make me stay a moment longer than necessary.

The night went off without a hitch; everyone had fun with the sparklers and enjoying the festivities. I stood back plotting my escape, not paying attention to what was going on around me, until a few pairs of hands grabbed me and lifted me in the air.

I screamed at the top of my lungs and saw Nathan looking up in shock, surrounded by his father, mother, and sister.

"Shall we throw the mortal into the fire?" one voice called out as I squirmed and wriggled.

All the onlookers laughed and joked around, "Sure, go on then!" said another voice, sounding maliciously amused.

I was carried closer to the fire, screaming and wriggling, but not one person helped me. Nathan stood transfixed in horror as I gasped as the heat from the fire tickled my feet. Feeling my feet blistering, I cried and tried to work out how to use my powers again, as Nathan's dad stepped forwards.

"ENOUGH!" he bellowed and they moved me back from the fire slightly. "I have already given an edict about touching my mortal. Do you want me to remind you, Nicholas, who is in charge here?"

"No, sir," Nicholas answered. I gasped in pain. The agonizing burning was right up to my calves.

"Nathan, Jenny, take the mortal into the house and treat her burns. The rest of you go home. Tonight is over!"

Gasping in pain as Jenny raked her nails up my legs, Nathan looked down at me, hissing, "Jenny, cut it out. Dad's angry enough."

I could feel tears stinging my eyes as they carried me into the house, but I refused to cry, not making a sound as Nathan attempted to get me into a chair. However, when they tried to take off my shoes, I screamed in agony. My feet were on fire. Nate brought over a large bucket almost full of water. The water was freezing cold and I screamed and writhed as they placed my feet and legs into the bucket, submerging them.

After ten minutes, of water changes, ice and shivering, I felt lightheaded and dizzy, retching. Nathan was the first to notice and jumped out of the way as I vomited. Unfortunately, Jenny was not as lucky and I was sick all over her.

"Oh my God, were you actually just sick on me?" she asked with malice in her voice. I couldn't answer her. She drew her fist back and punched me full in the face, knocking me from the stool I had been sitting on. The ice water went all over me and mixed with the vomit on the floor. My head was swimming with what felt like a million different aches and pains. I closed my eyes and rested my head on my arms.

"Jenny, what do you think you are doing?" Nathan's father demanded from what sounded like the kitchen door, making me jump in surprise.

"She was sick on me, Dad. I have mortal puke all over me. Ugh, I'm going for a shower!"

Nathan stood back watching me as his father walked closer, looking at my legs and feet. As soon as he touched them, my eyes rolled backwards into my head and I flitted in and out of consciousness.

"She has gone into shock," Mr Stevenson's voice said as I regained consciousness for a moment.

"Dress the wound in this, Nathan," Mr Stevenson commanded, followed this time by a foul smell, like seaweed, burning rubber and dirt, all mixed in together with a few other scents that I couldn't identify.

"Help her over to the barn. Nick, help your brother and since you did this, you can take the watch tonight with Nathan. Her dressings will need to be changed in a few hours."

As I was carried, I could feel a hand rubbing my back in circles, but that was all I was aware off, until I came to a short while later, lying in the barn on top of my sleeping bags, feeling as though my skin was being eaten by fire-breathing dragons. The fire burned right up and down my legs, and I made a small noise as I tried to move.

Nathan appeared at my side but when I went to open my mouth to speak, he shook his head and pointed in the direction of the barn door. Outside, I could just make out a conversation Nick was having, "No baby, I'm sorry. I have to stay and mortal sit... I know it's awful, but there is nothing I can do... the old man is making me stay... Yeah, me too... but I best get back. I've left Nathan alone and if she wakes, one of us needs to hold her down while the other rewraps her legs... Okay... see you tomorrow, bye."

The barn door opened and I looked around for Nathan, but saw him leaning against the fence post, playing with his phone. As his brother approached, Nate nodded in my direction, "I think it's walking up, shall we?"

"Sure thing, little bro. What do you want to do? Wrap the burns..." he said with an evil glint in his eye that I could see from where I lay, "or hold the stupid thing down while I wrap?"

"I'll do the wrapping. I think you're too much of a sadist and my work would be much harder if I hold her."

"Haha, you are correct, little bro. Now let's get this done so we can get to bed. I'm fucked up and I have to drive back to Birmingham tomorrow. I need some sleep."

They walked towards me and I flinched as Nick's hands bit into my shoulders with a tremendous force. As Nathan unwrapped the bandages, I suddenly understood why Nick held me so tightly. My whole body vibrated as

I shivered, shaking like a leaf blowing around in a strong wind. When Nathan applied the salve to my burns, I sobbed. My whole body vibrated so hard as I screamed in agony.

Suddenly, Nathan stabbed me in the top of the leg, causing a soothing sensation to flow around, allowing me to relax.

"What are you doing? Dad said to use that only if we felt it couldn't cope."

"To be honest, I didn't think she could cope. I decided to give her some pain relief so we can finish this quicker and get to bed."

"You are too soft-hearted, but get on with it."

I could feel Nathan applying pressure and adding another coat of this salve along with a cling film dressing. As soon as he was finished, Nick stood. My head felt fuzzy and I relaxed as Nick said, "Clean up, Nate. I'm off to bed mate. See you in the morning."

"Okay, no worries. See you tomorrow," Nate answered, watching him walk out of sight. "Are you okay, Jas?"

I shook my head. "I still hate you..."

"I know, baby, but this will heal and I will fix us. I can't tell you how sorry I am." He stroked my arm, gathered up the supplies, and turned around to leave. "Relax, Jas. You can go to sleep now, baby. I'll be back to watch over you shortly."

With that, I slept soundly for a solid nine hours. I awoke the next day to my legs feeling rough, blistered, and stiff, but not as sore as they should have been, the only relief I would get for a while.

I didn't see or speak to Nathan for over a month, and the longer he left me, the angrier I got. How could he do this to us? How could he say he loved me and then mess around with her? I couldn't think straight about him, so I blocked everything out, ignoring him completely. It was a long, lonely month and I felt more alone than ever.

The next time I saw Nathan properly was on the fourth of December at a family dinner. I helped serve, but he didn't speak to me at all. I occasionally caught his eyes lingering on me and, glancing at his expression, he looked frustrated and sad.

I tried to speak to Nathan in the kitchen between courses, but as usual, Lisa appeared. She had been following him around for the past month. He ignored me and walked over to stand with her, giving me a pointed look that shattered my already broken heart into a million little pieces.

His eyes hardened as he looked at me. He turned away and followed Lisa. His posture was the only thing that showed that he wasn't happy, but I couldn't watch him any longer. I turned back to the task at hand. I loaded the dishwasher and as I closed it, I heard the whisper in my mind, "I'm sorry."

CHAPTER 11
CHRISTMAS CHEER

On the fifth of December, I walked behind Nate and Jenny, not thinking about much, but reliving all our moments when I realised that he hadn't properly spoken to me in over a month and I missed him. No matter what he did around that awful time, I loved him, and I couldn't turn it off. As I thought about this, I noticed his head shift slightly in my direction, but he still said nothing.

Perhaps he didn't want to speak to me or perhaps he wasn't ready. As we walked, I heard footsteps coming up behind me and a girl with long, blond hair shoved me out of the way.

"Are you ready, Nathan? We have to hurry if we are going to make dinner." Lisa asked him, turning my stomach.

"Yeah, Lisa. Just need to drop my bag off, then I'm all yours," he answered her, emphasising those words. Shaking my head in dismay, continuing to walk was difficult as I tried to think of a way out. *I am so done with this shit.*

I didn't think about anything else and, as I walked away into the freezing barn, I turned back and glanced at them. Nate held her hand, but looked behind her at me. As I glanced at him, I saw a tear escape his eye and he quickly brushed it away. Turning back into the barn, I set up my school bag for the next day. Running away was the only option I had; I decided to visit my friends in Glasgow.

Planning everything took all night, but I managed it. As I fell asleep, I was comforted by the fact that this was my last night in the barn and I would never again have to see Nate and Lisa, or his family, ever again.

During the night, I felt a rustle beside me, but I refused to open my eyes. Eventually, I could only hear my breathing and I fell back to sleep. Nathan awakened me in the morning with my breakfast of cereal and toast, with a cup of tea. He never said a word to me — just turned and walked away.

A little over an hour later, I got on the 500 bus, which would take me towards Dumfries. Then I would change over to the x74 in Dumfries after half an hour. I couldn't wait to get away from them, but especially Nathan.

Sitting on the bus, I felt a huge sigh of relief building as the bus pulled away from Carlingwark Street and moved along the countryside. I closed my eyes and focused on the future — getting a job, finding a flat of my own, and getting over Nathan fully.

As we reached Dumfries, I got off the bus smiling, and walked straight into Nathan and Joe. Almost crying in frustration, I turned to run away as Nathan grabbed my arm. "Jas, listen please. I know I don't deserve you, and that you hate me right now, but you need to come back. If they find out you've left, they'll kill you. I have never stopped loving you, but after the look on your face last month, I don't know how to fix us..."

Turning back towards him, I opened my mouth to say something about how it was too late to apologise and fix us, when I felt a sharp prick pierce my arm and I fell into blackness. The last thing I saw was Nathan standing over me, looking down at me shaking his head, mouthing, "I'm so sorry..." He said something else, but his face went fuzzy and the next thing I knew, I awoke in the barn, shivering, sneezing, and coughing.

Crawling under the sleeping bags, I allowed myself to grieve for the life I planned away from them, but things had changed with Nathan. I didn't trust him at all anymore; the slight trust he had built was gone as he betrayed me and then took me back to hell.

The next few weeks passed slowly with Nathan and Lisa breaking up again. This time was for good, though I didn't know it at the time. Nathan also visited the barn every night, between one and three a.m., but I refused to awaken and speak to him.

Eventually, after five nights of him sitting there, I gave in. "What do you want, Nathan?"

"Just to talk, Jas. I miss you."

"Missing me doesn't fix us. It doesn't mean anything to me, not anymore. You've said it too many times now."

I turned away from him and tried to go back to sleep. I hadn't opened my eyes at all, I heard him sigh, lean over, and kiss my head. "I have been here every single night watching over you, willing you to talk to me, but this cold indifference you have is breaking my heart. I love you so much and I am trying to protect you but I know you deserve better than anything I can give you."

He breathed the words against my forehead and sat back, taking my hand in his, ignoring my flinch as he touched me. His voice was hoarse as he continued,

"If you want to leave, I will help you get away from me. Every move I make seems to hurt you and I can't bear to see that look on your face again. No matter how much it hurts me, I have to do what's best for you. I know you won't ever forget Halloween; neither will I."

He shuddered and drew in a shaky breath before continuing, "Walking towards you, I realised what I had done as I looked at your face. Knowing I had destroyed us almost killed me, so I stayed away, trying to give you time until you could look at me again, without feeling as if I had broken your heart. It hasn't happened yet." His breathing was uneven as he finished and he squeezed my hand harder, gasping in a breath.

I lay there listening to him, with my eyes closed, but I shifted my head around and peaked through my lashes at him. He was turned away from me and I watched his chest rise and fall harshly and tears glisten in the moonlight. I didn't say a word, because I didn't know what to say to him. I didn't know if we could ever go back to where we had been. Halloween had wrecked me, destroyed us and demolished my trust in him. As I thought about what he'd said, he shifted, whispering in my ear, "Look in your book." With that, he vanished.

I turned around, sadness engulfing me, and picked up my book. Leafing through it, I saw pieces of paper folded between the pages.

Jas, I love you.

Jas, I'm so sorry, please

Baby, just talk to me. Don't shut me out anymore.

Twenty of them... went on and on, over and over, all saying roughly the same thing.

Baby, I need you. Please talk to me.

Some were just hearts with kisses, while others pleaded for me to forgive him or at least try to speak to him. I didn't know if I could, if I ever would forgive him for what I had witnessed.

Burying the notes at the bottom of my school bag, I went to sleep with my mind going over and over things he had said and done. Waking up the next morning, I felt sluggish and tired, but went to school and powered my way through the day, not paying close attention to anything until walking home.

Nathan walked up to me and grabbed my arm. I looked into his beautiful green eyes, but said nothing. He turned away, pulling me from the road, where there would be too many witnesses of us talking, into the woods and towards a stone circle. He passed right through the circle, causing my mouth to drop open.

"Jasmine, please. I can't take this anymore. Please just forgive me? Or talk to me! Scream at me! Tell me you hate me, but don't, please done ignore me anymore" His eyes filled with tears, and he closed them as his breathing came in gasps. I stood immobile and he dropped to his knees, "please, Jas. Just give me a chance. I know I hurt you and I betrayed you. I fucked up okay. I'm a demon and this is all new to me and I'm trying."

He ran his hands through his hair and was rocking back and forward as he spoke again, "God, I need you, baby. You make me better and I can't do this anymore. I can't stay away from you anymore." My feet moved me over to him unconsciously as he spoke and I dropped to my knees beside him, having decided that he had one last chance to prove that he loved me. If he screwed this one up, I would leave him and I would never come back.

I placed my lips on his and felt the kiss deepen, intensifying and electrifying us. The air around us seemed to crackle as we kissed until I felt lightheaded. He pulled back, kissing me on the top of my head and breathed into my ear, "I am so sorry for everything that has happened. I will never, ever deserve you, but I promise to spend every single moment of forever making it up to you."

"Nate, if you touch her again, look at her again, we are done and I am leaving... I cannot live through that again, no matter the consequences. We cannot survive it."

"Okay," he answered in a small voice, "it was only because I was on a demon high that it happened. I will never ever touch her again. I promise on my life."

The next few weeks passed and all too soon, it was Christmas. A major snowfall allowed me to sleep in the house again as the stables were freezing cold. This all changed on Christmas Day. Waking up on Christmas morning, I had no presents and not one member of the family spoke to me, as I served them breakfast and coffee. I walked around feeling invisible as they laughed, exchanged gifts, and enjoyed Christmas morning.

I spent the morning in the kitchen where one family member or another assigned me tasks to complete — clean the silverware, tidy the dining room, do the dishes, and stock the fire, but don't light it.

I hadn't seen Nathan all morning and by lunchtime, I was exhausted. I went into my bedroom and closed the door, feeling the tears come as I remembered last Christmas. Being awakened by Jack, eating cookies and cream with Anna, and laughing at the silly Christmas jumpers we all wore. I stood, walking over to my wardrobe, and dug out my jumper from last year. It was a snowman and a penguin; the snowman had a carrot nose that stuck out, and the penguin had a Christmas tree hat with bobbles on it. The jumper was bright red and I held it tightly, smiling at the memories.

The door slowly opened and I turned around, ready to face whoever was at the door. Nathan walked towards me and pulled me into his arms. "Come downstairs please."

He walked away, saying nothing else, and I swallowed with difficulty, thinking about how cold he was being.

He turned back, whispering, "They are watching you. Come on please."

I nodded, threw the jumper back in the wardrobe, and followed him downstairs, walking into the dining room just a few steps behind him.

"Nathan, we are going now. Make sure the dining room is set up. She will help you," Mr Stevenson said, ignoring me completely as he barged past me, pushing me into the handle of the door. I yelped in pain.

No one paid the slightest bit of notice and Nathan glared at me as he passed by me with his sister. As they left, I felt like screaming, but kept it inside. As soon as their car was gone, Nathan flew into the house, grabbed my hand, and pulled me out the back door.

"Hurry, we don't have long and I have a surprise." He pulled me through the woods, leading me to the cave and as soon as we arrived, he made me stand outside, covering my eyes as he ran inside. After a few moments, as the wind bit into my exposed skin, Nathan pulled me into the cave and into his arms.

"I'm sorry. We were supposed to come here before dawn, but since you were moved into the house, my plans were scuppered." He leaned down and pressed his lips to mine, "Open your eyes, baby."

I obeyed and looked around at the scene. The cave was decked out in candles all lit and in the middle was a gift, wrapped in gold, with a bow on top.

I walked over in a daze, picked up the gift, and opened it to reveal a small intricate angel wing, with an inscription written along the inner wing. *Contego.* I fingered the fine writing on the white background.

"Contego means protection in Latin and the angel wing should protect you from all evil. I charmed it so it would be a protection charm for you." Watching him speak, he seemed nervous. "If you don't like it, we can swap it for something else, but I just thought it was fitting."

I smiled up at him with tears filling my eyes, "It is perfect. Thank you."

"That's not all. Look again in the box..." Doing as he said, I noticed a small heart in the box with the words, *Versus Amor*, inscribed on the white background. "It means true love."

I beamed up at him, he placed both pendants on my bracelet and kissed my wrist. His eyes took on a look of hunger that reminded me of Halloween and made me shudder, breaking the moment.

"We have to get back."

He leaned down, kissed me gently, and then waved his hands to blow all the candles out. We ran through the woods and just finished setting up the dining room as his family arrived home. We didn't speak for the remainder of the day; I hadn't realised then that we wouldn't speak again for some time.

The dinner was eventful as Nick punched me repeatedly for spilling some soup on him. He was over me, and I could see Nate wincing with every blow, but he couldn't do anything. After a few moments, Nick dragged me into the kitchen and threw me in the pantry, locking the door. It wasn't opened again until the next morning where I was led up to what had been my room.

CHAPTER 12
DISCOVERY PAINS

No one had spoken to me at all since the dinner in December, not even at dinnertime. I went back to sleeping in the barn. Even Nate had stopped speaking to me, in any way, and I had no idea why. Usually, he was in my head all the time talking nonsense at me. Weeks had passed and I internally debated whether to say something, anything to get a reaction, but I wasn't sure he would answer.

I realised after a few minutes that I was walking along without keeping pace with Nate and Jenny, but they were only two steps ahead. While I debated whether to walk faster, a sudden movement flashed up in my peripheral vision. The next thing I knew I was flying through the air and I banged my head on the concrete pavement so hard I heard a sickening crunch.

I looked up to see what hit me, but all I saw was Nate glaring down at me with such disgust and loathing. His hand was still drawn into a fist. I was not feeling any pain at all, just stun and bewilderment as to why he did this. My thoughts were interrupted by a throbbing in my head.

I could only watch as Jenny walked over to Nate, put her hand on his shoulder to restrain him. "Come on. Let's leave it and go home."

She looked at me like a piece of dirt and walked him away with her hand on his arm. *Okay, it's time to get up. Come on, get up now.*

I was already soaking wet and the rain was getting heavier, but when I tried to get up, my head spun and my knees gave out. Spitting out some blood, I checked with my tongue that none of my teeth had broken and sighed in relief when I discovered none had. I tried again, more slowly, to get up, rolling over onto my knees, and gingerly felt at the tender spot at the back of my head.

Bringing my hand around I could see it was covered in blood and I felt woozy looking at it. The more I tried to focus, the more my vision swam. I knew if I didn't get back soon, there would be worse to come. I started walking but could barely see; my eyes kept blurring and my head felt like it weighed a ton.

Pushing my feet one in front of the other even though each step caused a clanging sensation in my head, I managed all of five steps before I crumpled under a big tree. The tree covered me from most of the downpour and I fell unconscious before my head hit the ground again.

I was aware just before slipping under that I could feel more pain, which Nate promised, would never happen, and just before the haze of pain and discomfort took me, I wondered if this meant he had gone back on every promise he'd ever made me. I wondered dully why this wasn't upsetting me more, before I finally slipped under.

Now I was somewhere, but felt very unsure of where this was. As I looked around me, it was a familiar place, but I wasn't immediately sure why. I looked down at my hands and saw stuffed toys, a pink bunny and a green bear, but this made no sense to me at all. I was almost eighteen and I was now trying to remember them, but couldn't. Then I looked up, my heart rolled over, as my parents looked at me, with faces filled with such love. I could remember their faces as though it was yesterday and this memory made me feel safe and loved again, but the logical part of me shouted that this was not true anymore.

"Jasmine," my dad called, "we have to go. Come on. Let's get in the car. We are going to Nana and Granddad's today." He lifted me in the car and ruffled my hair before putting on my seatbelt. I just looked at him and Mum, trying to rememorize their faces.

I looked at my mum, with her tummy swollen. I remembered in that moment that my mum was pregnant just before the accident. A woozy feeling started in my head and I closed my eyes, trying not to remember the pain I had lived through. My dad shook me awake again. I could hear his voice saying, "Wake up, sleepy head. Come on. Wake up, angel."

My throat burned and I swallowed against the lump in my throat. I had forgotten my dad's silly nicknames for me. I didn't open my eyes, so my dad unbuckled me and carried me into the house...

Waking up to reality again, it took me a while to place where I was. How did I land myself in a hospital room, not five years old? Why was I in here? I couldn't quite remember and looking down at my body, all I could see was bruising. As I tried to lift my head, I felt so heavy. I drifted off again, dreaming of my parents.

As the morning light broke, the smells of the hospital became more prevalent — antiseptic, bleach, and sickness. As I tried to move my head, the pain caused a sick rolling feeling in my stomach. I jumped as a gentle hand touched my shoulder.

"Don't try to move; you fractured your skull."

Opening my mouth and swallowing convulsively, I tried to keep the bile rising from my stomach and spilling over. I looked up at his wide green eyes, looking at me in concern when the memories cascaded through my head, Nathan standing over me with his fist raised, the look on his face as he stood over me, and the hateful expression behind his eyes. The images battered like a sledgehammer and my stomach rolled again.

"Let me explain please..." he pleaded.

"No, just leave me alone." My voice sounded hoarse from lack of use and I closed my eyes, trying to rid the memories of him standing over me.

He stood, scraping the chair on the floor, and he leaned over me, to kiss my head and place something cold and small into my hands.

"I am so sorry, baby."

As the door closed behind him, I lifted my hands up to my eyes to examine what he had given me — a small pair of open hands, touching with the word *Memoria* inscribed on it. I placed it onto my bracelet, touching the charms and smiling at the memories before drifting off to sleep again.

Drifting back to my parents, memories of my past crept up on me, making me smile. I saw my aunts, uncles, cousins, and grandparents through my five-year-old eyes, playing with my family and sitting on my dad's knee. Awakening later in a cold, dark hospital room, a nurse peeked her head in.

"Oh, Jasmine, you're awake. The Stevenson's will be so glad. They have been so worried about you. The police have a few questions for you when you feel up to it. I'm sure Nathan will fill you in on everything that you have missed these last few days, but you look tired, dear. Try to rest. I'm sure when you awaken in the morning, you'll feel better."

Smiling and nodding at her, I hoped she'd leave and take Nathan with her. I really didn't want to play more mind games. His gentle squeeze of my hand made me shudder. As the door to the room shut, he spoke, sounding more than hurt. I tried to block out his words, trying to fall deeper asleep. I felt more hurt and betrayed by Nathan than I had ever felt in my whole life.

"I'm so, so sorry. I know you hate me right now and I don't blame you. I love you. Sleep well, angel, and know that I'll be here when you awake..."

Part of me knew that my injuries were Nathan's doing and as angry as I was with him, I felt grateful; even though it hurt so much going back there and seeing my parents.

As tears ran down my cheeks, his soft fingers wiped at my tears and his lips gently touched my cheeks. Butterflies rose in my stomach and nausea rose at my reaction to his touch. He had put me in here, but my body still reacted to his and I wanted to hate him but I didn't. I was so confused as my thoughts swung on a pendulum and I groaned softly as I tried moving my head.

I opened my eyes searching about for Nathan. As my eyes found his, sitting in a darkened corner, he watched me but I couldn't make out his expression.

"How long I was out this time?" I asked him, trying to see through the darkness as he answered me with a catch in his voice.

"Two days, babe!"

My head throbbed as I tried to sit up, which reminded me what he did to me and why I was here. I opened my mouth to say something, but when I turned my head to look at him, he was reading a book. I closed my eyes, but the sound of the door opening almost forced them open again. Footsteps soon sounded in the room and a voice asked Nate, "Has it awakened yet?"

He rustled the pages of his book before he answered, "Not really. It awoke crying a few days ago when I was here, and she was awake a few minutes ago, but she's out of it again."

I realised it was his dad, just by the evil aura and the way he walked, and my whole body stiffened in response. I tried to relax, but my heart jumped into my head. I felt him leaning over me and was so terrified that I almost started shaking, but for some reason it didn't happen. I realised that Nate's charm prevented me from shaking and kept my eyes closed.

Mr Stevenson walked over to Nate and said, "Come on. It's time to go home. We can come back tomorrow. I expect her to be awake then."

The nurses came in just as they were leaving and I realised that I wouldn't ever be left alone — the nurse was a demon. I could smell it from her, the cloying scent of blood and the fetid aroma of darkness. Before I could open my eyes, pain drugs hit my system and I fell into a deep sleep.

Waking up well after midnight, I opened my eyes and saw Nate leaning against the door of the bathroom. I looked to the left side of me and the nurse who was in earlier sat in my bedside chair, reading. Her beeper went off, breaking the sleepy silence like thunder.

Watching Nate, I could tell he was desperate for her to leave. His foot tapped on the floor and as soon as she was out the door, he was by my side, kissing my head. Looking at him, he seemed unsubstantial, like a shadow, but much darker. Trying to clear my throat to ask him why he was here, he shook his head and I watched as he disappeared. The demon nurse came back into the room a second after Nathan vanished and I couldn't shake the suspicion she was looking for him as she switched on the light and walked into the bathroom.

Deciding then to go back to sleep was easier than lying with the demon nurse watching my every move. I closed my eyes and I felt myself being shaken awake almost instantly. "Wake up, sleepy head." my dad's voice said over me. It was still dark with the moon high in the sky. "We need to go meet Nana and Granddad at the hospital. Mummies in labour and your little brother and sister are about to arrive."

He carried me out to the car, where mum already sat, and he buckled me into my seat. When we arrived at the hospital, a face that was all too familiar to me greeted us. Nathan's dad stood there, and I began shaking. My nana took my hand and said, "It's all going to be okay."

My nana allowed my dad and mum to go into the hospital. While we were in the waiting area, I fell asleep and when I awoke, I was back in the present with the demon nurse sitting beside me. I opened my eyes and looked around the room, unable to believe that I had just remembered that I had a brother and a sister. The demon asked me, "Where is Nathan?" I just looked at her and she growled at me, and again asked, "Where is Nathan?"

In that moment, I couldn't even think of who Nathan was. My head was too stuck in the past, when suddenly her hand swiped across my face. I felt the sting and my eyes began to tear up. I just shrugged at her.

Closing my eyes, she yelled at me in frustration, but it was too late. I managed to fall asleep once again. I was a lot more cautious as I awoke and let my other senses roam before I opened my eyes. I felt tension and heard a person pacing around. I could hear the voice of my nana talking to someone. I opened my eyes and crawled into her lap. She told me not to worry and to go back to sleep. I looked around the room and saw a sight I had completely forgotten about. My whole family were there. My uncles and aunts were all present and the pain hit again that not one of them wanted me.

My dad came out and I awoke with him carrying me while talking to someone I couldn't see. The person my dad spoke to was Mr Stevenson. As he passed through the double door, he turned back and looked at me with an undisguised hunger.

My dad had stopped walking and turned left into a single room. Looking around the room, I saw my mum, who pulled me towards her and gave me a tight hug. "What's the matter, Jasmine?" I just looked at her and shook my head. Suddenly the door opened and a nurse that was oddly familiar to me, walked in wheeling in a cot.

My mum lifted one of the babies out of the crib and helped me to hold her. She told me her name was Abbie and I was a big sister. I started crying again, unable to believe that I had forgotten a moment as beautiful as this was. My dad snapped a picture of us and then he asked the nurse who was still in the room, to take a picture of our family. "Of course, I will," and when I looked at her again, I realised that this nurse was beside my bed in the present.

I smiled as I was handed the other baby, Aiden, and he was my little brother. I smiled down on them both and swore at that moment that I would find them; no matter what had happened to them, I would find them. I noticed a newspaper on my mum's bed dated the twelfth of April nineteen ninety-seven.

Now I had a date to work from. The accident happened three days after this and I was alone. I knew I had to go back and find my brother and sister. As I stared down at them, both babies gripped my fingers and I knew why Nathan had sent me back. He knew about Aiden and Abbie, and he knew I needed to know about them as well.

After a while, my dad took me home and as he tucked me into bed with my favourite stuffed animal, I made a promise that I would find my siblings. No matter what, Aiden and Abbie would be back with me soon enough. Anyone that had hid them from me had better watch out. I was out for blood.

CHAPTER 13
ATTACK OF THE GORGONS

The next few days passed without any more visits to my past. Nathan never returned but the demon nurse stayed three of the days. Eventually, I was discharged and Nate's dad had come in at nine a.m. to pick me up. I was terrified. I didn't want to go back with them. It was mid-February and freezing cold. I could see the snow from the hospital room window, in the few minutes I was on my own.

I worried about how Nathan would react when I was back in the bedroom across the hall from him, as even Mr Stevenson admitted I wasn't strong enough to go back into the barn yet. As he came back into the room, he banged the door off the wall, making me jump and spin around so fast I had to hold onto the chair for support. He wasn't alone either; my doctor stood beside him, with a look of confusion on his face as he took in my face.

He walked over to me, handed me a prescription. "You take care now. Take one of your tablets three times a day, or when you are in pain, but no more than four a day, maximum."

He smiled at me and left. I didn't look at Mr Stevenson, but picked up my bag and walked towards the door. He held the door open for me and placed his hand on my arm, leading me to the lifts and finally out of the hospital, giving me no chance to run away like I wanted to, not that I would or could in this moment.

We walked out into the cold February air, headed towards the car park, and finally reached the car. Mr Stevenson then helped me in, even though I didn't require it. I knew why he did this; he didn't want to leave me alone for a second, just in case I bolted.

I didn't pay that much attention to him. I was busy thinking about my brother and sister, wondering where they were and how I would get them back to me. I sat in the car all the way back to the house, not speaking. As we went into the house, he stopped me, "Are you okay? You seem very quiet."

As he asked that, I knew I could go off on him, but Nathan's voice appeared. "Tell him your head hurts; do not tell him you know."

I cleared my throat and spoke, "My head is hurting."

He scrutinised me and then said, "Go to your room. Do not leave it; food will be brought to you."

The wind blew my hair around, causing the dull ache in my temple to get worse. As I walked up the stairs, my head felt as though someone had tied weights onto my ears. I tried four times to open my door before stumbling into what had been my room and collapsed onto the bed.

The next few weeks passed very quickly and before I knew it, April arrived and we were studying for our exams. I couldn't believe how quickly time passed between school, researching my family, plotting revenge, seeing Nathan at school, and studying. As the first exam hit in May, I was ready and felt that I had done very well. English was always easy for me and although I struggled with the exams, Nathan studied with me and as he had applied and been accepted to Oxford University, he took it all very seriously.

One day we were sitting in the library studying and I watched him under my lashes while I was supposed to be studying. His face was set as he sat across from me, his hair curling around his ears and his green eyes staring at his textbook. He was there, but only in person and I missed him. I hadn't thought about my feelings for Nate in so long, after everything that had happened between us, I wasn't sure how I felt about him anymore. I was bored, lonely and just wanted some interaction with him.

I passed him a note.

I miss you

I miss you too, but we need to study.

Why don't you speak to me anymore?

You know why. They were so close to guessing about us.
We needed to cool things off.

Yeah, but it's May. Why can't we talk?

Because they will kill us. Now quit bugging me and study.

I pouted and went back to work, with one hand sitting on my knee, reading about the Russian Revolution for my history exam. He reached under the table and squeezed my hand, running his finger over my palm. I glanced around and saw everyone else with their heads buried in books in the dark library, but the librarian looked right at me. Nate noticed me tensing and glanced up, moving his hand away just as she walked over. As she got closer, the most disgusting smell reached my nostrils, like putrefying flesh. Her face changed, from kind and homely to sharp, with a beak for a mouth, and murky, mud-coloured eyes. She had a clawed hand that she slammed down on the table and as she breathed on me, I felt as though I would pass out. My head spun as she asked me in a high-pitched squeal, "What are you looking for Jasmine?"

My head swam as her voice caused my head to feel as though it was ringing. Nathan nudged me with his leg and I asked in as strong a voice as I could muster, "Are there any more books on the Russian Revolution?"

Suddenly the smell vanished and she spoke in her normal tones as she answered me, "Of course, deary. Why don't you come with me? Nathan can watch over your stuff and we can find other books for you."

I shuddered but got up and followed her. As we reached the bottom of the library, I glanced back and saw Nathan watching with a concerned look on his face. Turning the corner, I walked forwards and leafed through different texts as a clawed hand swiped over my back, cutting the skin and tearing off some flesh.

"Now to taste you, little warrior. We shall see, we shall see!"

I gasped aloud in pain and fell forwards, paralysed. I couldn't move but saw something in my peripheral vision. Nathan stood a little away, watching in shock and horror as she raised my skin to her lips and sucked on it.

"Mmmm, very juicy. How tasty, I need more."

She moved to stand over me again and I could see her face, smell the awful stench from her. As her hand came down again to peal more skin off, I booted out and kicked her so hard she bounced off a bookcase.

I scooted backwards and sat up shaking. Looking over at Nathan, he now looked astonished but still didn't make any move towards me. He seemed frozen and as I stood for the fourth attempt, I managed to stay upright. As I stood, I saw Nathan turn and walk away from me. Following him from a distance, he gathered all of our belongings and walked out the door.

As soon as I reached the door, I broke into a run and caught up with him. He just kept walking, not speaking. He looked at me a few times, opened his mouth, and closed it again.

Walking with my clothes open, the sunshine stung my back like crazy, but I kept pace with him, until we reached the woods. He reached over and grabbed my hand, pulling me into the shade of the trees. For a few minutes, the only sound was the snapping of leaves under foot. When he suddenly stopped, he pushed me into a circle and stared at me as though I intimidated him. He looked terrified and again opened his mouth a few times to speak, but closed it without saying anything.

After watching him for a few minutes, I felt sick and dizzy again. As I sat, my foot slipped and I fell sideways, but before I hit the ground, he was there and I landed on him. He oomphed and pulled me in tight to his chest.

"There is still venom in you..." was all he said to me, before I blacked out for a few seconds.

"Jasmine, wake up," he shouted at me. As I became more aware, I realised why he shouted. My breath came in short, sharp gasps. I felt as though I could barely breathe, as though a steel band tightened over my chest.

"Jas, speak to me. What's going on?" He reached behind me and as soon as his hand touched my back, I bolted across the clearing, feeling his skin burn like nothing I had ever felt before. It was ice on my skin.

I wondered why I made a noise like a wounded gazelle, but when I tried to calm down, "What... wh..." I tried again, sucking in a breath, "what is... is happening... to me?"

"I don't know, baby. Please let me look at you."

"I can't move. I feel..."

As I fell forwards, Nathan caught me and lay me down softly, as he looked at my back, "Oh no, we need help with this. I can't heal this..."

I floated along beside Nathan and he walked while talking on his mobile. I almost blacked out again, and closed my eyes as I heard him say, "I have no idea... yeah, she just kicked out at it... I think it was a Gorgon... Yeah, I know, but she's lucky to be alive... Yes, she's still breathing, but it's faint... We're on our way... Okay..."

I drifted off again and awoke as we arrived back at the house. Walking down the garden, Nathan kept to the trees and had me floating beside him until we went through the back door into the kitchen.

His mother stood there, staring down at me open-mouthed. "How did she fight off a Gorgon?"

"I have no idea how she was strong enough, but I just hope no more come along. If any of the others appear, she's going to be in trouble and by extension, so are we..."

The next few hours passed with me drifting in and out of consciousness, hearing disjointed voices talking overhead and smelling antiseptic and bleach that made my nose burn, my stomach flip, and head ache.

Nathan still sat beside me, idly playing with his sleeve, saying nothing. As soon as his mother left the kitchen, he leaned over and whispered in my ear, "Jas baby, wake up please. I can't do this without you. I didn't know how dark my soul was until you walked into my life in a burst of colour. You lit up the darkest parts of me, bringing me into the light and guiding my way while I adjust to the brightness."

I fought to open my eyes, wanting him to know that I was gonna be ok. I managed to move my hand, and a breath in my ear tickled me, as Nate continued,

"You claim every part of my heart, mind, and soul, and I can't and won't go back into the darkness..." His voice broke off and he sniffed, shuffling back on his seat and scrubbing his eyes.

"Nathan, has she awakened yet?" his mother's voice asked from the hallway.

"Not yet, Mother," he called back, standing and walking away. The sound of the tap running made me realise I needed to go to the toilet.

"Nathan..." I croaked out softly, my voice crackling over the word. He didn't hear me over the running of the tap so I tried again, jumping slightly as a terrifying sound battered against the windows.

A rattling sound followed by a screech made the hair on my arms and neck stand. My heart froze and dropped like a stone as I lay there trying to get my muscles to react and move.

"Stay still..." Nathan bit out at me as I tried to push myself up from the table again. I heard an ungodly laugh and my heart began thudding in my ears as some voices called in voices that were so high pitched, they made my ears bleed.

"We want her little demons, so send her out to us now and you may live. Refuse and you will all die; we can assure you, there will be pain as we strip flesh and muscle from your bones."

I opened my eyes and looked up at Nathan in terror, as his mother ran into the kitchen, "Use the emergency escape. We'll hold them off. Go on; hurry. She can regenerate us. We can't die, but she can..." She turned to me, "Up. Get up, girl. Come on; hurry up." Her impatience was palpable as there was more cackling laughter and scratching sounds on the windows. Suddenly all the lights went out.

Nathan grabbed me over his shoulder and turned, running into the utility room. He ran along to the wall between the washing machine and dryer. He placed his palm flat on the wall, muttered the words *aperio* and *pateo*. He drew a shape on the door, but with the battering on the windows and the cackling, I couldn't concentrate on what he was doing. Blood ran from my ears, dripping steadily onto the floor.

His mother came running in. "Hurry, Nathan," she whispered, grabbing the mop and bleach, to clean the blood from the floor.

Nathan moved forwards into a dark, damp tunnel and I saw a wall close behind us. Just before it closed, I could see his mother scrubbing the floor and heard the screaming get louder before cutting of altogether as the wall closed.

Nathan stopped a little ways along the path, huffing out a breath as he pressed his lips to my own. My heart was thundering in my chest and I leaned into him, breathing in the smell of him to try and calm me down, but every time I almost succeeded I remembered the evil laughter and wondered about what would happen if Nathan's family couldn't hold them off.

CHAPTER 14
THE DEMON HIDEOUT

It was dark, dank, and the blackness was suffocating. Nate didn't stop walking again for around ten minutes, looking side to side occasionally, with me still perched over his shoulder. I gasped for breath as we walked in silence and he stopped, put me down, and took my face into his hands.

"Jasmine, listen to me. Just breathe!"

My breathing still came in short, sharp gasps, and I saw lights popping in front of my eyes. He held my face tighter and came close enough that his breath tickled my face. He leaned his head down and touched his forehead to mine, his breath speeding as our skin touched.

He pulled me into his arms, and then just as quickly, pushed me back. "We have to move. Come on now. Hurry up."

He grabbed my hand, squeezing tightly, and pulled me alongside him, eventually breaking into a run uphill. Darkness surrounded us. How he knew where we were going was beyond me.

"What's a Gorgon, Nathan?" I asked, panting along beside him.

"Not here, wait. I'll explain soon."

We kept moving for what felt like an eternity, but eventually we saw a light and as we got closer, it became blindingly bright and all encompassing. I couldn't see anything beyond this light and I couldn't think about anything but the light, as it burned my eyes, skin, and made me feel like my blood boiled under my skin.

I panted and Nathan held on tight to my hand, urging me forwards. As we walked further into the light, shapes appeared — an old fireplace, marble and stone, a large set of patio doors, and an old-fashioned wicker chair. As the light receded, more of the room became clear and I was stunned to see Nathan and his parents in a photo on the fireplace. The photograph looked much older, with outfits that made me laugh. Nathan looked at me as I giggled and followed my gaze to the picture.

Shaking his head, he walked deeper into the room and sat on an old couch. He patted the seat beside him and I felt nervous. My legs shook again as he walked over, grabbed my hand, and pulled me over to sit by him on the couch.

As I sat, a cloud of dust puffed around me. Nathan looked nervously at me and as I opened my mouth to speak, he shook his head. "Not here," his voice sounded in my head, clear as day. "My family will be here soon."

"Where is here?" I whispered softly and he pressed his finger against my lips.

"The safe house. My family comes here from time to time when we are under threat."

He stood and walked away from me, stopping at the window and looking out the glass into the trees beyond. As I followed his eyes, the building shook. Light coming through the floorboards crackled under what sounded like electricity. A strong smell like singed hair and burnt skin filled the room and made me gag.

The smell got stronger and stronger and a drum beat on my forehead. My eyes watered and Nathan stood at the window watching me shaking and shivering, but made no move towards me. Seconds later, it was clear why he looked at me disdainfully.

His family had arrived, all of them looking a little worse for wear, with the exception of his father.

"Well, what have we here?" He asked with venom in his voice.

I just shook my head, not understanding what was going on as Nathan stepped forwards, "I brought her here, sir."

His father glared at him loathingly and he drew his hand back, punching

Nathan onto the window. I sat there numb with shock as Nathan's head flew onto the glass. I couldn't move as I watched him laying into Nathan, hitting him over and over as he just lay there taking every blow.

As I tried to move, I realised a hand on my shoulder held me in place and I looked into the face of Nathan's mother. Her eyes were on her son, and her voice, when she finally spoke, was cold and unaffected by the fact that her son's face was a bloody mess. "Mr Stevenson, stop. That's enough."

Mr Stevenson stopped hitting Nathan and turned his black eyes towards me. He said nothing, but walked over and grabbed my hair, dragging me out of the room with him. As we passed Nathan, he stirred slightly, but didn't move. Dragging me across the dusty hallway into a disused dining room, he threw me from his grip and my thoughts scattered as I scrambled across the floor. He shut the door, closing off the lights.

I banged into things I couldn't see on the floor, as a hand closed again around my neck, forcing me backwards onto the cold dusty floor. I gasped, trying to catch my breath as another hand punched me repeatedly. He grunted and eventually let up with his hand. I couldn't see, could barely breathe. It was painful beyond measure to breathe and he just sat there.

"You caused a Gorgon to attack my family; you are ripping my world apart. I now have to deal with that. It would be easier to kill you now than to leave you alive and have to fight these constant battles."

He dragged me over to a radiator, tying my hand to it, while I just lay there trying to take in burning breaths. He walked away and returned a moment later, dragging a semi-conscious Nathan into the room, tying him to the radiator as well. My eyes stung with tears as the blackness threatened to return, but I couldn't cry.

I must have drifted off. I had dreams where I was underwater and my lungs burned when I tried to breathe. I came around when I heard Jenny enter the room, the door opened creakily as she made her way to Nathan to give him some water. She didn't even look at me as she tipped a glass up to his swollen lips. A lantern in the room showed a basin of water, cloths, and a towel. When Nathan finished his water, his sister cleaned up his face and dried him. She left shortly after and I wanted to cry. My throat felt like it was on fire.

Nathan shook his head and turned to look at me in the darkness. "My light," he whispered so softly before drifting off, but I couldn't close my mind down. The darkness was too thick and I couldn't get comfortable as my thoughts ran rampant. *What was it about me that caused all these creatures to appear? Was Mr Stevenson right? Did I bring this on them?*

With no answers and more questions consuming me, I sat awake all night and into the next day, with no way to measure how much time passed. Nathan would reach out and touch my arm occasionally, but it seemed more like he was checking if someone was in the room with him.

After what felt like an eternity sitting there, unable to see, my breathing became more laboured. I saw lights popping in front of my eyes and my skin felt cold. Nathan awoke at this point and shouted out, "MUM!!! DAD!!! JEN!!!"

His voice sounded panicked, but I couldn't focus on it as I drifted and the oddest sensation came over me, as though I was floating above, watching as the door flew open and his family came running in. His father pulled a knife and cut the bonds. I watched myself slump forwards and land in a heap on the floor, but I was unresponsive as they shook me and shouted my name. I watched Nathan's face as he tried hard to mask all of his emotions, but I could see the tears in his eyes and the struggle he had swallowing.

I looked back at me and watched while his dad went into doctor mode. He cut a small hole in my throat to let air out and put in a straw. As soon as the straw went in, I floated back to my body, but I fought it when I realised I couldn't leave without Nathan. He said I was his light, but he was my fire. He kept me going and gave me the energy to fight every day that we lived with his parents.

I was blue lighted to the hospital with Nathan, where they said some other children attacked us. Attached to a ventilator, I sat almost right beside my body, watching as it healed from my injuries. Watching and listening to the exchanges of the doctors and nurses amused me, but the only conversation I really paid attention to was between Nathan's parents.

"The Gorgons have rescinded their claim on the girl. You were right, the threat of your father worked." Nathan's mum said to his father.

"Good. Once she is healed, we can get back to normal. Keep an eye on her and Nate. I can feel something there."

"I will, but I don't think we need to worry about that. He's loyal and loves Lisa. She's been by and they have been hanging out since he's been in here."

The door closed and I sat there for an inordinate amount of time, waiting to get better. Later that night, at 3:20 a.m., according to the clock, Nathan slipped into my room.

"Jas, I need to speak to you. Please wake up. Come back to me. I miss you. I'm drowning in this darkness and I need you to come back to me. I love you more than my own life. Please just try to come back."

He sat there for a few moments before standing and kissing me softly on the lips. I felt myself come back together and gasped as I struggled to breathe around the tubes coming into my neck. Nathan disappeared and chaos descended. Nurses and doctors surrounded me as they took out the machine and stitched my neck.

The following week, I was moved to a ward and was eventually after another few days in there I was allowed back to their farmhouse. I had to sit my exams on my own, since I had missed them, but I managed okay. June passed too quickly. Nathan was leaving in July to set up for university. We had been spending as much time as we could together, mostly late nights when his family was asleep. He would teleport over to me and we would hug and kiss, talking and laughing for a few hours.

The start of July saw us sitting one night in the barn discussing what would happen later that year.

"After a few months, I will be back to rescue you. When October hits, we will go on the run. I will have money and I have a plan for us. You need to trust me though. I cannot tell you the plan, but I will be back for you."

He kissed me, and lay down with me in the tent. His fingers stroked my face softly and he ran his fingers through my hair. "Jas, I love you." His lips met my own again and his tongue slipped inside my mouth. I wrapped my arms around his back pulling him down to me and we made out for a while. He pulled back, licked his lips and kissed my forehead, before he tucked me under his arms, "sleep now, baby." He snuggled in with me and held me tight until I fell asleep.

That was our last night together, but he never said it and in the morning I reached out for him, finding his spot empty, I was alone and I knew he was gone. He had left me without even a proper goodbye. As tears stung my eyes I tried to reach out to him, but I couldn't. There was a distance between us and when I tried again, just wanting to speak to him in my mind, I met a wall. He had closed me off, leaving me without him completely, broke my heart. I missed him almost straight away and when he didn't speak to me again for over three months my hurt and anger at him consumed me

CHAPTER 15
AWAITING RESCUE

I couldn't believe it was October already. *Where had the year gone? What would happen now?* Nate had said he had a plan to get us away from his family safely, but I hadn't spoken to him since that morning in July. He had completely closed me off and anytime he visited home, he made sure I was gone before he arrived and that he was gone before I got back. One day in mid September I saw him, but as I rushed to try and speak to him a force pushed me away from him and my heart thudded painfully as he looked through me, before getting into his car and driving away without a backwards glance.

October was the dreaded month, the month I was to die unless we could find a way out. I hated being there without him, and not speaking to him was unbearable. I missed him so much and couldn't wait for him to come home.

In twenty-seven days, Nathan's family were due to arrive and then it was bye-bye time for me. I jumped as a voice sounded behind me, but it was just Nick checking that I was working and not skiving. That would have been bad, very bad indeed. The last beating I took was in July, so bad I wasn't allowed to leave the house for four weeks, until the bruises had faded.

Nick watched me so I figured I better stop thinking about things like that, or I'd get into trouble. He just stood there watching me for ten minutes, and then he walked over and whispered in my ear. "Not long left now," and with that, he hit me, catching me right in the centre of my chest. I dropped the vase I held, but it just bounced on the carpet, making such a loud banging noise that his father came in to investigate.

Mr Stevenson just looked at me once, turned to his son, and asked him what happened. Nick looked towards me and said in an even voice, "I don't know. I turned to leave and she dropped the vase on purpose. I saw her from the corner of my eye."

Mr Stevenson turned to look at me and said in his most threatening voice, "If you make any noise again, you'll be beaten with the belt and left in the barn until you learn your lesson." I just nodded along; I knew if I didn't, I would be beaten worse. Inside, all I felt was chagrin.

Both of them turned to leave, but Nick winked at me, making me think that his torture wasn't over. I was unsure how much more I could take before I snapped back.

Going back to cleaning, my hands shook so hard and I felt so alone. Since Nate left, his visits had gotten fewer and fewer until, after the time I spotted him, he stopped visiting completely. I missed him like crazy, but I knew he didn't miss me. If he had, he never would have left me like this. I could feel the tears coming and since I couldn't stop them, I sat on the floor and broke down completely. I cried over missing him, loving him, being afraid of what would happen, and whether we were actually going to escape.

After a few minutes, I felt his arms go around me as he whispered, "Please don't cry. We are leaving in a week. I promise. I love you and I miss you too. I have to go. Be safe please." He pressed one kiss to my head then disappeared so quickly I wondered if I imagined the visit. I realised after a few minutes that I couldn't have. I had felt him press a note into my back pocket and I could smell him on my skin.

I smiled and continued working until well after dark, when my arms ached and my back hurt with all the effort. Sometimes I felt like Cinderella and the thought made me laugh, which I instantly regretted when I saw Mr Stevenson standing over me with a look of pure rage on his face. He just glared at me and then hit me with the belt, again and again, until I lost consciousness.

I awoke in agony a few hours later and found Nate once again by my side, in the barn. I tried to ask him what he was doing home, but he firmly placed his hand over my mouth. "You are not awake, but if you speak, they will hear you. Listen to me please. I know how hurt you are and I am sorry. I needed to get you out of the house so I could visit again. If they knew I was here, I think they would kill me as well." I asked him through my thoughts how he was here and his answer shocked me. He just looked at me and murmured, "The same way I've been here every night since I went to university. I have been teleporting myself into your head when you sleep. I wanted so much to talk to you and on some levels, I have. I have missed you being awake. I miss holding you so much."

The next minute I felt Mr Stevenson and Nick shaking me. They made me get up and walk into the house. I heard Nate saying goodbye in my head and that was the last time I saw him until he actually came to get me.

The next few days passed very slowly. I was in so much pain and moved much slower at cleaning than normal, so much so that Jenny had been assigned to help after she finished school. I could tell she was not amused but, in light of her father's mood, she didn't dare argue. She realised that they were supposed to keep me happy; my soul would have been brighter if I was happier. When she got home on the first day, I was in the kitchen with the entire cutlery set out.

I had been instructed to clean it all for the feast on the thirtieth, the prelude to the feasting on the humans on the thirty-first. It was a long, tiring job and I had been at it all day, my arms moving that much slower. Jenny came in to see what I was doing.

"Goddamn it, you've been doing that all day. What the hell is wrong with you? Why haven't you gotten more done?" I just looked at her, but then went back to what I was doing. I felt a whack across the back of my head. My head spun. Trying to get back up, I was pushed down. I tried to speak, but I was hit in the mouth. I fell flat on the ground and managed to roll over onto my side, as I became violently sick. I realised after that it was all over the cutlery I had spent all day cleaning, and Jenny was there still watching me.

The next moment, her mum walked through the door. She just looked at the mess and said, "Well, you are going to have to finish this job and until you do, there will be no sleep or food for you. Now clean up this mess!" I just looked at her and thought about how awful my life had become. If I thought it was bad before, it had become a whole lot worse, at least before Nathan was around to help cheer me up

I had to spend the whole night cleaning and by the next morning, I was completely exhausted. The day from hell was hardly over. They kept me busy, cleaning the wooden hall floors first, then the banisters and bedrooms. I finally had a lunch break, but it was nothing more than a piece of toast, which left my stomach growling for more. I couldn't remember the last time I had some proper food to eat.

Jenny came in from school at four thirty, only to torment me, instead of help me. I was cleaning Nate's room and I could smell him on the covers and pillow when I changed the bedding. I was so sad being in here without him that it was taking longer than necessary to clean. Jenny quickly realised this. She whispered, "Missing him, are we? Why haven't you finished in here yet? He's not here, you know. He doesn't even care about you. Why don't you just drop dead? Oh yeah, I forgot. You will just as soon as the thirty first comes." I just looked at her instead of answering her, and in response, I got a kick in the teeth.

My mouth gushed blood and I ran into the nearest bathroom and spat out the blood from my mouth. I felt a little sick so I drank some water from the faucet and waited a few more minutes to make sure my mouth stopped bleeding. When I was sure it had, I rinsed my face under the cold water. As I was about to return to the room, I could sense Mr Stevenson in Nate's room, and could hear him very clearly ask Jenny why there was a trail of blood on the cream carpet.

She just shrugged as I walked back in the door with a wad of toilet paper in my mouth to keep the bleeding at bay. Mr Stevenson just spun around and looked at me, "Well, I think you are going to have to clean this carpet until the blood is gone. Then when you have finished that, move out into the hall and redo the floor all the way up this level."

At this point, I could feel my spirit snap. I was exhausted, in copious amounts of pain, and famished, but I was not allowed to stop working. I cleaned the floor in his room and finally got the blood out at twenty minutes to twelve that night.

When I finished, I went down to the sitting room to tell Mrs Stevenson that I was done. Mr Stevenson was nowhere in sight and I wondered where he was until the next second, when I felt my knees being knocked away from me. I half-turned around and saw him standing there with the look of pure rage. I knew what was coming. He grabbed me by the hair and dragged me out of the house into the rain. He then started to hit me and I had no idea why, but when I slipped under for a few minutes, it felt like relief. I came to after a short time and I knew he was saying something to me but in my sleep deprived, painful state I missed what it was.

That was a mistake. The barn was freezing cold; the October wind bit but I didn't feel a thing. I only realised just how cold I was when I heard the footsteps coming into the barn early the next morning.

Mr Stevenson came into the barn at six the next morning with the local doctor, who also happened to be demon and asked him what he could do to fix me. His answer was simply, "Bed rest, fluids, and a bath would help." I was only half-listening as I could hear Nate more clearly. I heard Mr Stevenson ask the doctor if I could stay in the barn with a heater and the doctor agreed, but also suggested that they give me a thicker sleeping bag as the weather was to drop to minus five, making it the coldest October on record.

I waited until they were gone before allowing myself to ask Nate to repeat what he said. He told me to keep focused and that, in a few more days, we would be out of their lives forever. I wanted to ask him what he meant, but the barn door thudded open, making me jump as Jenny and Nick barged in with a look of the utmost contempt on their faces. They said nothing as they dragged me up and into the house.

Nate asked me what was going on and I told him I had no idea at all, as it got stranger by the minute. He sounded worried but assured me that there was no way they could have figured out what was going on. We got into the house and I was taken into the downstairs bathroom and thrown down unceremoniously, landing on the floor in a heap.

The next minute Nick left and the doctor came into see me. He looked unpityingly at me and instructed Jenny that she would have to sit with me while I was in the bath. I would definitely not stay above the water in the state I was in. Jenny again gave me that look of deepest loathing, as if she wished me a slow and painful death. Then she smiled as she dumped me in the roasting hot bath fully clothed. I almost slipped out of consciousness again as my skin flamed.

As I sat in the bath for a while, my whole body ached and my brain fought to close down. The bath became slightly cooler while I began to relax and let the water seep into my soul, healing me. I checked the time and it was eight fifteen. I had been in the bathroom for over an hour.

When I turned my head to see Jenny sitting on a chair looking bored, she spotted me looking at her and shouted for her dad. Mr Stevenson came into the bathroom and told Jenny to help him get me out of the bath. I wanted to protest but I couldn't seem to find my mouth. I started to cry and they both just laughed at me, seeing me so distressed. In the next few moments, I was dumped onto the floor and given a towel, told to dry myself and change into clothes.

I tried again to ask what clothes to wear but my mouth felt as if it had been glued shut. I started to scream in my head when I heard Nate telling me to calm down. I could hardly breathe and he told me to calm down? I wanted to scream at him as well. He told me I was screaming at him and if I didn't calm down, I wouldn't open my mouth. Feeling as if I was hyperventilating, after closing my eyes and concentrating on his voice, I managed to do what he said, although both his dad and Jenny smacked me on the head, telling me to move.

He told me to focus on his voice and remember how to open and close my mouth. When I had focussed on what he'd advised, he spoke again, "Look in the mirror and draw a finger across your mouth. Do this three times clockwise and four times anti-clockwise, then repeat three times."

I had to change my clothes before I could get up and a swift punch in my back reminded me I wasn't alone. Moving was agony; my bones were on fire and when I looked down, I saw why they were. My skin looked red raw and I could see licks of flames dancing up and down my arms.

I looked at Mr Stevenson and he smirked looking more like the demon he was. I had never seen him look so evil before. He told Jenny to leave and informed me in a whisper,

"Jasmine, if you get aren't better by the thirtieth then that feeling of your skin burn and blood boiling will become all you feel as we kill you." His eyes met mine in the mirror and my whole body shook at the malice in them.

I glanced down, unable to maintain eye contact with him and for a second, I experienced a moment of pure agony, worse than anything I had ever experienced. As I fell forwards, gripping the sink, it stopped. He laughed and left me alone in the bathroom where my breathing was shallow as I tried to control the memories of the pain.

I changed and dragged myself across to the mirror to do as Nate said, but I could hardly get myself into a standing position. I still felt extremely weak. I could feel Nate helping me as I sat there and finally managed to stand upright, looking at myself in the mirror. I could barely recognise the person standing there.

My hair was matted with blood and dirt, my face swollen and bruised, especially around my eyes and mouth. I stared at my reflection for a few minutes and heard Nate's howl of rage, ringing in my ears, as he saw my reflection. I followed Nathan's instructions as he raged and stormed inside my head, saying over and over again, "A few days, Jasmine. I will be there for you in a few days. We will have a plan. I won't leave you there much longer. I promise."

I dropped to my knees, hitting the floor like a sack of potatoes as I heard

Nathan telling me he had to go or he'd be late for class. I knew he was lying. I could feel how sick he felt and didn't want to think about the way I looked because it was a result of his family's viciousness.

I managed to scramble out into the foyer when Nick walked by, accompanied by his Barbieesque girlfriend, and although they just glared at me, I could feel the hatred emanating from them in waves.

Mr Stevenson walked out of the dining room and over to me, unsealing my lips. He called Nick back to help him and they dragged me into the barn where they threw a thick sleeping bag over me. It smelled old and dusty, but I could smell Nathan's aftershave on it, which soothed me some. I finally thought I had a few minutes to myself when Nick walked back out with a beaker of soup. He spilled some on me and laughed as I winced in pain.

He then turned to leave, but before he reached the door, he walked back with a bucket of ice-cold water, that had been catching the rainfall into the barn. He tipped it over my head. I was soaked through and shivering, but he laughed again and walked out, slamming the barn door behind him. The barn was freezing, the wind chilly, and my clothes soaking wet.

What had my life become? I couldn't imagine how I would survive a few more days of this. I crawled into the sleeping bag, shivering so badly that it felt like convulsions that hurt my aching body more than I thought was possible. I was still in pain all over, but eventually I drifted off to sleep.

The beaker of soup was leak-proof and I kept it beside me for extra warmth. When I awoke with the sound of the door banging open, I felt groggy and unsure of where I was. I looked down at the flask and felt so hungry my head spun. Waiting on eggshells to see who had come in, no one was there. I scrambled into a sitting position and took a mouthful of soup, gagging at the coldness of it, but thankful that it was filling and not freezing cold.

Somehow I imagined that Nate around me, but I knew that it was impossible. I took another drink of soup as Nate spoke. I gagged on my soup and jumped again, wincing as the movement pulled on the parts of me that were in agony.

"Jas, I'm sorry. I didn't mean to scare you. I had to take an enchantment off that soup or you would submit to my family's orders. Forgive me." I began to ask him why he did something so risky, but he cut me off. His answer shocked me to the core. "I couldn't let you submit to my family. They would ask you about us, about me, and it would end up with us both being killed."

"I don't understand, Nathan," I answered in my head, whispering just in case anyone was listening in.

"You would tell them whatever they wanted to know, and they would have killed you before coming for me."

CHAPTER 16
INVISIBLE ATTACKERS

I fell asleep again, wishing I could have seen Nate when he was there. I missed him so much; having him hold me for a second would have made the torture in that moment much more bearable.

I was in that state between waking and sleeping when the barn door slammed open once again. I didn't have the energy to open my eyes, but could feel a presence there. I tried to force my eyes open; lying like that made me feel very vulnerable when I a hit caught my back, right between my shoulder blades. Still struggling to sit and open my eyes, the hits kept coming and some sharp claws cut at my eyebrow. Suddenly from the other side of the barn, I heard a yell. When I finally managed to open my eyes, no one was there.

I glanced over to see Nick and Leanne looking silently at me as if I was insane. I could feel the blood flowing from a cut above my eye and my hands were scratched. Even when Mr Stevenson appeared at the door and looked in askance, Nick categorically denied knowing what happened. "When we walked in the door, she was writhing about on the floor and struggling to get up." I said nothing, feeling numb. It seemed as though I was being beaten by not only the family, but by invisible creatures as well.

This was getting ridiculous. Mr Stevenson walked over to me and asked me what happened, but I had no idea. When I told him that, he just gave me a look filled with rage and I knew what would happen next, except it didn't.

He just walked away from me and it had me wondering again how such a beautiful man could be so inherently evil. I still found it hard to believe, as I looked at his green eyes that crinkled at the corners, so much like his sons, and it caused me a pang as I realised just how much I missed Nate.

Watching him walk out the door, he stopped just outside, saying something to Nick that I didn't quite hear, but I got the gist of it when Nick walked in and placed a stool on the floor by the door of my barn.

I just looked at him as he growled at me. Leanne walked in, sat on his knee, and kissed him, which was not something I wanted to see. I crawled into my sleeping bag and blocked out the noise from three feet away.

Normally I would have found this difficult, but I needed to tell Nate what had happened. Tentatively, I reached out to him and said hi. He didn't answer straight away so I started to run through that day's events in my head. It became more difficult to block out the noises from beside me as I heard the stool being thrown away as they moved onto the floor.

I could hear unzipping and fast breathing, but I concentrated on my own dilemmas and ignored Nick and Leanne's astounding lack of ethics and morals. The smell in the barn changed from the normal small of decay and wet hay to the unmistakable smell of sex. The wind howled and suddenly Nate spoke to me, making it even easier to drown the other sounds out.

"Hey baby," his voice crooned softly in my ear.

I told him about my day, "Well hi," I answered him softly and I began explaining what had been going on. "I was attacked this morning, but there was no one there."

He interrupted me, startling me. "Jas, I know and I know how you feel. I miss you so much and I can't wait to get you out of there and back into my arms where you belong. God, this is so hard. I miss holding you, kissing you and knowing you're safe."

The noises beside me got louder, I scrunched up my eyes and my thoughts must have shown what was happening beside me because Nate started speaking again, disgust colouring his tone, "he's actually having sex while you're there? Oh my god, that's sickening, but we need to talk about the thing that attacked you okay?"

"Okay," I whispered, "but I don't remember much."

"How about I just ask you questions and you answer them with as much detail as you can remember?" His voice was soft, gentle and soothed my soul. Tears stung my eyes as I thought about the previous few days and how bad things had gotten.

"Jas, I need you to focus, please? What happened when you were attacked?"

I closed my eyes and tried to breathe through my mouth as I thought about the attack. "I was half asleep and the barn door flew open, but I didn't bother opening my eyes. I thought it was one of your family, come to torture me some more."

"Did it have fists or claws? Do you have any cuts or scratches on you? Did it have really sharp nails?"

As I answered his questions, my head spun; he fired them at me like bullets, not giving me time to look at my arms, hands, and face to see if I had any new wounds. "Slow down Nate. I don't know if it had claws or fists, but I have a cut on my eye? It did have sharp nails though, I remember that much."

"Okay, do you feel sick or dizzy? Does your head hurt?" His tone was gentle and I reached out and touched my cheek, feeling the sticky wetness that told me the cut on my eye was still bleeding. My stomach rolled and I lay back down slowly,

"Yeah I feel sick and dizzy, but my eye is still bleeding. Nathan what did this to me?"

"I don't know baby, but I will find out. Why don't you try going to sleep?"

I didn't want to move; I could still hear the unmistakable sound of sex beside me. The howling of the wind got louder and the tree in the barn creaked and scraped on the wooden roof, making me jump. It sounded like claws dragging along the wooden roof. The noise terrified me, but Nathans voice soothed me as he spoke softly to me, "Sweetheart, you're completely safe. Nick's there and as much as he's a total dick, he'll protect you. He has too, so go to sleep and get better."

"Okay. And Nate, I love you."

"Yeah, you too babe. Sweet dreams."

I relaxed and allowed myself to fall asleep. I knew by the light of dawn that I'd slept through another night and when I looked out of my sleeping bag, I saw Nick looking at me defiantly. He looked exhausted, with bags under his eyes. My eyes moved to the figure beside him and I noticed Mr Stevenson looking down on me as if I was a piece of dirt stuck to his shoe.

The drip, drip, drip of the water from the roof landed softly beside me and I was stunned at how well I could hear. I didn't say anything to either of them, but my heart leapt for joy at the thought that in one day's time, I would be out of there and with Nate.

Mr Stevenson looked at me and came right down to my level. As I still struggled to get up, he handed me a new flask of something hot. He asked me where the other one was and without thinking about it or meaning to do it, I transferred the contents from yesterday's flask into that day's and vice versa. He took the flask away and I had no idea what I had done until Nate's voice sounded in my head, asking me how I had managed that.

I heard him as if he stood right beside me, but I instinctively knew he couldn't be. Jumping a little as an almighty roar sounded, I crouched down into a ball, looking around painfully. I couldn't see clearly, my head buzzed, my skin burning, and I shivered with the freezing cold wind blowing into the barn, but still I was alive and getting out of there within a few days if all went according to plan.

At two in the morning, I awoke again. I knew I shouldn't be alone but I felt as though I was being watched by eyes I couldn't see in the darkness. I reached for my lantern when a hand shot out of the darkness and just as I was about to scream bloody murder, the hand clamped over my mouth and a voice that made my heart leap hissed in my ear, "It's me, Jas. Shush." I exhaled in relief, but I still wanted to cry. It was so hard not to cry out as he held me tightly until I fell asleep again.

"Why are you here? It's so dangerous."

"Jas, you were crying out to me in your sleep. I couldn't leave you here alone again, but I have to go now. When I come back tomorrow, I'll tell you the escape plan. Then the next day, we'll be off. Good night. I love you." With a kiss to my forehead, he vanished as I fell into a deeper sleep than I would have thought possible.

I awoke the next morning and realised my hands were gripped onto something. I opened my palm and saw a note pressed there. As I opened it, I glanced around and saw that for once I was finally on my own.

When you go shopping today, get on the bus towards Dumfries. I will be there to meet you.

Going to the shops that morning proved difficult because Jenny accompanied me, but as we got closer, I was almost bouncing in anticipation, waiting for her to go away. Then Lucca appeared at the checkout as we entered the supermarket. Jenny walked out, leaving me. I abandoned the trolley and walked outside to the bus stop, noticing that the bus to Dumfries was just leaving. I climbed on, paid my fare, and hid in case anyone noticed I was missing. As the bus pulled away, I saw Jenny walk into the coffee shop and I sighed in relief.

The bus took forty minutes to get to Dumfries. When we arrived, I walked off the bus and into Nathan's arms. His smile when I was in his arms was contagious and although we had never been in more danger, I finally relaxed because no matter what happened next I was with Nathan.

He stepped back, kissed my forehead and my nose, before he leaned back and growled at me. "Look at the state of you. Let's get out of here." He dragged me outside to his car; we got in and drove off, weaving in and out of traffic, for just under two hours. He didn't speak the whole time and his eyes were on his rear view mirrors as we drove down towards the south. He squeezed my hand when we reached Birmingham, and smiled over at me. His smile was breathtaking, and his green eyes rested on me a moment before he pulled into a car park on the motorway.

He pulled me out and we swapped cars. He left his car, a brand new BMW sitting with the keys in the ignition as he transferred our bags to a ford focus with tinted windows. It wasn't a new car and I wondered how he had arranged everything.

"I'm awesome, haven't I told you that before?" he answered lightly as I dived into the other car. He started the car and began driving northwards.

"We need to drive up to Edinburgh and we are gonna hide out there for a while if that's okay with you?" He sounded nervous and I nodded slowly at him. I didn't trust myself to believe that this was real. I thought I was in a really good illusion or dream, but I didn't wanna wake up from it.

Nathan hummed along with Ed Sheeran on the radio and smiled as he watched me, sitting looking out the window. We got caught in traffic and Nathan made me hide on the floor in the event any demons were about. He had glamoured the car so that if anyone looked in, they would see him and another girl. He knew that no magic was fool proof and a strong demon would see through it.

After five hours of driving we finally pulled off in Edinburgh and headed towards Campbell Park. We parked the car in what looked like a large boulder. The boulder closed behind us and Nathan ushered me from the car, leading me around in circles for about half an hour.

We finally arrived at what looked like a shack in the woods, invisible to mortals but made of what looked like oak with runes carved into the sides.

"I hope you're ready, Jasmine. They are gonna come after us with everything they have." He put his arms around me and as he did, I knew I could fight whatever they threw at us as long as he was by my side, fighting in my corner.

PART TWO

CHAPTER 17
A SHACK IN THE WOODS

We approached the shack and my eyes widened, it was small with two rooms, no cooker, or bathroom or any appliances. There was a half tent set up in the second room. It was full of drafts, from different angles since there were random holes in the woodwork.

I moved around taking in the space as Nathan set up the two camp beds from the corner, placing sleeping bags over them. I also noticed a camping stove and four buckets. There were tins stacked and a few cool boxes stacked in the corner beside them, with water bottles sitting beside them.

"It's not much," came Nate's voice from behind me, "but it's safe and we're together." He slipped his arms around me, kissing me softly. "I've been setting this up for months."

Since he didn't have his phone, and there wasn't any electricity anyway, we had no idea if the hunt was on for us. As night closed in, we sat beside each other holding hands, and we were both too tense to speak. When the dark became pitch black, Nate pulled out a torch and ushered me into bed.

"Your body needs to heal, go to sleep my angel. I'll be right here keeping watch over you." He kissed my head as I snuggled down in the sleeping bag and held my hand while I dozed off to sleep.

After a few hours, I awoke, hearing voices outside, but Nate just pressed a finger to my lips and I shuddered. He leaned close to me, touching my forehead with his as his words formed in my mind.

"They don't know where we are baby. It's okay, go back to sleep." I tried to sleep, but it eluded me so I decided to switch over with Nate. He needed to sleep too.

"Babe, you go to sleep. I'll keep watch for a while"

He nodded at me, kissing me softly as he passed over the torch and lay in his bed, pulling the covers up to his chin. "Wake me if something happens, okay?" he whispered as I turned away from him, shaking in the darkness. "Sure, thing."

For a while, I just sat staring into the blackness and eventually I nodded off. My head was on my arms as I dreamed that they found us. Nathans dad coming first, they broke in and grabbed him, pulling him outside and tying him to a tree. My whole body shook as they prowled towards me and I woke Nathan up screaming and writhing as they tore at my skin while he watched helplessly.

A hand shook me awake and I sobbed onto Nathan's chest, "Oh my god, they found us." His arms tightened their hold, as he spoke soothingly into my hair, "no, they didn't babe, we're still here. It's okay, we're okay." His hands rubbed my back in circles as I calmed down and my breathing returned to normal.

He didn't speak to me for a while, just sat on the cold floor holding me and I closed my eyes, knowing that he was beside me and that we were safe however temporarily it seemed. "Jas," Nate's voice broke into my thoughts as I began to drift off once more. "Yeah, Nate?" I answered sleeping trying to force my eyes to open.

"I love you. Now why don't we both go to sleep since all's quiet? I'll be right beside you and when you wake up, I'll be here holding you okay?" He kissed me softly on the forehead, on the nose and finally on my lips. "I love you too, Nate. Thank you for saving me and for everything."

"I wouldn't have it any other way, baby. You are my whole world and I wouldn't be able to live with myself if something happened to you." He helped me up and tucked me in, zipping my sleeping bag up and kissed me gently before stepping back and pulling his bed right beside mine. I fell asleep as he curled his hand around my own and woke up with the noises from the birds outside in the early morning.

Nate slept soundly beside me and I looked at his face, he was tense, but in sleep he seemed more relaxed and more at peace than I'd ever seen him before. It was amazing watching him as he slept.

"Jas, are you being a creep and watching me sleep?" He peaked over at me and smiled as I answered, "yeah, Nate. I guess I am." His eyes turned hungry and he closed the gap between us, running his hand up my neck and pulling my face to his. As his lips met mine, he sighed, "god, I missed you every single day I was away, don't let me leave you again."

He pressed more firmly to my lips and I met his tongue with my own. There was a sudden noise and Nathan fell onto the floor, his camp bed collapsed and at his wounded look I burst out laughing. He stared at me angrily for a moment, before he joined in, pulling me down to the floor beside him.

He tickled me and I laughed, looking into his eyes as he smiled down at me. His eyes shone with the love he had for me and for one moment I saw our futures together, entwined as though our future was a tapestry yet to be written, but one where we always found each other and had to be together.

There was a loud cracking sound from outside and Nathan jumped up and ran to the window. We were well hidden in this shack, but his spine stiffened and I made to move towards him, "stay there. They'll sense you." His tone was ice as his words shot into my mind and I shivered, rocking back on my heels until the danger had passed.

Nathan walked back towards me, shaking as he moved and his eyes darted around and around. He sat on the chair as far away from me as he could get and looked out the window, watching without glancing at me once.

"Jas, we need to be careful. I let my guard slip there momentarily, and they almost found us. We can't be intimate until this is over, because our love acts like a beacon and they are drawn to us. I need…" he took a deep breath and swallowed before continuing softly, "God, I want to, but we can't risk it."

His eyes closed as he swallowed and I nodded at him, but I could respect that. "Okay, Nate. It's okay; we won't go any further until it's safe."

Over the next few weeks the temperature plummeted even more and we ended up sharing our sleeping bags to keep warm, but that lead to more temptation, although we coped well with it, never straying and knowing what would happen if we did, but just being with each other was enough and as the shack became colder and snow fell, we were both exhausted and sleeping without trying because my nightmare about Nathan's family finding us became more a more frequent and I worried that it would eventually become a reality.

Running was harder than I ever imagined. I couldn't believe it had come to this. What were we thinking? The shack was just so damp, old, and risky. I felt like at any minute we could be caught. I had to stop myself right then. I definitely did not want to jinx our temporary safe haven.

Some of the past few months had been the best of my life. We had been so happy and content. We lived off of the land and only shopped when we had to. Nate usually went and came back loaded with tins to last us until the next shop.

Nate had gone to get a few thistles and leaves to make some sort of potion and I felt extremely on edge. I just wanted him to come back straight away. I knew the shack was protected, but I felt as if they were closer than they had been before. We had been hiding for a few months and we hadn't been caught yet, but still it felt as if they were somehow closer.

Sitting at the window, looking out into the forest, I could see nothing out of the ordinary when a face appeared in front of me. I almost screamed in terror. A face straight out of my nightmares! Oh my God, they found us. I could see them tying up Nate and I heard the wood of the door creak open. My heart raced and my breathing sped.

I awoke drenched in sweat, and shaking. I moved swiftly and quietly into the other room, trying hard not to wake Nate. I could hear him restlessly moving around. When he walked through a few minutes later, he found me curled in a ball on the earthen floor, crying. He said nothing but sat on the floor and pulled me into his arms, holding me until I stopped crying. I looked at my watch and could see it was three a.m. We were both exhausted; I had been having this exact dream for the past week and it was freaking me out.

Eventually he asked me, "What happened, baby?" His tone was soft, but his eyes were tense and I could see just how much this worry was wearing on him and I didn't want to add to it. "I had that same dream where your dad finds us." His eyes closed at my words and he ran his fingers over my cheek, breathing in and out and for a moment it was the only sound, until he broke the pre-dawn silence.

"I can feel it too. We're leaving here at dawn."

It was a freezing cold January morning outside, but as soon as dawn broke, we got our things together and left. He teleported us to a road a few miles away from where we had been staying and we then took a bus to take us towards the town centre, although we got off well before we reached the town.

Finally, after an hour of silence, I asked him where we were going. He didn't answer my question but handed me a bottle of water and took me into the nearest McDonalds, just a few feet from where we were. He handed me a change of clothes, brand new by the look of them. "Drink the potion quickly, and then change your clothes." It was very early in the morning with only a few people about and the server on the counter didn't even look as we walked to the bathroom.

Going in separately, continuing the conversation in our heads, I asked him, "Why do I have to drink the potion?"

As he changed, he answered softly, "This potion has added thistle and holly. It will change our appearance." Just as I was about to ask where we were headed, he said, "We'll head for Glasgow first and then head somewhere else after that."

I stopped asking questions after that. I watched my face change in the mirror. My face was thinner than before, my skin darker, and my eyes changed from piercing hazel to dark blue. I was stunned and when I looked at the sizes in the bag, I noticed that my clothes were two sizes smaller than the ones I normally wear.

As I put them on, I noticed that they fit pretty well. I couldn't believe how much thinner I was. Living on the edge with all that worry must do that to a person. I walked out of the bathroom and a stranger looked directly at me. Even though I instinctively knew he was Nathan, I still felt a little freaked out. He looked over at me, smiled as he said, "Are you ready to leave?" Even though he spoke with a voice that was strange to me, I could still hear Nathan through it. I just smiled, walked over to him, and took his hand. We walked out of the McDonalds, crossed the road, and began the next stage of our journey.

We were on the bus from Edinburgh to Glasgow, and as we passed the woods where we had stayed hidden for those few months, we both looked out, watching the cold morning drizzle. The bus ambled slowly along when we saw something that had us both tensing in panic. His dad's 4x4 parked at the side of the road. I could see his dad in front of me, menacing and evil. My body started to shake. The bus stopped directly across the road from where it was parked and we both looked out the windows to see a crowd of people gathered at the edge of the woods.

Nate just stared at the group and put his hand around my shoulder, giving me a squeeze. "Calm down, Jas." His voice whispered in my head and he brought his lips to mine since my breathing was becoming a little erratic. I found it hard to calm down, but as Nathan deepened the kiss, I had erratic breathing for a whole different reason. I shuddered as the bus moved off, stopping at traffic lights up the road and I could see in Nate's face how tense and worried he was. We both stared out of the window wondering if the bus would ever move away from those woods. Looking back, we could see his family shimmer into their demon forms, to find us.

Finally, after what seemed like an age, the bus moved and we stared back to make sure we were safe. I didn't feel safe and I could tell Nathan didn't either. If the way he held my hand was any indication, he was terrified. After about half an hour, we relaxed, and as we got closer to Glasgow, my heart stopped racing. I still felt on edge. We decided to go for breakfast and talk. We walked away from the bus, heading across to Buchannan Galleries, where we headed to the top floor food court. We ate in silence, just looking at each other. Eventually, I broke the silence, asking if he had a plan on where we were going. His answer surprised me.

"We need to find an internet cafe, and get out of here. It's too close to the bus station and if they find us, we are both dead."

Looking around, I could see a few computers and we decided to check them out. As we walked over towards them, I shook again and asked him then how long the potions were due to last.

"Thirty-six hours is all the cover we'll get on these, baby."

At the endearment, I looked questioningly at him and he shook his head gently. I saw a demon child staring at us. Nathan followed my eyes and snarled under his breath as the child walked away, making me jump.

Nate typed quickly, cursing under his breath the whole time he checked his alias email and as he found one from Joe, who was in hiding as well.

"Fuuuuuuuuuck!!" he muttered.

> Nate,
>
> We had to run, mate. We are hiding out in Glasgow, but I'm not sure how long we'll stay here. Lisa is getting so worried. I hate this. Why can't our families be normal?
>
> Anyway, we are staying at a youth hostel in the city of Glasgow.
>
> Let us know what you are doing
>
> And take care of both u n Jas
>
> Joe.

I looked over at Nate and he shook his head before asking me to get him something to drink. As I walked over to the counter, I could see him typing furiously from where I stood, leaving me wondering why he didn't want me to know what he was saying. Nate met me halfway as I walked back; leaving the three bags we had on the floor next to the computer.

He kissed me on the head and told me to go online. "There is still credit left. I have to disappear for a short while."

I felt stunned by that since he hadn't left my side since we had run. Why now? What did he say to Joe? Had we been made? All of those questions ran through my head as he kissed me softly, before turning to go, ignoring my questions.

I walked over to our belongings just to stop myself from thinking before the terror of being left alone incapacitated me. I could feel him watching me as he went down the escalator. I could see him from the corner of my eye. I saw him shake his head and look at the ground with a heartbreaking expression on his face. I turned back to the computer to distract myself and logged into an email account I hadn't used in the previous two years.

I found an email from my childhood friend Gwen. I had met Gwen when I was in the children's centre and we had become fast friends, but I hadn't spoken to her in the longest time so her telling me that she had a boyfriend and a baby boy named Abe was a surprise. She told me she stayed near Glasgow and that I should go and visit her. The date on the email was two months previous and Gwen had given me her mobile number to call, if I fancied a meeting.

I wrote the number down and I noticed another email had just come through. I looked at it and saw that it was from Nathan. Seeing that email caused my heart to stop beating. My breath caught in my throat, making me sound like I was choking. My eyes burned with tears.

I stared at the screen for a moment. I couldn't find the courage to open the email. I shook before finally moving my finger towards the button to open the email. I stopped halfway and thought, if I could take the beatings, monsters and hurt from before, I could open an email. No matter what it said, I knew I would be okay. I was lying to myself and I knew it; my head and my thoughts were in complete disarray. All I kept thinking was that he left me.

Why would he do that? He didn't want me anymore. What was I going to do?

After a few minutes of thinking like that, I mentally slapped myself and opened the email.

> *Jas*
>
> *I love you so much, but I have a few things to do and I need to leave you for a time. I'm sorry for doing this to you, but I have to keep you out of this.*
>
> *If you still want to be with me, meet me at the bus station on Saturday morning at half past seven.*
>
> *Be safe, all my love*
>
> *Nathan xxxxx.*

I couldn't think straight. I was deathly afraid and couldn't understand what had happened to make him leave me, even if it was just as he said, for a few days. I had nowhere to go and I was in a strange city. What would I do? I thought he loved me. Why would he leave me here like this? Eventually, I realised I had to leave and when I looked down, I noticed that only my bag of clothes were there. It felt like a kick in the stomach.

Suddenly I felt sick. I walked towards the escalators. I noticed a letter sticking out of my bag. I sliced my finger as I opened it and tried to examine the contents — money, a note from him just saying to stay safe, and my alias passport. I walked blindly along, not noticing where I was going. I did that for a few hours before eventually crossing a bridge. I just sat at a bus stop in the pouring rain, not looking around. I felt too numb to take in that I was alone and I needed somewhere to spend the night. I shivered but I couldn't even be bothered to move to warm up. I just sat there in this suspended stupor for over an hour.

CHAPTER 18
MISTAKES COST DEARLY

I was so cold after an hour sitting like that, that I could barely think. My breath came in gasps and my fingers were bright red. I noticed a telephone box beside the bus stop. I remembered that I had written down Gwen's number. I didn't think it through any more than that. I called her, surprised that she answered on the first ring. I suddenly didn't know what to say. I started to speak, to say hello, but she cut me off.

"Oh my God, Jas, is that you? How are you? Where are you? How is your life going?"

I waited for her to stop. "I'm in Glasgow somewhere and I got lost."

"Wow! Where are you? I'll come get you and you can stay here."

Because I was freezing cold, I didn't think about how irresponsible it was or how it could be dangerous. I told her that was outside a train station facing a railway bridge as she said, "Stay there. I know exactly where you are. I'll be there in a few minutes!"

I waited fifteen minutes and finally saw a blue Ford KA pull up beside me. I didn't notice any other details and while she leapt out, looking around her. She didn't recognise me, and I used my powers to allow her to see my true face. I stepped towards her and she ran over to give me a hug, I looked around, feeling more than a little sick. Eventually, I just looked at her and cried. She didn't ask what was wrong with me, but looked at me curiously. I lied and told her it was because I was so incredibly happy to see her. Getting into her car, she started chatting at me, telling me all about her life now. How much she loved being a mum and how her wee boy was the light of her life. I didn't talk, just listened in amazement at how her life had turned out.

I felt so happy for her. We got to her house after about twenty minutes and went in. She made us both a coffee and while we sat in her pristine living room, I tried to listen to what she told me, while I warmed up.

Suddenly I fell asleep and when I awoke, I was in a dark room, chained to a wall. I had no idea what happened, but I felt pain and began to get flashes of the day. I hadn't really fallen asleep. I was charmed into unconsciousness, but I managed to stay awake. I remembered her partner coming in and hearing him say, "Ah, you got her?"

Her answer shocked me more than anything, almost opening my eyes as she told him, "Yeah, I did, but she's on her own. I think he's left her. She cried all the way here and she looks so sad."

I couldn't believe she'd betrayed me like that. When I went to sit and let my eyes creep open, I felt myself being beaten and heard a snapping sound so loud that it echoed through the dark, damp room. As I went unconscious again, I felt Nathan, but I was sure that I was mistaken; he had left me. Waking up much later, I was in a different room, dark brown with no furniture in it, except a hard-backed chair.

While I looked around and tried to catch up with what was happening, he stood over me. I jumped up in terror. His face was one I had seen before. He had a face like the bark of a tree, eyes black as night and his hands were like claws. He was there Halloween I found out about the horrors of life with demons.

He questioned me for what felt like hours, asking me the same questions, "Where's Nathan?" I didn't answer and he growled, his fist flying into my mouth. I heard the crack of my teeth, but I couldn't feel it. I still didn't speak, just shook my head at him, spitting some blood out of my mouth.

"Where is my cousin?" His voice was getting angrier and this time he kicked me full force in the stomach. I grunted, but didn't answer and he grabbed my hair, yanking my head back as he punched me on the cheek, "I'm gonna try this again, Where is Nathan?"

I still wouldn't answer and the beating went on for ages. Starting to fight back, I kicked out at him, eventually connecting with his knee. He walloped me in the stomach and then began beating me again. Finally, he stopped, walked out, slamming the door so hard the wall shuddered. I slumped down, exhausted. I realised that it was a deadly situation, but I refused to be killed. I tried to figure out a way out of there.

Jumping in fright when I heard Nate speaking to me, "Jas, you have got to get yourself out of there. Now! I can't get to you, but you have some of my transportation powers. Use them with yours and try to come to me!"

Closing my eyes and concentrating as much as I could on getting to him, I again slipped under and when I awoke once more, I was not alone. It must have been about three o'clock in the morning and I felt thirsty and sore. My lip hurt but my arm was killing me, throbbing and aching. I gingerly tried to move it, but it was broken again.

I noticed Gwen watching me. She was supposed to be my friend. She looked at me with disgust in her eyes and told me she was planted in the home to keep an eye on me.

"The elders realised you were being bullied and were unhappy. They worried about you running away, so they planted me in there and told me to be your friend. I missed my mum and dad terribly. I was separated from my family for so long, two years in fact, and I will never, ever forgive you for that."

She then walked over to me, gripped my hair, and slapped me across the face. I felt so angry I could scream. I felt a rage building in me, like a fire I had never felt before. My family were dead or missing because of her precious demons. The love of my life had left me because I was a danger to him. Everyone I had ever trusted had betrayed me, yet there she stood bitching and moaning about her life. She got up, walked out, and locked the door.

Fuming for a few minutes, I abruptly felt like I had been wrenched away. I was free of the chains. I grabbed my bag, sitting on the floor beside me, and allowed myself to be overcome with rage. A moment later, I stood in a strange unfamiliar room, looking at a stunned Nate. The last thing I saw before I collapsed onto the floor in a heap.

Feeling him working over me and hearing other voices I didn't recognise made me uneasy and I started shaking before sinking back into the warmth of the blackness. The next time I was able to wake, I managed to open my eyes even though they felt sore and swollen. My arm was stiff and sore, but surprisingly not broken. I looked beside me and saw Nate, completely exhausted. He just glared at me without saying anything and I didn't know what to say. Then the tirade started.

"I thought I asked you to take care of yourself. Look at you. I almost lost you again. We're leaving in an hour. I booked something to take us away. I managed to get your passport. Alan almost caught me, but I managed to get away. My parents are here in this city now. Jas, what were you thinking? How did you not know she was the daughter of demons? She was at my parents' house that Halloween."

I couldn't speak yet. My voice was lost. I was hurt and angry that he thought I would intentionally put myself in danger. I felt as if he had just punched me in the gut. The tears filled my eyes and I turned my head away so he wouldn't see me cry. He got up and I heard the door close. I sobbed so hard it hurt, but I had pushed my face into a pillow so no one could hear my tears. Nathan walked over to the bed, climbing in beside me and pulling me into his arms. "I'm sorry, baby. I know it wasn't your fault, but I almost lost you. I know it was my fault. I should never have left you alone. Please forgive me."

I was still too upset to speak and as he hugged me, I broke down further. I couldn't tell him why yet; there would be time for that when we got where we were going. I looked at him and asked if I could go for a shower. He surprised me, saying, "No, I'll help you get washed."

It wasn't until we stood in the bathroom, in front of a mirror, I understood why I couldn't go for a shower. My face was swollen, bruised, and puffy from crying. I looked at him in horror and he understood my terror. He reassured me that no one would see what my real face looked like; they would only see the illusion he had created. I got dressed into a polo neck and jeans, slowly and painfully needing his help.

"Your arm was broken. You had a broken jaw and rib, but when you got here, we managed to mend the breaks. We can't cure the bruises or the stiffness. They will heal on their own, but the bruises at the breaks will take longer than normal bruises."

He helped me pull on my polo neck and we walked out of the room slowly together. He gave my hand a gentle squeeze, leaning down to kiss my head. "I love you," he whispered as we walked out of the room holding hands.

We left the place we were staying at seven in the morning and I wondered how long we had been there. Looking around, I could see a familiar part of Glasgow. We had spent the night in a flat just next to Buchannan Street and we walked to the top of the town. Nate didn't speak to me, just occasionally glanced sideways as I winced, feeling the pain shooting through me over and over again. Feeling exhausted, Nate assured me that we would sleep.

The pain in my chest increased as we walked and I could feel that we were in immense danger. I saw him look up tense and agitated, but he kept a firm hold of my hand as we walked casually by Nick and Leanne, who were looking straight through us as if they couldn't see us at all. I felt myself shake and then jumped suddenly as Nate reprimanded me. As we got by them, Nate kept looking back and said to me in a stern voice, "Jas, baby, we gotta move. They are all here. I can hear them. If they catch us, they will kill us."

I just nodded along as our walking picked up speed and I could feel the fear leak through. We got to the Thistle Hotel at the very top of town, meeting the transport, along with Joe and Lisa. I panicked as I spotted them, pulling on Nathan's hand. He turned around and looked at me, as I backed away, pulling him with me. He followed my gaze and his eyes softened, as he understood what scared me.

"It's okay, Jas. They escaped too and are coming with us. They were in the apartment with us and helped me heal you. It's okay, baby. Don't worry."

I was still shaking a little as we walked towards them, but Nathan and Joe shook hands and Lisa smiled tentatively at me, before walking onto the bus.

"It's good to see you awake again, Hun."

Nate left me standing alone as he loaded our bags onto the bus and we boarded. He paid the driver for all four of us and we followed Joe and Lisa, finding a seat at the back of the bus. The bus wasn't busy, but if felt more dangerous. As I tried to hold it together, Nate put his arm around me, quietly whispering in my ear. "You have to keep it together for just a little while longer. Okay?"

I buried my face into his chest and tried to breathe in through the panic. His hold tightened unexpectedly as though he expected danger. He was seated nearest the aisle and a 'police officer' climbed aboard the bus, spoke with the driver, and moved slowly to look at all the passengers.

His face was hideous — grey in colour with eyes a vivid green and skin that looked rough and jagged. I felt myself shaking with fear, but he looked right through us and stopped at the row in front of us. A girl with dark hair slept in the seat and we both gasped in horror as he grabbed the sleeping girl by the hair, dragging her face back to look at it.

He then grabbed both of the passengers directly in front of us, helped by an unsuspecting human colleague, and pulled them off the bus. As he passed the driver, he nodded, giving the signal that we could go.

I wondered why the humans couldn't see him for what he was, but we could. "I put a charm on us so we can see demons, but they can't see us at all. It will last until sundown and should hopefully keep us out of sight."

I shook again so hard I felt like my teeth would to break, but I made myself relax and allowed myself to fall asleep. The relief of unconsciousness lasted only minutes and then I was awake again. Nate pulled me out. "They can sense you if you are unconscious. We need to stay awake for now while I set protection around our unconscious minds. Can u do that? I have to concentrate hard to make sure this works. Please try to stay calm."

I nodded at him and looked out of the window at the exact same moment he did. We both saw his father looking enraged and yelling something at Nick.

Nathan looked at me, walls completely down, and for the very first time, I could see just how much this hurt him. I felt so bad. This was entirely my fault, but at that thought, Nate squeezed my hand to reassure me and began again to concentrate.

An hour later, as we passed through the washed out, green, Scottish countryside, he looked sideways at me. "Sleep, honey. I have put as much protection around us as I was able. So you can go to sleep. Okay?" I looked up at him from where I lay on his chest and kissed him, working my way up to his lips. He kissed me back, followed by him saying, "I love you so much! None of what happened is your fault. We shouldn't exist." I could feel the tears building and I closed my eyes. I felt him tense as he saw the images my mind brought up. He held me tight, allowing me to finally fall asleep, but not before thinking if we could survive this, it would be more than a miracle.

I slept for a few hours. As I awoke, he was asleep. All the pain, worry, and angst gone from his expression, and he looked so innocent. I needed this Nathan back, somehow I had to protect us. I was through with him protecting me. I knew I had powers and it was time to start using them. His skin was smooth as I moved my hand up, touching his face and kissing him softly before turning to look around. The countryside rushed by and I wondered where we were going. I heard Joe speaking in a low urgent voice behind me and I wondered why they sounded tense. I wanted to look around, but I stopped myself. I wondered if Nate's life would have been better if I had never entered it.

"Babe, stop being ridiculous. I love you more than my own life and if you hadn't come along, my life would be worthless. I would be a soul-sucking monster with no conscience. You are my world and I don't need anything but you to feel complete."

Smiling over at him, I couldn't think of anything to say to that statement. Instead, I asked him where we were going. "Ireland!" he answered simply. I didn't understand the reluctance in his features. I could tell he had realised that I was puzzled. He nodded across the aisle, his eyes tight and mouth in a small line. Following his line of sight, I noticed the demon on the bus for the first time. His skin was dark brown with green running through it. His eyes were purple and he looked right at us. I asked Nathan in a whisper, if he could see or hear us. He assured me that he couldn't because of the protection charms, but it wasn't a good idea to talk about or plans aloud. I still didn't feel safe at all and at this moment, I wondered if I ever would.

We reached the ferry port soon after and jumped off the bus. We then boarded a massive boat. Once aboard, we found so many demons on the boat, stunning Nathan.

"You and Lisa can't leave our sides. If you have to go to the bathroom, go together. Don't... just stay with us please."

Watching him, we agreed; his expression and tone scared me. As we went to get food, I noticed that he had a new bag. The bag was inconspicuous but as he opened it up when Joe and Lisa walked away, I noticed it was full of cash.

"What on Earth do you need that for?"

"Later!" he hissed at me, his face tensing as he put his hand on my back and gently pushed me towards the food. When we paid for the food, we left the warmth of the boat going outside, onto the top deck. The January sky looked grey, almost black, it was raining and freezing cold. We were all alone outside with no one around. The boat rocked as Nathan finally decided to fill in some holes. I could barely hear him over the roaring wind.

"We are going to Donegal and are going to hide out there for a while. The bag has eleven thousand pounds in it, all the money I had saved up. I was supposed to use it for university but I saved it for running away ever since I realised I loved you and wanted to save you. I knew it would come to running away and hiding."

The boat journey seemed to take an age. The sea was choppy and the rain bounced. Eventually, we reached Larne and got back on the bus to Donegal. The bus was warm and cosy, but I looked around and noticed a demon couple sitting on the red seats, three rows away from us.

On the bus, we felt on edge as we could see the demon couple look around. The man texting on his phone had us all exchanging looks of panic. After a few hours on the bus, we finally arrived in Letterkenny where we left the main bus and went onto a mini bus. Thankfully, it was only our group and another two mortals.

The bus driver, Charlie, was a good natured, happy guy who made us laugh with his witty comments and jokes. As he drove, he questioned us on where we were going to be staying. The other people, a man and his son, ages about forty-five and sixteen were visiting family and would be staying with them.

"So where you all staying then?" Charlie asked us, looking around at the four of us and smiling.

"We'll sir, we're on a gap year from university and one of my friends was from here, and he suggested we should visit so here we are." His tone was bright, but his hand had tensed in mine as he spoke. I stroked the inside of his thumb and he shuddered. .

"How long are you over?" he probed and Nathan shifted slightly in his seat, the only sign he was uncomfortable with this line of conversation.

"Probably a couple of months. We plan on staying here till May or June and then head to Dublin before flying to Spain for the summer."

"Ah, that sounds grand."

The rest of the journey passed in relative silence and we didn't look at each other; we all felt slightly awkward and on edge with worry. As we reached the diamond in Donegal Town, the driver spoke in a low voice to Nate.

"My sis has a wee cottage not far from here that she lets out during the winter months. I don't think she got someone this year. It's probably sitting empty if you're interested. I can text her and ask."

"That would be amazing. Thank you."

"Don't thank me yet. I haven't got it for you yet," he answered as he texted his sister.

Nathan looked around at me, hope lighting up his features. He looked at

Joe who nodded and Lisa was smiling, as the bus driver walked back over.

"It is free and would be fifteen hundred pounds from now until May. If you stay until June, it's another five hundred. You would need to pay from now until May in advance."

"No problem," Nathan answered with a smile in his voice. "How do we get there?"

"Sure, I'll take you over now. Get back on the bus." Charlie answered, looking around us. Our faces paled, but we all nodded, getting on the bus and strapping ourselves in. We all worried again. This could have been a trap and we had no way of knowing for sure that it wasn't. We just had to trust Charlie and pray that he wouldn't betray us. Looking out of the window, we arrived after thirty minutes in a small village called Inver. As he drove closer to the beach, we relaxed and as we reached the row of houses facing the sea, he pulled over. "My sis lives in the first one. I will take you in now to meet her and you will need to pay her for the cottage. It's the second one in and runs on a one euro meter, which you'll need to top up to get electricity and gas for the house."

As we walked towards her house, I saw something flicker in the field behind, but I shook it off, thinking it was just another worry manifesting. I saw Lisa looking at me with wide eyes as though she had seen something as well.

After twenty minutes, a cup of tea, and some soda bread, we were finally given the key for the house. As we crossed the threshold, Nathan put down a line of salt, thyme, rosemary, and some rose petals, with stones marked with the runes for protection and safekeeping. As they sunk into the ground at the front door, he walked into the lounge doing the same on the window and repeated the protective enchantments at every door and window of the house.

As we walked around the house, the furnishings were old-fashioned, but more than adequate for our needs. There were two bedrooms, one facing the sea, with a double bed and a single. The other room had just a double bed and a wardrobe. We sat downstairs drinking tea while warming up on the sofa. It was so nice to have a home that was furnished, warm, and felt safe, although safety was a relative term. It only lasted a few months before the war and battles started again.

CHAPTER 19
A SAFE HOUSE

After a few weeks in the house, we planned our next move which involved a lot of going in circles. For me having Nate trying to shield me from decisions was difficult. He'd always been honest with me and to have myself sidelined as he discussed things with Joe annoyed me. It became unbearable in the house and all I wanted was to escape. I was frustrated with Nathan, angry that he was sidelining me and hurt that he couldn't see how much I was suffering being stuck in the house.

One night as Nathan and Joe discussed moving into a caravan on an island to protect it; Lisa confided in me that her period was late.

"Jas, have you ever, you know, been late?" her low voice asked as we watched the boys sitting at the table discussing the caravan idea. "No honey, I haven't, we haven't... I mean we can't..." I opened my mouth to say more when she interrupted me, "wait you and Nate have never?" Her eyes were opened in surprise and she spoke again softy, whispering in my ear, "but you're so intense?"

I nodded at her, watching Nate as he shifted and caught my gaze. He smiled at me, running his fingers through his hair and looked away after a moment. "I love him more than my own life, but we haven't ever you know."

She smiled at me and watched Joe as he bent down, speaking to Nate in a voice so low I wondered what he was saying as Nate's face tensed and he glanced over at me, shaking his head at his friend.

I shook my head, trying to dispel the worrying thoughts and looked back at my friend, "so, you're late huh?" She nodded at me with tears in her eyes and looked down at the carpet.

I touched her arm gently, and she swallowed before speaking again, "I know it's not great timing, but I really love him, Jas." I nodded at her and smiled at the thought of her having a baby at eighteen, but she'd be a great mum if we could just find a way to keep her and Joe safe.

"You'll be fine. We'll get a test tomorrow and then you can know for sure." She nodded at me and the boys walked over to the sofa's, sitting down beside us.

"So, what are you talking about?" Nate asked us, glancing between the two of us with a smile on his face. Lisa shook her head gently, and I answered, "Not much, what's happening with the caravan idea?"

Nate's face lit up and even Joe smiled, something he didn't do very much. He seemed not to like me, or at least to distrust me.

"We've decided to try and find a cheap caravan, move it to a secure location and protect it with spells and enchantments." Nate sounded so excited as he spoke and Joe continued, "It should be safer and more protected than this place which means we can relax a little."

I smiled at Nate, Lisa at Joe as we contemplated being able to relax a little. Nate pulled me by the hand up to bed and as we lay down he kissed me hard. Our kisses were getting a little firmer and our hands were beginning to wander, but after a few minutes of kissing me, he pulled away panting, "Jas, we can't. Not until we're safe."

He rolled over on his back and faced the wall away from me and disappointment welled up inside me, at the rejection. I knew he wanted me, but I also knew why we couldn't, but it didn't make it any easier. I lay down facing away from him, trying to swallow the pain that threatened to overwhelm me, when his hand snaked around my waist. "I'm sorry," he breathed into my ear, "I want you so much and it's so frustrating that we can't, but I can't risk your safety just to have some with you. I love you so much." He pressed a kiss to the back of my neck and pulled me towards him, holding me there until I fell asleep.

. Within a few days of these discussions, they went out and bought a second-hand caravan for a little over two thousand euro and a car for seven hundred euro from Charlie. The car was an old Volvo but Charlie was a mechanic and had just done a load of work to it.

The caravan was in a shed out back and they worked on it every day, buying things for it and putting them into the shed. Lisa and I were kept away from it; the boys said we couldn't leave the house just in case the demons sensed us. Nathan and Joe had scouted locations and had found an old deserted island not too far away. They went there for a few days to find somewhere large enough.

After another few weeks, on Lisa's birthday, the thirteenth of March, the boys came back exceptionally happy. One of the islands had a hidden cave. Owey Island was the place they had found and we were all praying that it would be our salvation. Every day, either Nathan or Joe would drive up to Cruit Island and get a boat across to Owey Island where they prepared the cave, putting all manner of protection onto it so when we moved there, it would become a safe haven. I could finally try to find my brother and sister.

Since we had escaped, I had begged Nathan to let me try to find them. I needed to know what had happened to them, but he told me that the minute I began searching, all manner of demons would be onto us and would come after us. I had to wait until we were safe.

After the first two months, I would often stand at the door looking out, thinking. The sea, grey and choppy, blew hither and tither in the freezing cold wind. I felt so worried that I was surprised I could feel the wind at all. We had another close call yesterday. Nathan went to the store and a demon almost spotted him. We could only hope they didn't see him or there would be more of them around before we could blink. The house was too open and our protection was minimal, but the island and the caravan simply weren't ready yet.

Nathan came to see me and I realised I'd been standing in the doorway, in the pounding rain for over half an hour. He pulled me up into his arm and guided me into the house to get warmed up. "Babe, come inside. You're soaked." His voice was gentle and his touch warmed me, "try to stop worrying, please?" He kissed me gently and led me by the hand into the bathroom where he turned on the shower.

"Nate, do you think we are safe here?" I asked him in a small voice as I waited for the shower to heat. He turned towards me slowly, his eyes running up and down my body as he stepped closer to me. His fingers reached out and he ran a finger over my cheek, caressing me, "I don't know, Jas, but I can't think about it just now. I've redoubled the protection around the house and it should hold up for most demons, but if my dad or Jack find us then, I don't know."

His lips turned down and he looked down when he finished speaking. I knew just by watching him, it was weighing on him. My powers we're so unpredictable and were a magnet for demons which that meant that we couldn't use them, so everyone was relying on him and now that Lisa was pregnant, he felt it more. I stepped into his arms, feeling his warmth through the soaked vest I was wearing as his arms circled my back. He rubbed my back and kissed my head, avoiding my eyes as we stood embracing.

"Nate?" I whispered with a question in my voice. He shuddered and kissed me once on the lips, gently before answering me. "What Jas?" He was still avoiding my eyes, so I touched my finger under his chin and brought his eyes up to meet mine, kissing him once more before speaking.

"We know you are doing everything you can. You need to try and calm down, we trust you and if the worst happens, it won't be your fault." His eyes filled with tears as he looked at me and he bent down kissing my fiercely, dragging his hand down my back and cupping my ass.

Suddenly, the door banged overhead and footsteps sounded above us. He stiffened and stepped back, while I groaned inside. The moment was gone again, every time we'd even come close to cementing our relationship, something happened to put a dampener on the moment. I knew we couldn't and why we shouldn't, but I wanted him so damn much it hurt.

He leaned his head on mine, breathing hard, kissed my forehead once, before he turned and left the room, closing the door softly behind him as he went. I stood there for a moment thinking that I knew I loved him and that he loved me, and all I wanted was for us to be together fully, but it seemed as though some higher power was enjoying messing around with us.

As I stood in the warm water, I knew we had to get away from this little village, into somewhere we could be protected from everyone. Being on the run was harder than I ever would have dreamed. We had to conserve every penny. Barbs, the lady we stayed with, was lovely, always buying us things and trying to give us some money back.

"He charged you too much. I don't want all that money. You kids should take it back and spend it."

It was the end of March and the house was freezing cold. When we started living here, the gas pipe was frozen and it occasionally happened then. It took us a week of pouring hot water on it from the kettle to use the cooker. Only two of the rings worked, but it was much better than the shack. It was warmer even though it was freezing; the shack would have been much colder.

We could use a little magic in the shack though, but in the cottage, it felt too risky to even conjure heat. We were so worried about being caught. It had also been confirmed that Lisa was pregnant, which meant we had to be so much more careful. She was four months gone. Joe wandered around during the night, checking and re-checking the doors and windows, making sure they were secure.

Joe and Lisa had just gotten up and I went to start breakfast for them. Sausages were the only food not turning Lisa's stomach, but they look a long time to cook. The kitchen was so cold I could see my breath. I wished they'd cooked faster, without really thinking, when I looked back at them, they were cooked.

Looking at them, I thought it was odd, though it wasn't the first time that had happened. I needed to speak to Nate about it while keeping an eye on it. A scream from the lounge made me run in. A demon was looking in the window, but he couldn't see us. He must have sensed the magic I inadvertently used. I closed my eyes and thought him away to the empty house in Ballyshannon, the one we thought about moving into, but decided we wouldn't have had enough protection.

We did lay a fake trail there though, and I hoped that would be strong enough to keep us safe for the moment. When I opened my eyes, he was gone and everyone looked terrified. I didn't know what to say. I had no idea I had this kind of power. What was I supposed to do? I didn't realise I'd voiced this aloud until Nate walked over to me, hugging me. I turned out of the hug, walked into the kitchen, and heard his voice asking, "What have I done? Talk to me, Jas. Please don't shut me out. We are in this together."

I couldn't answer so I just concentrated on getting the food out before it got cold. I walked out and found them all sitting around the table, talking about me. I heard only snippets of the conversation.

"We need to do something about her. She's getting too powerful!"

"What do you suggest we do? We don't know how to bind her powers, and even if we did, could we afford to? Though they are growing so fast, it's really beginning to scare me."

Joe just looked at him and said without feeling, "The only way to stop her is to kill her."

I couldn't believe I heard that they were considering killing me. I had no idea if I sent that thought to Nate. I turned around and walked out the back door, placing the food down on the counter on my way out.

Marching into the fields, the rain poured down so fast it bounced up from the grass. I kept walking through the field even though I felt wetter than I ever had in my life. I could feel Nate trying to get through to me, but I decided to block him out and hid myself in the stump of an old tree in the middle of the field behind the house.

I just needed some time to think, or so I kept telling myself. I didn't admit to myself that Joe's words or my own powers scared me. I never realised that the powers were growing stronger and I thought back to a time when I never believed in any other magical or mythical creatures. While I sat here with the rain dripping and the mud slopping around, I realised suppressing my powers could be a mistake.

CHAPTER 20
NEW FRIENDS OR FRENEMIES

I fell asleep thinking about it all and when I awoke, I realised I was no longer in the tree stump, but in a dark cave and I was dry but stiff. I couldn't understand what had happened, I could feel Nate worrying and I couldn't help wishing he was beside me.

As a light flashed in the cavern I was being held in, I saw Nathan arrive but he was unconscious. I looked at him to check that he was breathing when a voice behind me made me jump around, hiding Nathan with my body.

"Don't need to be afraid, we had to get you out of that house. We have brought your clothes and the caravan you were planning to live in has been finished. We also brought your friends as well, but they protested. We have sent them into the dream realm for a while."

I was dumfounded. I couldn't even think of a question to ask, but within seconds, the presence and the voice disappeared. When Nathan awoke, he hugged me, kissing my forehead. As my eyes became accustomed to the darkness, I could see a cut on his cheek with a black eye above it. "Nathan, what happened?" I asked, worry evident in my voice. He just shook his head.

"Not yet! I am so glad you're okay, baby. Why did you run away?"

I ran my finger over the cut, watching it heal as my finger touched it. I touched his eye, which healed as well.

I had no idea what was happening when all of a sudden, a gong sounded from deep beneath the ground, making me jump up.

Knowing we needed to follow it meant the explanation would have to wait. We saw a lantern hanging to our right, which I picked up. Almost as soon as I picked it up, the light flickered and went out, making it so dark I couldn't see my hand in front of my face.

With Nathan right beside me, I felt that somehow I knew the way. I allowed my senses to lead me. Nathan shivered beside me. He didn't say anything, but he didn't need to. We were together and that was all that mattered.

Hearing that thought calmed me and as we walked down a dark, musty corridor, fear threatened to overwhelm me. His presence kept me calm. I heard him curse under his breath and I went back a few paces to help him as he had stumbled.

The stones beneath our feet were small, but occasionally we walked over boulders and although I managed to stay upright, sometimes using the walls, Nathan wasn't so lucky, and he stumbled falling over a few times. His grunts as he fell made me go back to him to make sure he was okay. We walked on for a long while, holding hands again for the final part of it. Eventually, we walked through a hole in a wall, covered in a sheet so dark that it looked like part of the wall.

The moment we went through the curtains, we walked into a room so bright that we couldn't see anything. I looked around, trying to figure out whether to be scared.

"Where are we?" I turned around, but I didn't see Nathan. I could only see my own shadow. I dropped my hand to my side.

Turning around slowly, I would never forget the sight in front of me. There were creatures so small you could step on them without realising it, and creatures so big that they could squash a human being between the thumb and forefinger. I felt far from being reassured and when an old majestic voice asked us to step forwards, I just looked in awe at the most beautiful face I had ever seen. Her skin was translucent, with flowing locks of golden hair, eyes blue as the sky, and rosy cheeks.

Looking down at her feet, I could see Joe and Lisa, who was visibly pregnant now, lying there. I could feel my face change and I looked at her in defiance, feeling the power building in me like never before. I wanted my friends safe, even though they thought I should die. Nate placed a hand on my arm, pulling me back to him as the beautiful lady spoke.

"Calm down, little one. Your two friends are in an enchanted sleep and will awaken soon. We are leaving here because of the influx of demons, but we want to give you some protection before we leave." Looking at Nate, I finally breathed out, but I was still worried and Nathan could see it. He ran his fingers over my cheeks, calming me with his touch.

Turning back, I asked, "What kind of protection do you mean? What's happening? I don't understand! Who are you? What are you?"

At this, she looked mad and her face changed from a face of beauty to the face of a witch, with a long pointy nose, green eyes, ebony hair, and a wart at the end of her nose. She didn't realise that I could see that and when she spoke again, it was with care, and as if what she said was of vital importance. I felt her trying to get to Nate again, but I shadowed him again, intentionally this time. Even though I was unsure of these new powers, my instinct was to protect him. I looked at her and she answered me, "We are a mixture of mythical creatures who have gathered here to protect you, impart some wisdom and teachings to you. You must live. You are our only hope for survival, superstes."

"I'm sorry ma-am, but I don't understand what that is?"

Her eyes appraised me coldly and she tried to get to Nathan again, but I was standing in front of him. Her answer scared me a little, and her eyes drank in my expression greedily as she stared at me.

"You are the survivor, the warrior and the witness. You will free us from the eternal night we have been subjected to since the fall of Lucifer."

Nathan stiffened at the mention of Lucifer and I glanced round at him, but he shook his head at me. I pulled his arms around my waist and relaxed onto his chest. His lips pressed against my neck and I smiled round at him, as she spoke again.

"Haven't you told her, young demon?" Her sharp tone stabbed at me in the strangest way and Nathan groaned, "No, I haven't." I stood up with my back straight, and spoke with as much authority as I could muster, "STOP IT!"

As soon as the words left my mouth Nathan relaxed against my back and his breathing slowed from a pant to normal. She smiled over at me, and I could see her teeth crawling with insects which made me shudder, "you have more power than you know young superstes, but can you use your powers to protect those you love?"

I nodded and looked around the cave, taking in details. Lights hung to the ceiling, way too high up for a person to reach. Five or six smaller caves led from the huge cavern with about fifty or sixty different creatures, besides our friends, Nate, and me. I saw seats carved from stone and a waterfall behind the creature. Looking back at her, I felt Nathan right behind, touching my shoulder as he asked, "Can we trust them?"

"What choice do we have? Either we trust them or they kill us."

I turned around to ask the lady a question, but the cave went dark as I turned. All the lights flickered out and the creatures disappeared. I didn't understand what was happening until I felt a sinister breath on my neck.

Turning around in time to see an evil looking creature replaced Nathan. Taller than I and twice as wide, with green eyes and a brown face, it looked as though it was made by someone who had never seen human or animal features. The creature had a mixture of both. Looking at the creature, I had no idea what to do.

It swiped at me and the claw bounced off some sort of sphere around me. It swiped again and bounced off, but this time I noticed that it had made a small hole. I knew if it managed to hit me again, I'd die. I didn't know how I knew this, but I did. I looked at it and flicked my wrist towards the leg. A gash appeared there and the creature looked enraged. Flicking my wrist with more power this time, towards the hand that came towards my face, I heard the bone break and the creature screamed a horrible, gravelly scream and lunged at me.

This time I flicked my wrists towards the knees and I heard the horrible sound of them breaking. The creature fell to the ground inches away from me, howling. I felt sick and exceptionally worried. Speaking to the creature, directly into the mind as it twisted and snarled at me from the ground, I asked it, "Who are you?"

The creature didn't answer, just glared up at me and I flicked my wrist gently across the arm. As I moved my wrist, I saw a gash appear. It was deep, right down to the bone. I again tried to speak to the creature, "I'll ask again... Who are you? What do you want?"

As it lunged at me again, I threw it across the room, but it sprang up faster than I had anticipated. As it reached me, I fell backwards cracking my head loudly on a rock and the creature trapped my hands. I looked into the face of the creature who wanted to kill me. Realising I was stronger than the thing, I froze it with its teeth bared an inch from my face.

I could feel the shock flit across my face, but I needed to get up. Just by thinking it, I looked down at this frozen beast. I entered the mind of it again, but managed to keep a portion of my mind on the freezing power, to allow me to question it without it attacking me again.

"Who are you?" I asked.

The beast looked up at me maliciously, but didn't answer. I froze its brain for a second before releasing. Feeling horrible, I knew if I wanted to survive, I had to find out what this creature was and who sent it.

I could sense that the creature knew the answer. I pushed again. Eventually, it spat an answer out at me. "You are an abomination who must die. You cannot be allowed to live. No one should have power like you."

"Where did this power come from?"

He didn't answer so I removed his tongue. I heard it choking but I waited a moment before giving it back. His answer shocked me to my core, "You gain power from those around you. Why do you think the demons wanted your soul? The power you can gather, shared between all of them, makes you mouth-watering."

Looking down at him with pity, I asked a question to which I already knew the answer. "Will you kill me if I release you?"

His answer shook me because he didn't beg, lie, or cheat. "Of course I will. If the demons get you, all creatures will die. I am the great assassin and you must die."

Shock became my prevalent emotion as my power receded and he lunged again. This time, he made it only halfway before I placed him in an enchanted cage. I didn't want to kill him. I needed to know where he came from and why he was after me. I heard him growl, puff, and pant as he tried to find a way out, but I knew, without knowing how or why, that he wouldn't.

Suddenly the lights came back up and I felt Nathan behind me again. "What happened there?"

I was so exhausted that I collapsed in a heap at his feet. I was still conscious and I heard him ask, "What is that creature? Where did it come from?" Unable to answer, I drifted away, dreaming of my brother and sister, knowing that when I woke, I had to seriously consider how to get away from the hell that was the present and focus on finding them, before other demons did.

When I awoke, I was still in the bright cave with loads of creatures around me. I wasn't interested in them; I only wanted to see Nate. I looked around for him, or for Joe and Lisa, but I couldn't see any of them. I walked around blindly, looking for them.

Then I heard Nate calling me and I followed the sound of his voice. Finding him in an anti-chamber, eating with Lisa and Joe, I felt exhausted as I asked him, "How long have I been out?"

"A day, give or take a few hours."

I asked him what happened and he told me that I had a test to take, but he couldn't see me. He felt like he was taken to another dimension to allow me to complete the test. I realised I was famished and I couldn't remember the last time I had eaten. I had some grapes, bread and butter, and yogurt, but the food tasted like ash. After a few mouthfuls, I stopped, feeling more than a little queasy.

I heard the voice of the lady again and I knew I had to go back through to the main chamber. As I left Nate with a kiss and a hug, I decided I wanted him to come with me, pulling him up by the hand. His instincts told him to stay and he dragged his feet, looking at the ground. I acted on impulse and overrode that command so he could come with me. I needed him with me; he kept me sane.

Walking through the wall into the main chamber, I turned to look back into the anti-chamber the door bricked over. Nate looked shocked and I just felt angry. I could see plenty of pixies, fairies, white witches, wizards, and some Asari. Walking into the middle of the room with Nate right beside me felt like walking into a snake pit. From some of the looks I was getting, it was as though some of them were poised and ready to strike.

As I looked into the chief's face, my anger began to resurface, "what the hell is going on?" She smiled an evil smile at me and laughed as the room abruptly went dark again. I felt Nathan's fingers slip through my grasp. Turning around in a circle, I realised that once again I was alone.

A hand caught me on the back, sending me flying across the room. I bounced off the wall and landed in a heap on some rocks. I was not impressed by this. I saw a harpy flying at me. Her arms were winged and clawed and she had feathers on her legs, but her body was the shape of a woman. Her face had a beak and a cruel mouth. Her eyes were a burning orange, narrowed in delight and disgust at me. Stopping her in her tracks with a look, I waved my arm slightly, sending her falling to the floor.

"Who are you and what do you want?" She just looked at me as if she wished I were dead, then I realised that I picked that thought right out of her head. I looked at her and she disappeared into the blackness again.

Standing very still, closing my eyes, I tried to figure out what direction she planned to attack from. Pissed off by this point and more than a little exhausted of all these games, I sensed her above me and I reached out to grab her. As my hand closed around her, she was no longer there but at my back. Spinning around as quickly as I could, my footing was precarious and I lost it, stumbling down to the flat ground again. I scraped my hands and my knees.

Grabbed from behind, her hand closed on my throat. I struggled to breathe. I relaxed and told her to freeze as I did before. Only it didn't work this time; she laughed in my ear and said in her hoarse raggedy voice, "Your mind tricks won't work on me, young one. Just die."

As she spoke, I realised I wasn't powerless. I could still use Nate's power of projection. I moved myself to the other side of the cave and my breath came in raged gasps. I heard her cackle, but I figured she couldn't see me or sense me. In the few moments I had, I took in a few deep breaths and moved slowly towards her. All of a sudden, she flapped her wings as if she would try to fly, but I knew I had to stop her.

"You can't fly." I almost felt like saying "Nanananana," but that would annoy her more and the odds were tipped slightly in my favour. I looked at her, seeing her wriggle like a worm on a hook, as she was half up in the air, flapping around but not going anywhere. *How do I deal with the harpy?*

I stared at her and could feel her hatred, but I couldn't figure why she hated me. I decided to ask her a few questions while she just hung there. "What do you want? Why are you trying to kill me?"

She looked at me as if she loathed me and I searched through her head for the answers I sought, but she blocked me. I wasn't aware of the power harpies had. I looked at her, trying to force her to talk to me. I decided to give her a little shock. I closed my mind down so she couldn't possibly see what was coming next. I struggled to think what to do that would shock her into giving me some answers. I decided to be nasty and make her feel like her bones were on fire. Made me feel nauseas to do it, but I needed answers.

I heard her scream, yell, and flap about but I didn't stop. I couldn't stop! I needed to know why all these things were after me and how to stop them from finding me and by extension, Nathan and our friends.

Looking at her, I could finally see what I wanted to know. This was another test. Those creatures wanted me dead because I was destined to bring about the end of their rule. But their rule where? And how could I bring about the end? I didn't even know what these things were until they tried to kill me. Things I would need to think about later; I needed to deal with her first.

Keeping us both elevated without moving drained me. I let her drop and she tried to run, but knowing I had power over her, it was no problem to make her stay. I knelt down beside her because I knew she couldn't hurt me, even though she wanted to, and asked her some questions.

"I need you to answer me and I swear I'll let you live if you do."

"Sure you will! You're just a lovely innocent human! Ha!"

I tried to figure out what she meant when she broke free of the bonds I'd placed on her, flying towards me. I managed to stop her with a look. It froze her while I tried to think what to do. I decided to unfreeze only her head, which was a big mistake. I let the bonds fall away from her face to allow her to talk. She looked at me in loathing and hissed as I spoke, "Okay. Let's try again!"

A bolt of fire hit me square on the chest, sending me soaring across the room. As I sat there in shock for a minute, the harpy landed on me trying to suffocate me again. Unable to think and breathe, I succumbed to the feeling of darkness before an image of Nate appeared in blinding light. Sending a wave of fire up my body threw her off and I used the fire to throw her across the room into a cage.

Walking over in anger, I could feel power spread through me, from the tips of my toes to the bottom of my hair. I hit her with fire after fire until I saw Nathan in a vision.

"I want answers now."

The cave shook in my anger; meanwhile the harpy looked terrified. I was too far past reason to acknowledge the fear in her expression. Walking slowly around her, I asked, "Who sent you?"

Her answer terrified me and I began shaking myself.

"The devil himself sent me to find you. I am the first of many who will find you and kill you. One of us will succeed."

I felt contempt and the urge to kill her, but I warred with myself as the good in me was disgusted. I was beyond livid and completely terrified, but I decided to use her for information. Reinforcing the cage around her, I slumped down, waiting for the lights to come up. I sat there for a while and every time she shouted at me, I just glared at her and shot her through with fire. I was not happy and I got tired of waiting. I decided to bring everyone back.

The power in me scared me. When I saw Nate's face, I realised that it scared him as well. I wanted to reassure him, but I couldn't think of what to say to him. I just wanted a hug but as I made my way over to him, he walked away without looking back which felt like a punch in the gut.

I turned around, searching around for the chief, but she looked completely dumfounded. Feeling confused, tired, and hurt, I decided to go for a walk to clear my head. I threw the harpy's cage across the room into a free anti-chamber, sealing it up tight so that only my magic could unlock it.

Walking out, faces turned towards me, but they turned to blurs as I felt more and more scared. My breath came faster because I didn't understand why Nate walked away. I found myself walking onto the beach where I stumbled upon Nate and Joe talking about me. I stopped listening intently.

"Mate, she is scaring me. Her powers are coming on too thick and too fast. Soon she will have no control. She is attracting the beasts and fairies. The other creatures are getting too tired to keep shifting us all dimensions. Did you know that she that pulled us all back there?" Nate's words caused me to stuff my hand into my mouth to stop myself making any noises. Tears ran down my cheeks at hearing him say I scared him, he was supposed to love me, not fear me. Never fear me. My heart splintered painfully as I crept along towards them.

I could see them standing a few feet from me. Staying hidden behind a big rock, Joe looked terrified, and his voice cracked as he spoke. "Was it really? How did she do that? Where have these powers come from?"

I heard Nate's answer in my head before he voiced it. "She copies powers and stores them, without realising what she's doing. She pulled us back because I think she got bored waiting. I'm so worried about her."

Joe then asked him the question I dreaded most of all. "What happens if she loses control? How do we stop her?"

I didn't need to hear the answer. I could see Nate's face and I read it there, but he said it anyway, "We have to kill her. In fact, it's me that has to do it. I'm the only one who can get close enough to her to kill her."

As he said it, tears ran down his face. Joe put his arm on Nate's shoulder and said, "Mate, I'm so sorry. Isn't there any other way?"

Nate just looked at him and shook his head. "Not that we've found yet and believe me, I'm looking. The last thing I want to do is kill Jas. I love her with my heart and soul. But if I have to stop her, I will."

I felt my heart crack right then. Within seconds, they walked right by me, and back into the network of caves. Feeling numb for hours, I tried not to think, but the words didn't leave me. Repeatedly, I heard Nate saying, "I have to kill her." My head felt like it would crack open and eventually, the tears stopped. His betrayal was worse than I could have ever imagined. He didn't have faith in me. He thought he would have to kill me? How could he love me at all if he thought that? Was his fucked up idea of love so messed up that he had to kill me?

When they realised I was missing, I could sense the panic that I wasn't where I was supposed to be. They were searching for me, but I sat by myself. The ocean began to sneak up on me, bashing against the ground around me. After everything we'd been through, I trusted him with my heart, my life, and my soul and now he plotted to kill me. I didn't realise he had heard me. I was so lost in my numbness that I didn't feel him beside me. Looking into his eyes, I could see the pain and regret on his face, but I couldn't feel sorry for him. I didn't betray him.

Walking away from him and wishing I'd never met him, he reached down to help me up. His hands shook as I looked at him wordlessly. Making no move to take his hand, he sighed softly. Leaning down, he went to put his hand around me to help me out of the freezing cold water, but I flinched as his hand neared me, "Please get up, baby? Jas, please, for me, get up?"

He touched me gently and as I jerked away from him, I had never seen him look so hurt. He fell to his knees, landing in the water with a splash, "Please Jas, talk to me?"

"No!" I answered, surprising myself with how strong I sounded. I looked once more at him, seeing tears building in his eyes, pushed myself up, and walked away from him, leaving him kneeling there.

"Jas," his voice followed me like a broken whisper, "please don't leave me." His voice was breaking, but I had to keep moving. I had to keep him from becoming a murderer, no matter the cost. I wouldn't give him the chance to kill me, it would destroy him.

Hearing him call out my name, begging me to come back, almost destroyed me. He had saved me, fixed me, healed me, but now had broken me beyond repair. I could hear his desperation as I walked with tears running down my face. I reached the farthest part of the beach, hearing his voice in my head, pleading with me to go back. My answer cracked out a whip, "Why, so you can kill me easier?"

He didn't answer, he didn't have to. All I could feel was our hearts breaking in unison as I walked away from the boy I had loved with my whole heart, the boy who had saved me on so many occasions, and the boy who crushed my heart into pieces. I needed to be strong and move on; I couldn't forgive the betrayal. I could never trust him again.

CHAPTER 21
THE BEACH

I walked up the path leading away from the beach, climbing over the rocks, with the waves crashing up and the spray hitting me. I walked up the hill towards an old cemetery nearby. I needed shelter from the pounding wind and the rain. I was soaked through.

As I reached it, about half an hour later, I heard a scream from the beach and I instinctively knew that it was Nate but I was too hurt to care. I climbed into the graveyard, huddled under a gravestone, and sat for about an hour contemplating what would happen now. Through the fence, I could see demons taking Nathan away. He was unconscious, with a bloody lip. I couldn't help him and I knew it. Even if I could, I didn't know if I would. I just watched them lead him away!

The next second I witnessed Joe being led away, finding that I didn't much care about the boys. Lisa was another matter. I just had to help her. I pulled her away from them and put her inside the mausoleum, placing protection around it. I made the guards forget all about her and glamoured all the demons into thinking they were only after Nate and Joe.

I waited until the coast was clear before heading into the mausoleum to check on Lisa. She was okay but it was pitch black. I lit the room some so I could see. I awoke Lisa and she just glared at me. I was just about to open my mouth to ask her what was wrong when a sound outside the door stopped me. I heard voices and a scuffle. When I went outside, some demons were beating up Joe and Nate. The boys regained consciousness and had escaped back into the graveyard. I looked at them and anger took over for a few seconds.

I sent the two demons flying over the fence and cracked them off of a wall. I threw the two coming towards us right out into the sea and sent Nate and Joe flying backwards into the mausoleum with Lisa. I marched in, securing the graveyard against the demons. I checked them over for injuries and healed any that they had. I didn't look at Nate even though I could feel him looking at me.

"What happened?" My voice shook the mausoleum with the power in it, and I worked on calming down and trying to get my powers under control.

Joe and Lisa both just shrugged and looked at Nate. I needed to look at him to get the answers, but I didn't want to. It took me all my time to turn and when I did, I knew he had heard the internal struggle I was going through. With his head bowed, he refused to look at me. I needed to know what happened though so I gathered all my strength and asked, "Nathan, what happened?"

My voice cracked when I uttered his name, but I couldn't help it. His words came out through his teeth and I knew he struggled to keep it together. "When you left me, I was standing on the beach. I got a message that I was needed back inside. In a daze, I walked to the main hall. It was quiet, except for the chief and me. She gave me, erm something..." I looked at him in disbelief as he stood, looking me straight in the eye. "I'm so, so sorry, baby. I only ever wanted to protect you." He moved towards me, and I instinctively reached out caressing his cheek. I thought about how much I loved him, but if he was willing to kill me, there was no way I could be with him. I knew he heard me, because his breath caught and I looked up at him, straight into his hazel eyes.

I drank in his face, as tears poured down his cheeks, and missed the blade in his hands. I looked down in shock at the burning pain between my ribs, gasping and watching the blade as he stabbed it into me three more times. I fell to the ground, looking down at the blood pouring out of me. When I looked up, I saw him and Joe helping Lisa out of the mausoleum. Neither of them looked back as the door swung closed on me and I lay there gurgling and feeling my body become lighter as the pain eased.

I was there just waiting to die when I heard a little voice beside me. I looked to my left and saw a little man sitting there, about a foot tall, all dressed in green, with ginger hair and a ginger beard. He had a little bottle in his hand and from how he looked; I assumed he was a leprechaun, as silly as that sounded. He jumped onto my stomach and said something quietly. "Listen, lovey, you need to get up. Here drink this; it's a potion to help return your strength."

I shook my head at him, closing my mouth tightly. The movement caused a searing pain to shoot through me and I let out a scream of agony. There was a pounding on the door, but I couldn't focus on it. Then distant screams, but I could only think about the bright light hovering above me.

Did I really need to drink the potion, I wondered, because if I didn't I would die? Was that not a good option? My head was in disarray. Nate had just stabbed me. I opened my mouth to ask the little man something and he poured the foul tasting potion down my throat, choking me. The little man jumped off me, while I coughed and sputtered on the floor. Seeing blood and the knife, it hit me, again, that Nathan had stabbed me. He tried to kill me. I looked at the little leprechaun and sat up.

"Slowly now, easy does it. Too fast and you'll be last."

I managed to get up onto my knees first. Then, even though my head spun, I pushed up onto my feet and walked over to the blade. I snapped it into thousands of pieces. I looked at the little leprechaun, but he didn't say anything. He just watched me walk around before I checked the stab wounds. They seemed fully healed. The little man seemed eager to get out of the mausoleum, bouncing up and down at the door. "Okay, are you ready to go?"

"Time to go, princess. If you dash, there'll be no need to smash."

He bounced over to the door, opened it, and jumped through it. I began to follow him, thinking he was insane, but knowing that I didn't have any options. My heart thudded painfully, when I thought of the look in Nate's eyes as he stabbed me. I shuddered, wondering where we were going and jumped when the little man laughed, singing, "You don't need to know that yet!"

His voice sounded further and further away, as I took a step out the door. I fell into a hole in the ground. As my eyes adjusted, the room lit up and I saw the wee leprechaun, Nathan, Joe, and Lisa tied up against a wall. Nate looked right at me, as if he couldn't believe his eyes. He struggled with the ties. I could hear him trying to say something, but I refused to look at him, turning away from him to speak to the little leprechaun, "Where are we and what're we doing here?"

"Not here!" the little guy said and he motioned for me to follow him, while he moved ahead whistling and humming. I left the three of them behind, so angry that I couldn't bear to even think about taking them with us. My anger protected me from the pain, and I knew when the pain of what Nathan had done, hit me, it would be crippling and all consuming

Nathan was trying to speak into my mind, something we hadn't done in a while, but I reinforced the block and stopped him. I didn't want to hear what he had to say, it didn't matter. He'd tried to kill me. I had to stop myself thinking about it again, and tried to find numbness, but my mind wouldn't let me. On our way towards our destination, I tried to block him out and find the numbness, but his pain broke through and I could feel how desolate he was. He thought he'd lost me forever and the pain of his heartache almost brought me to my knees, but I straightened my spine and made myself take one step after another.

We walked further uphill for about twenty minutes and finally reached a hole, which I had to pull myself through to get out. I was covered in dirt and blood as we emerged, into a dark room. It took my eyes a few moments to adjust, and all I could see initially was trees through a broken window.

Upon inspection we had arrived in an old dusty house, with broken and mismatched furniture, a huge fire in the range, and windows covered in planks of wood. The wind whistled through and I looked around with interest. There were lots of little men and the one nearest me, being the one who rescued me, introduced himself again as Pierce. He was small, but fierce, and had a bluebell on his cap.

The next one up was Paul, with a daisy through his cap, followed by Seamus, Charlie, Noah, and Patrick, all wearing different flowers — a rose, a daffodil, a chrysanthemum, and a sunflower. I looked around them and heard more voices from other rooms, but none were distinct enough to make out any words that they spoke.

I looked at Pierce with what must have been a glare; he stepped backwards and said, "Now lady, don't be like that, after I just helped you."

Looking more softly this time, I decided to be nice. "Thank you, Pierce. I really appreciate you saving me there."

"You're welcome then, says I!"

"What happened? How did you find me?"

He started to tell me the story about trying to find me before I disappeared.

"I was in the field that day. You remember the day that you hid under the tree stump? We heard a rumour from some fairies and pixies that an Asari and her followers had been turned evil by a hag. This meant that they existed to do the bidding for demons, hags, and other creatures of darkness."

"We found out from our fairy friends that when you hid under that stump, an evil fairy from that coven found you and took you to their cave. But the cave was protected and for two months, they kept you in an enchanted sleep. You awoke on your own before they could arrange for the first assassin and the harpy to get to you."

I nodded as he spoke, his words making sense. It was never a test; I had been used to find out how much power I had. Pierce clicked his fingers in front of my face and I started before looking back at him, murmuring, "sorry."

He smiled, before continuing, "The demon boy thought you had been caught, or had left him, but we didn't trust them enough to tell them what we knew, for fear that we too would be captured and killed. He walked through that field day after day, but we knew it would be too dangerous for us to talk to him. We kept watch and tried to make sure that no demons found them"

My heart thudded painfully at the pain Nathan must have went through, not knowing what happened to me and for a moment I wondered if that was why he'd betrayed me

"Your powers grew again in that cave, Jasmine. You are now more powerful than the evil ones could have ever imagined. When you awoke, you, yourself brought the demon boy to you and this showed your one weakness — him! The evil ones knew this, but decided to test you against the evil assassin and the harpy. They transported you into another dimension to take these tests, but on the last test, when you pulled yourself back and put the harpy into a cave that only you could open, they decided to try to kill you with another approach. The demon boy..."

At this point, I interrupted Pierce. "Do you mean Nathan?"

"The demon boy who stabbed you?" His eyes widened as he looked at me, and he bounced on the balls of his feet as he nodded, before continuing, "Yes, that's who I mean. Anyway, don't interrupt. Where was I? Oh yes, so the demon boy. Nathan had already been fed the idea from the chief Asari. They told him you were so powerful that the only way to stop you would be to kill you. If the demons got a hold of you now, they would be the most powerful things ever, more so than ever before."

"Nathan did not want to kill, and defied them for weeks. He looked for answers on scrolls, sought other magical creatures to consult, but he found no answers. All the creatures he saw were under the Asari power and lied to him. Even the scrolls said it, but they were bewitched to tell him that. He didn't want to believe it, but yesterday he realised how powerful you were. They told him he had no choice, he had to stop you. He still fought it when you heard him and his friend on the beach. But they had told him you would leave him, as you did.

"He was told that you would leave him, and if you did, he must kill you before you gained anymore power and killed all of the cave dwellers, including himself, Joe, and Lisa. You only left because there was a plot to kill you and that plot might have worked had Nathan not still loved you. He was bewitched by the Asari when she gave him the knife. She bewitched him to follow her orders and stab you with the power-draining knife.

"When you left, he was beside himself, but the call for him to go back in was too strong. You see she had control of his mind. Anleasea is exceptionally powerful and had the demons she had summoned drag him back into the cave. She could see where you were going, so she summoned the demons to capture the escapees and take them up the same path as you. It was all a set up. Nathan loves you, but he had no choice over what he did.

"As soon as he stabbed you and got outside the mausoleum, the mind control wore off, but you were protecting the mausoleum. He couldn't get back in. He didn't realise that because he still loved you, you would survive. The knife wouldn't work as was intended. Another thing he didn't know was that your wounds were healing and when I got in, all you needed was a little poteen and that would get you back on your feet, and moving again."

When I asked him how he found all of this out, he answered, "Well you know that leprechauns are tricky and powerful?"

I just nodded to allow him to continue and he did. Leprechauns loved to talk.

"We captured a few fairies and turned them back to the right side, but we cloaked them so they would stay undiscovered. They have been reporting to ourselves and some other trustworthy creatures for the last three months, and from the information we gathered from them, we have managed to cloak you and this lair which is impenetrable. Although, we did have to steal some of your blood to make it stronger, but that's by-the-by now. You have to go back there and fix them, feed the others some poteen, and then come back up here." I told him I needed a moment, but he forestalled me.

"Come on, come on, we have no time. We need you to free them from the enchantments. Be quick. Down the hole with ye." I just looked at him, mumbling under my breath as he handed me a little red bottle glowing like fire. As I lowered myself through the hole, I wondered about everything he said. *Had Nate really been bewitched to kill me? How was it possible that he hadn't had enough power to fight them off? He was always my strength?* I loved him more than my own life but I was wasn't willing to die to prove my love to him.

As I reached the ground underneath the mausoleum, I could feel eyes burning onto my skin. I knew Nate was looking at me, but I couldn't look at him yet. Walking over to Joe and Lisa, I gave them a little poteen, which smelled like whiskey.

As they swallowed the poteen, coughing a little, I turned around to face Nate. He didn't need to see my face to know that he had hurt me, more than he ever did while we were staying at his parents.

I couldn't look him in the eye. I just knelt down before him waving off the rope binding him. I handed him the bottle of poteen as Pierce shouted, making us jump. "Hurry up down there. God, you'd think there wasn't something evil afoot. Oi! Move your bahooky and get up here."

Turning away from him, he grabbed my arm saying, "Jasmine, please wait. Please let me explain... I am so incredibly..."

Pierce yelled again, galvanising me into moving. I turned back to look at Nate, pulling my arm away, "We don't have time for this. We have to get moving. Come on."

Helping them all through the hole in the floor, I pulled myself through and walked over to the window, peaking through a gap in the planks of wood. I had no idea you could see the graveyard from where we were. We looked out the window and saw the Asari and other creatures breaking down the door into the mausoleum. In the next moment, a scream of fury and anger rang clearly through the night from the mausoleum, making everyone jump.

"Well, now they are looking for you. We must be off," Pierce's voice sounded from behind me and as I turned around, he handed me a piece of gold.

"Sure if you ever need me, just give this a wee rub and I'll appear."

Suddenly the house went deathly quiet; all the little leprechauns had disappeared. Nate came over to stand beside me, but there was nothing he could say to me that I wanted to hear in that moment. I just looked out into the sea, tears stinging my eyes as I avoided Nathan's gaze, when his hand touched my arm. He moved away when I flinched and I stood like a statue, waiting for them to check our hideout.

As the creatures searching for us came in the door, they looked right through us as if we weren't there, finding no traces of our presence. Nate walked over, closing the door, but I had a warning sensation that something more dangerous was coming. We could sense his parents and he began shaking beside me. Wanting to help him, I found I couldn't even touch him. I was still hurt and even though my wounds were healed, I could still feel the pain of them and the burning from where the knife cut me.

I saw a sword propped up against the mantelpiece. Walking over to look at it, I heard Joe and Lisa leave the room. Turning around, I looked at Nate, shaking my head as he approached me. I walked into the room where Joe and Lisa were hiding, seeing terror in their expressions as soon as I arrived. I realised that I had to move them, just in case there was a showdown. Lisa pregnancy meant I somehow had to protect her.

Closing my eyes, I opened up my mind, searching for the old shack in Inver. Taking a few minutes away in the shack, I turned it into a liveable home, re-glassing the windows, fixing the roof, and placing basic furniture inside, along with a note, money for food, and a working fire. I also placed a charm around it that would protect it from all creatures. No one would see or sense it. Placing six stones marked with protection and safety runes around the house to make a protected circle, I prayed it would be enough to save them. Going back, I couldn't look at Nate. Since there was no time to explain to him, Joe, or Lisa, I touched their arms and sent them into the shack.

"What have you done, Jas? Where are they?"

I shook my head at him, speaking in a voice that betrayed my emotions, "Safe. I moved them away from us." My voice cracked as I tried to rein in my emotions and I could feel danger gnawing at my concentration. Walking over to stand beside Nate, he turned towards me, "Jas, please let me explain. I couldn't control..."

"I know, but we really don't have time for this just now. Nate, we can talk about it later w..."

He pulled me into his arms, and kissed me with more passion than he had ever before, cutting me off. "Just in case we don't make it," he whispered breathlessly against my lips, and my soul shuddered. Warmth spread from my lips through me and I kissed him back with a fire, as tears rolled from my eyes, "I love you and every moment has been worth it to be with you." I pulled away from him, closing my eyes as the levee threatened to break, but he tugged me back into his arms, his tears mingling with my own as he sobbed out brokenly, "Jas, if we live through this, I will spend every single day showing you how much you mean to me. I promise that I will not hurt you ever again."

He turned away, leaving me stunned as we watched the procession of demons make their way up the garden path towards the house. I looked at Nate, still not meeting his eye, whispering to him that although the house was impenetrable we were by no means safe.

Out of the space between the planks covering the windows, I saw his father, brother, and uncle trying to break down the door, but I knew they shouldn't get in for at least a few minutes. If they found us, we would have to fight. I wasn't strong enough to take on Nate's father yet, which posed a problem. I was far from ready for that battle.

I needed to think of a way out and as my eyes darted about, I noticed the hole in the floor. Looking over at Nathan, all I could see in his expression was fear so I took his hand, leading him over to the hole. I gestured to him to go without saying a word. He turned to me, looking like he thought I was crazy, but there was no time to explain.

I could feel the house weakening; the demons outside were seconds from getting into the house. Shoving him into hole, I followed blindly, sealing it up as the door of the house cracked and splintered open. I had protected the space around us, but wasn't able to take us out of there or go back down the tunnel.

Taking Nathan's hand, we could feel the ground shake and hear footsteps running around the house. The demons couldn't sense us under the house, but in no way did we feel safe. We could hear them stop in the room above us. Nathans dad's voice sounded calm as he told the others, "I am sure they were here, but I can't seem to sense them at all, anywhere. We have to find them. If you find them, bring them directly to me. I will deal with the traitor and his whore..."

Nate looked at me and opened his mouth to say something, but I put my finger on his lips to quieten him; he acknowledged the warning in my head. It was taking all of my concentration to keep up the shield that was protecting us. Jack spoke softly to his brother, but his voice carried down to our hiding place,

"Should some of us go back to the mausoleum and keep an eye out from there, just in case they go back?"

Mr Stevenson prowled around the room and it took him a while to answer. He pushed again and again at our protection, stopping directly above us. Taking Nathan's hand, I squeezed it. After a few moments, he moved on, leaving me exhausted by the time he answered. Only just managing to keep the shield up around us, we heard Mr Stevenson say, "Yes, that is a great idea. Take Logan, Jonah, and Mitchell with you. Same rules, Jack. If you find them, they come to me..."

There were new voices in the room and we could hear Nathan's mum, brother, and sister all there, but I managed to deflect their scanning away from us and after an hour and a half, they left. Nathan's brother stayed and when I finally lowered the shield enough, I got a sense of him and he prepared to fight us. No matter what his father had said, he wanted revenge.

My strength wavered, which was dangerous, "Our only way out of this is to either fight your brother, even though I have little strength left, or to teleport out of here."

Just as I finished telling him that, I felt pressure on the shield and I was sure that Nick was testing the area again. I felt it pushing against me and for the first time, I felt weak. I knew this was just the demon magic. I knew I was stronger than them. I just had to prove it.

"What's happening, Jas? Are we okay, baby? Can I do anything?"

I nodded, asking him to be quiet because I needed to concentrate on deflecting his brother, but it was difficult. The look on his face said I had hurt him, but I had no time to try to fix the clusterfuck that was us. I had to try to save us both in whatever way I could.

I sat up straighter in the muddy, musky little hole, focusing all of my energy on protecting us, even though Nate and I were muddled up and possibly over, I would not, could not let him get hurt or killed by his family, because no matter what he had saved my life repeatedly and I at least owed him that much. He squeezed my hand and when I flinched at the contact, he dropped his hand, but not before a drip of water splashed onto my hand.

Forcing my eyes closed and concentrating harder than I had ever done in my life, we suddenly were no longer underground, but out in the woodlands. Having no idea how we got there unnerved me, but when I looked around me, I noticed a few things. We were in a protection circle, surrounded by a mix of magical creatures.

There was another abandoned shack up ahead and when we walked towards it, I noticed that the protection of the circle extended beyond the shack. Inside was pitch black, so black we couldn't see anything in front or to the side of us, but we heard a mixture of voices as the feeling of exhaustion that I was fighting back in the abandoned house came over me stronger than ever. I almost fell asleep, but first I needed to know that we were safe.

Knowing I had to question the motives of these creatures was hard, but the last time we had help, it turned out to be a trap. I looked around, seeing pixies, gnomes, fairies, and a few mystics. One of the mystics spoke to me in my head, telling me that it was okay to fall asleep. As I looked beside me, Nate had succumbed to sleep.

He looked so innocent in his sleep; his face smoothed of worry and stress. I hated him, but I loved him, and I didn't know how to separate my feelings about him. Feeling my eyes burn and roll, I sat up straighter knowing I wouldn't rest until I was sure we were safe.

I could feel the magic pressing in on me, trying to make me fall asleep, but I felt stronger sitting up from my slouched position on the ground.

"Who is the leader?" I asked in a firm voice, looking around at the numerous different creatures, seeing them dart between rooms. Some tall, some short, some with wings, some without.

"It is not the right time to see the leader," a voice answered me firmly, sounding angry.

"The hell it isn't. We have been tricked before so I need to know who is here and who is leading these creatures. Come out now please."

The room filled with light and a fair-haired man stood before me. Although I couldn't recall seeing him before, I knew he was familiar to me and I finally believed we were safe.

As I was about to ask him how I knew him, my instincts kicked into overdrive as I sensed a sinister presence, followed by more and more of them. The demons had arrived and we were no longer safe. It was time to fight again.

CHAPTER 22
FAMILY FIGHT

It had been almost a day that we'd been hiding out from the demons and I kept thinking that we would need to fight our way out if we wanted to survive.

Nathan's father was there, trying to break down our defences constantly. It cost me so much energy to keep them out and I had the backing of all the creatures surrounding us, but would it be enough? I doubted it very much and found myself wishing I could take Nate away from here, but he refused to leave.

"I will make it up to you. I know you don't want to hear it, but I love you. I am with you through it all; we will fight them together."

How could I make up with someone after he tried to kill me? And how would I ever trust him again? I knew he was under an enchantment and that I wasn't being fair to him, but I couldn't help it. He had stabbed me and left me for dead. I had to stop thinking about it though. Keeping the monsters out required all of my concentration.

Looking out of the window, seeing all the demons gathered there, felt like we had already been beaten. It was oppressive and depressing. We were outnumbered at least two to one, but we would fight because we had no other choice.

At that moment, I realised that these thoughts and feelings were just demon mind tricks. I had more power than any of them. However, numbers this huge could mean people (or creatures) would die. Nathan walked over to me as I tried to think of a plan, breaking my concentration, "Should we go out and try to compromise with them? If we handed ourselves in, they would probably leave all of these creatures alone."

He wanted us to sacrifice our lives and our freedom to save all of these creatures. I was stunned. I stood on my tiptoes and kissed him on the lips gently. Pulling away, I realised that it had been ages since he had last seen his parents and it was hard for him to think about fighting them. Thinking about it, I realised it could be an idea, but I told him, "Not right now, but it's definitely a plan we can use later on."

Nathan walked to the window while I heard an almighty growl come from outside. I looked towards the sound and saw Jenny growling at him. I tried again to think of a plan, but nothing was forthcoming. After a few moments though, I figured the best way was a spell, but I didn't know if I had the power to make it work. Leaving Nate in the front room, I climbed over the branches and broken floorboards that littered the hall.

Feeling Nate's dad trying to find a way through again meant I re-doubled the protection, causing me to stumble and fall. I didn't notice as I walked into a branch. I sliced open my hands as I slid down the wall, bracing myself as I stood back up, realising as I did so, that I had tripled our protection because of how powerful my blood was.

I wondered if the plan I was thinking would work; it was something we discussed in the small hours of this morning, but decided it was too risky. I could not let these monsters kill Nate, or me, regardless of what he had done to me.

Going from room to room, I could see a mixture of the creatures who rescued us, but not the ones I was after. I ducked under an old tree and walked into the back room. The mystics were in there, standing over a hole in the ground. Their black coats billowed in the breeze. "It will work, Jasmine..." a voice rose from nearest the flames.

"They will not suspect it and we should save most creatures through this plan of yours. However sacrifices must be made if we are to escape in numbers," another voice said.

"Call a meeting, but remember, you must warn all creatures of the consequences."

"Okay, thank you. Will you help me if they agree?"

Walking into the main room moments later, over twenty faces turned towards us expectantly. I shook inside; terrified I would lead these poor creatures to their deaths. I couldn't think of any other way out. As they looked at me, I could feel the hope they had that they would survive.

Nate looked at me and asked me silently if I had a plan yet. I just nodded at him, unable to articulate it yet.

Sending a shock out towards the demons, one that should knock them all out for fifteen minutes gave us a chance to escape. Knowing I wasn't strong enough to defeat all of those demons on my own left me feeling terrified, but I knew that I could defeat some of them. I sent out another two shocks just to be safe. Sensing after the third shock that all the demons were out cold meant we had to hurry. Nate's dad didn't succumb until the third shock, and would ultimately be the first to wake.

"Do you have a plan, Jasmine?" the voice asked and I looked around, trying to figure out where it came from. A little fairy tugged on my skirt; the fairies were all grounded, so to speak, which was odd. I looked at her mutely and she asked again, "Do you have a plan?"

She looked like a child and I felt guilty. It was my fault they were in peril; they were there because of me. Nodding towards her, I finally found my voice. I didn't look at Nate; I knew if I did I wouldn't go through with this. I looked around at everyone else while trying to tell them what we would be doing and why.

"Okay, people. The plan is that we copy ourselves. It's an old piece of magic, which involves placing some of your life essence outside the body and allowing this to take on another form. This form will look like you, talk like you, and have powers like you. But it will not be you. We will need some blood from each of you, along with sage, rosemary, rose petals, and conifer leaves. This will make up a potion that each of us will have to drink. Everyone will need to drink some of my blood though in this potion, as this is the only way I can think of to make it strong, to work well enough, and long enough, to fool the demons. We need them to believe that the other ones of us are actually us and this may well save our lives."

A voice interrupted, a gnome named Ned, his voice was gruff and gravely, "Why your blood? Will that not affect us?"

I looked at the little gnome, with his bright green eyes, rosy cheeks, and around belly, and thought about the answer I should give. "The blood should wear off in three hours, but you will see and feel everything your other self feels. If this person dies, a pain will affect you in your heart, but you will live. This is the only thing with even half a chance of helping us to survive."

Nate looked at me in alarm, raising his eyebrows and staring at me expectantly. I knew it was a long shot, but it was the only one we had at that moment.

Looking around at all of those faces, childlike and innocent to rough and older, I decided to put it to a vote. A majority had to rule; if anyone hid or didn't allow us to do it, then the plan would be ruined. I needed to tell them that. Just before I spoke again, Nate walked over to me and whispered in my ear, "We don't have long left. Five minutes or thereabouts. I can feel them coming back to consciousness."

Nodding in acknowledgement, I continued explaining the plan, "The other us, will be duplicates and they will come into being about three miles from here, near the river. Out in the open. At the moment the duplicates awaken, the protection here will fail. It will look as if we have gone, but we will be hidden in a room below this shack." I took in a breath as I looked around at all the tense and expectant faces watching me, and Nathan squeezed my hand gently, slipping his fingers through my own. His support gave me the strength to continue and I swallowed against the fear as I began speaking again.

"The mystics already have supplies and a room ready down there. It will be cramped and musty, but it may well help us survive. As soon as the demons sense us away from here, they should leave, thinking we have teleported there. But the duplicates will fight, giving us all a chance to escape. It is risky. If the demons don't fall for it, we have then exposed ourselves, and hiding in that hole will only be a temporary solution. As soon as it's clear, Nate and I will leave. It's us they want, and they will tear everyone apart until they find us."

After a glance at a nervous Nate, I rushed on, "We need to vote on this now. Are you all in favour? Or would you rather fight our way out?"

We heard a lot of mumbling and whispers.

"Reckless." A hoarse whisper to our left called out.

"Gambling with our lives," came another to our right, this time deep timber.

"No other plan," a high pitched voice across the room called out.

"May be our only chance," was another thing I heard and I closed my eyes, praying that everyone would agree with me, because I couldn't see any other way out of this.

Eventually, after a few minutes, everyone agreed. As we worked on the potion, the demons started to wake and tried to find a way through the barrier, but it was holding for the moment.

The mystics had brought along some of the ingredients and others, like the conifer leaves, were readily available. The potion needed about fifteen minutes to boil, which meant holding the demons off until then. They were all awake and I could feel them battering against our protection. I could only hope it would hold for another twenty minutes.

Once the mystics had started the potion in a huge pot, I cut my hand, let seven drips go into the pot, and then I left with two of the mystics, leaving one to watch over the potion. We went underneath the old shack and most of the creatures were clearing out the lower level so we could hide. I got seven stones, drew protective runes around them with my blood, and placed them in the walls, creating a huge protected space. It had to be I that protected this space. I was the only one strong enough.

Suddenly, a yell came from upstairs, which caused all of us to jump. I ran upstairs to see two of the little gnomes being held outside the front window by the demons. They had tried to run for it.

Very quickly, I wiped their minds of our plan and prayed that it wasn't too late, that we hadn't been given away. I could hear laughter and see the evil faces of the demons smiling and showing their teeth. Looking at the gnomes, one of whom was Ned. I saw the flesh being stripped from their bones, while they were still alive. They howled in pain. I felt awful for them and I wished there was something I could do to help them. The demons kept them alive and suffering for at least twenty minutes, peeling skin off as though they were peeling bananas.

It was obvious that the demons didn't need to know what our plan was; it was clear to myself and Nate though, what their plan was — to torture and kill every creature who helped us. They wanted to terrify all the creatures into deserting us, so they could get to us and kill us. What they didn't know was that by doing that, they made everyone more determined to stand with us and fight.

All of those who had moved back upstairs to see what was happening turned slowly and went back. This time I placed the rune stones of the mystics in a circle around the wall, making a doorway and a path open up underground. The only problem with this path was, that every person who entered it would have no idea where they were going to end up coming out.

I decided I would tell all the creatures this when we got down here. We had just ten minutes left and the space still wasn't big enough because of all the rubbish and debris piled up all over the place. I asked Nate to help them while I went back up to check on the potion. I walked up the stairs, out of the protection, and headed towards the back room. The potion was there, but none of the mystics were. God, I wish this would hurry up. The colour changed right then and the potion looked ready, but because I used magic to speed it up, our protection had lowered even more.

It wouldn't be long now until they could get in. I walked through the house, making sure everyone was downstairs, and when I was in the front room, I looked out the window and saw Mr Stevenson looking right at me. Any second now, they would break through. I ran towards the downstairs and just as I reached the trapdoor and closed it, they broke through. I ran down the stairs and two of the mystics ladled out the potion and handed people the knife. The potion required three drops of blood, and would take effect once everyone in the room had consumed a spoonful of it.

All of a sudden, a wail sounded from upstairs, and we knew that someone else had been caught. Damn it. It was one of the mystics. We could hear her scream in agony. I wanted to help her, but I knew I couldn't. I did manage to reach up to her and wipe her brain of the plan, but that was all I could do without jeopardising the twenty-odd people in this room. I watched the creatures take the potion, as they all glowed a little bit, and prayed that this would work. I hoped it would look like we tried to make a break for it, but I wasn't sure what would happen.

Finally, it was just myself, Nate, and the two mystics left to take the potion. I bled into my ladle and Nate did the same to his.

"Bottoms up," we both said at the same time, laughed, and drank the foul-tasting potion, feeling it burn and boil on the way down. I felt my other self inside, along with parts of over twenty others. I knew that when one of them got hurt, I would feel it. As I looked around the room, I saw the mystics drink the potion and felt two more join me inside.

The potion took effect as soon as the last person drank some and it felt as though we were all flying through the woods and appeared in a cliff side clearing, where the sun shined so brightly. The essences were surrounded by demons, outnumbered at least two to one, but somehow we were still in this dank and musty cellar. Most of the demons left to go find us and we had to make an escape plan. The danger became clear to us, almost as soon as the demons arrived. Our minds were split between here and our essences in that clearing. This would be difficult. How would we be able concentrate on getting out of here when we were fighting the demons there?

For the first few minutes, I felt sick and dizzy. It was as if I could only see the trees and hear the sea behind us. We could see the sky and feel the wind, but smell the dampness and the mustiness that was this cellar room.

We all realised at the same moment what would happen if the essences were killed. Some of the creatures in the room had just experienced the death of their essences; we would collapse after yelling in pain. I soon realised that there were still people here, looking for us. I heard footsteps upstairs, which meant we needed to get out of here, before we were discovered and captured. I walked around, through lots of the creatures who looked at me like this was my entire fault, and picked up the fairies that I had felt and seen collapse, for there was more than one. I gave them to others of their kind to carry.

"Okay, everyone listen up. You have to leave, hide in the safest place, the most secret place you have and don't come out for anyone. I will find you all if I need you. Thank you so much for helping us, but you have to go now," I said all of it in a rush. I could feel the demons upstairs prowling around. "Place your hand in the centre of the circle and two may pass through. If you have any unconscious friends with you, they will be allowed to pass as one conscious and unconscious. Go now, please!"

In the time it took me to tell them that, three more people had collapsed and my head felt as though it were being cleaved in two. I sank to the ground and groaned. When I looked up, I shouted at the creatures looking at me, "Go! Please leave! Hurry..."

I knew at that moment that I would have to concentrate on the fight for a bit. If I didn't, no one would get out of here alive. I focused my mind and fought, dodging blows, ducking, and diving around. I felt Nathan do the same beside me.

We both allowed our minds to be overrun with the fight. We began to dance around more, fighting back. I knew the demon powers wouldn't work on me, but that didn't stop them from trying. Every few seconds I would feel the pain of another creature's essence dropping, hurt or killed.

I tried using my powers, but quickly realised that they were not as strong as my real powers. They were strong enough to send Jenny flying into a tree and knock her out. I protected all the little creatures by shielding them and, out of one corner of my eye I could see the small creatures escaping from the cellar.

Out of the other corner of my eye, I saw Nate fighting Nick. It was so close between them that I realised the same rule applied to Nate. Another person charged towards me and I lifted my hand just as she reached me, flicked my hand towards the cliff face and she flew away, off the cliff. I looked around for Nathan's dad but he was nowhere to be seen for the minute. That momentary lapse in concentration almost cost me my essence as a figure I now recognised as Mr Stevenson charged into me and knocked me to the ground. I lay there winded, when he put his hands around my neck and started choking me.

He flew off of me, thrown backwards by Nate charging at him and they wrestled on the ground for a moment, but it seemed as though his dad was getting the upper hand. I reached out grabbed essence Nate and we moved together, fighting hard. We deflected from one corner, and I set a ring of fire around us that was impenetrable. It gave me a second to close off and make sure that the creatures were using this time to escape.

Within a few seconds Nate groaned, in my head and I saw his essence, hit with a flying boulder. I placed my hand on his back and power surged through him, just in time because his father managed to break through the fire and he lunged at me. I moved out of the way a second too late and I careered backwards, burning my shoulder on the flames.

The flames flickered and went out, and the demons surrounded us again. I moved some of them out of the way, but Nate's dad grabbed me from behind and threw me to the ground again and he placed his hands around my neck, tightening them with a look of maddening rage. I coughed and sputtered, unable to freeze him or get him off me when I started to lose consciousness.

As my struggling stopped I saw him pull out a ceremonial knife and draw it down my face, "I'm going to end you, you fucking little whore. You destroyed my family and know this the traitor will die, because you can't save him and you can't save yourself. This is over." He raised the dagger up and I tried to send a current through my body to throw him off, but before the current had fully passed over me, Nate grabbed him and threw him off the cliff.

Nate ran around grabbing demons and tossing them off of the cliff, while I used my powers to try and keep them down there. In the seconds that passed, he pulled me up and I was so angry that my powers increased in my essence and with one wave of my hand, all of the demons were thrown off the cliff and into the water. I made the water into a cage and trapped them all to allow us time to escape. I looked around and saw the 'bodies' of all the little creatures who had been killed, but I knew that they would be okay. I decided with one look towards Nate that we should retreat back into our proper bodies and get the hell out of there before the demons figured out it was a trick. He nodded at me and we both went to come back into our own minds.

Before we left, I told my essence to head for Sligo, to lead the demons that way, which would give us a chance to get to safety. As I got back into my body, I looked around the room and only Nathan, the mystics, and I remained. The mystics told us that they did not want to leave us as there were still demons prowling around above.

I decided to knock them out before we left so that we wouldn't be followed. Even though we were protected, I still didn't want them conscious as we left. I lifted my hands and pulled a beam of wood down on them, knowing full well that the house would crumble on them, the moment I did so. The mystics ran towards the doorway first and got through it as an almighty roar told us who prowled above.

Jack was up there, now trapped under the wooden beam. I heard another girl yell and a man grunt in pain as the house tumbled down on them. I looked at Nathan and he nodded. We ran to the door as the sound of the house falling became louder. We got to the doorway, almost too late; the ceiling fell in on us and I put my hand on it, grabbed the rune stones, and ran through the door, as the roof caved in, bringing the unconscious demons and a ton of earth falling into the room where we had been moments previously.

We ran along a low earthen corridor, coming out of a tree on a roadside, heading to God only knew where, but I felt we were safe for a few moments. We looked around for a road sign and saw only farmlands, all green and yellow, in the summer sunshine. We walked along the road, towards the trees only a little ways away, but the sun was scorching; my mouth was parched but we had no water and no supplies.

We kept walking and to distract ourselves from the bleakness of our situation, we talked about the last four days.

"Nate, I don't... I don't understand?" I stopped unable to go on, as he walked slightly ahead of me with his head down. His shoulders shook at my words, and his breath came in gasps as he fought against the emotion of what had happened to us.

"Jas, I can't. Please don't ask me..." He stopped and froze, swiping his hands across his face and he took a fortifying breath before speaking again, "I thought I'd lost you, for two months. I couldn't find you anywhere and then suddenly you were beside me and..." He shuddered and glanced towards me, tears flowing from his face as he drank me in. He shook his head and looked forwards again, "I knew you were more powerful than any sacrifice ever before, but I didn't realise how powerful you'd become. It scared me, I'm a coward. I couldn't cope with how powerful you were."

He stopped moving and I walked into him. He steadied me and buried his face in my hair, breaking down completely. I gave him a few minutes as he cried, holding him tightly, but I had to know what had happened, why he'd betrayed me and if I really could trust him not to do it again.

My thoughts must have registered with him, because he held me closer, "hurting you like that was the most gut-wrenching pain I've ever experienced. It felt as though I was being cleaved in two and I fought it. As soon as I was outside, I tried to get back in, to get back to you, but I couldn't and then I was in the hole in the ground, bound and gagged. I fought so hard, trying to get back to you and then you appeared right in front of me, but you couldn't even look at me." His voice shook and he leaned down kissing the tip of my nose,

"Jas, when I saw you were okay, I couldn't believe it and the relief was incredible. They hadn't made me loose you, you were still here and all I wanted was to tell you how sorry I was and how much I loved you."

He kissed me gently and turned to face the road, "we should keep going," he whispered kissing just under my ear, before he turned us around and pulled on my hand, urging me forwards.

"Nate, you didn't tell me how they convinced you to do it?" I spoke softly, and his back stiffened as he replied in a cold voice, "I don't know how they made me do it, baby. All I know is I'm glad it didn't work and that I still have you. I know you are confused and I don't blame you, but I love you with everything I am and if you never forgive me, then so be it. Just know that I will never go back to the darkness that you saved me from."

I knew I had a lot to think about, the past few days had been insane and although I still loved Nathan, I still had a scar where Nate had stabbed me and I was still upset about it, but still he had saved me again from his father. My feelings at this point were so mixed up and I didn't know what I wanted. I needed some time to come to terms with the fact that he stabbed me. The sensation of that blade as it entered me, and the look on his face tormented me and I didn't know how to move on from it. I just needed time to process it and everything that had happened since that moment.

It took us two hours of walking along this road before we saw any signs of life — a demon. We hid behind a tree as the demon walked along the road, whistling and humming. I looked at Nate in the shade of the tree and realised that no matter what I still loved him.

He looked at me and leaned in for a kiss when a yell from behind us made us both jump. We peered around the tree and there stood his father. Soaking wet and dripping all over the side of the road, looking towards the whistling demon with undisguised fury on his face as I felt myself shaking, Nate leaned over pulling me in for an embrace.

We peeked around the tree again and Mr Stevenson was nowhere to be seen. We walked slowly through the shade of the trees, watching for branches and roots that would trip us up. We walked through the woods for over half an hour, meeting nothing. The light was eerily green and there was a strong smell of wood. We kept peering out to see if there was any sign of demons or Mr Stevenson again, but there was nothing. We could see the woods thinning up ahead. We walked towards the thinning of the woods, but when we got there, we had walked into a farm filled with demons.

We looked around panic-stricken. We saw a bush large enough to cover us and dove for it. Two seconds later, Jenny stood where we had been standing looking around for us. The bush was jaggy, scratching at our faces and arms, but there was nothing we could do. We had inadvertently walked towards them and now we were stuck. I lay my head down on the ground and felt Nate lie down beside me. My breath came in gasps and I shook so hard. Why were things like this never easy? Why couldn't we just bloody escape?

Nathan gave in to exhaustion hidden in the thicket of a bush and woke hours later to the sound of car doors slamming. I jumped, feeling dizzy with how completely run down I was as I lay keeping watch to make sure that no one got to us as we lay so close to a demon stronghold. Nate had been sleeping with his arm across my stomach. He looked at me smiling, but we heard footsteps nearby and froze watching as a pair of feet walked right by our hiding place.

"Jenny," a voice yelled, making us both jump again. "Get a move on. We've got to get to Sligo before they leave."

Mr Stevenson walked over to Jenny and she turned back to her father, walking slowly back to the garden full of cars. Nate whispered in my ear, "We have to move now, baby."

The sound of more doors slamming gave us cover to crawl through the bush, seeing a plethora of demons piling into cars. There were so many of them and so much was going on that we didn't notice Mr Stevenson, until he spoke directly in front of us. He was talking about us.

"They were spotted heading into Sligo in a car. Head for the town centre and we'll split up from there."

The group nearest us walked towards the cars, all stopped, six or seven of them, and looked back. Both Nate and I held our breaths as they walked back towards us. They leaned into the hedge we were hidden under and pulled out something. We only saw the knives after they walked away. Nate's dad had one and Jack had the other. "The ceremonial knives", Nate whispered into my head.

They got into two different cars, a Toyota jeep and a Suzuki Swift. The cars drove off, leaving the front of the farm house deserted. We got out and walked over to the windows, still terrified that someone would be here, but thankfully, no one was.

We walked past each set of windows, checking in the rooms to make sure no one was there and finally, we passed the sinister farmhouse. We continued down a hill behind the house, onto some sort of main road.

As we walked, we felt lightheaded. We were hungry and stiff. We had slept on the ground with nothing covering us. We weren't really watching where we were going, just stumbling along as the rain started. The rain bucketed down and we had no jackets or anything with us. I wore a blue skirt torn in a few places, caught in a few others, a vest top that had a hole in it, covered in blood from where Nate had stabbed me, and a white blouse covered in cuts, blood, and mud. Nate wore a blue sweatshirt, that had catches, mud, and holes, a pair of blue jeans covered in mud, and a pair of trainers caked in blood and mud.

Finally, after half an hour, we saw a car. As soon as the driver saw us, he stopped, rolling down the window to offer us a ride.

"Sure, I can take you into the village or into Donegal. That's where I'm headed."

We jumped into the car as the thunder clapped. We were both exhausted as the driver asked us where we were from and how we were walking down a road during a storm.

I looked at Nathan, in the front seat, chatting with the driver. I turned and looked out of the window as the driver told Nate his name was Niall and he was from Donegal, but studied in Derry. He seemed nice enough so I relaxed a little, wondering how and when I would see my brother and sister. It had been ages since I had found out, but I wanted them out of the houses or wherever they were now. Nathan told me how dangerous it was and how the demons would expect me to go after my family. As soon as we were somewhere safe and impenetrable, I would find and save them.

Eventually, we reached Donegal and got out, but as we thanked the driver and left the car, we realised that our day was far from over. We needed supplies and money. Nathan had opened a bank account in a false name a few months ago, claiming that he'd rather the money was safe in a bank, which was a relief because we had nothing left. All of our plans had been scuppered and we were being stalked, followed and seconds from being killed.

We walked over to the bank and went inside, all the while praying that it hadn't been discovered. Luck was with us; there was still eight thousand in the bank. He walked over to the teller, who didn't even look at him, and withdrew four hundred euro and walked towards the shops.

CHAPTER 23
THE BOOKSHOP

Walking around the town, we figured we must look a mess because all the passersby stared at us as if we were Martians. We went to the nearest clothes shop, Magee's, and bought some clothes for us to wear. We left the store quickly though; we spotted a demon browsing the shelves. We went into a typical Irish pub and I walked into the ladies room and looked in the mirror.

No wonder people looked at us oddly; I was a complete mess. I ran the cold-water tap and washed some of the dirt off my face, and pulled the leaves and twigs out of my hair. My face, neck, arms, and legs were covered in scratches. My clothes were torn, from the twigs and the knife, and in some places, covered in dirt and blood. I walked into the cubicle and locked the door. I changed all of my clothes and put the others in a plastic bag that I would throw away. As I took my top off, I realised I was still wearing my handbag. I had a brush and some makeup that would come in handy, but I placed it on top of the cubicle.

As I was changing, I heard the bathroom door open and some females came in. I peeked out through the door and saw that they were all demons. I stepped back and to the side of the door so they couldn't see me. While I pulled on my shoes over my new jeans and my jumper, I heard what my demon bathroom companions were talking about. I was too tired to use magic, and too exhausted to talk to Nate, but I sent him a warning, telling him to stay locked in the cubicle in the bathroom. The demons told each other about the fight today, and how we were almost caught.

"The girl is very powerful, but she will be caught and we will all get a piece of her. During the fight, she sent all of us into the sea and trapped us but Mr Stevenson got us out. We managed to kill a few of those helping her and we will track down the rest of those responsible and kill them."

"Where are they now?" She seemed to have a young voice, around eighteen or nineteen, but sounded excited at the prospect of us being caught.

Her companion answered her, with a sneer and laughed as she answered her,

"They've been cornered in Sligo, with a net closing in around them to capture them, only they don't know it yet. They think it's safe, but as soon as Mr S gets a hold of them he'll kill them for sure. His traitor of a son first, and his whore will follow soon after."

"Do you really think they'll kill his son? Wouldn't it be better to try and fix him so he can do what he's destined to do a kill her?" one of the girls asked her breathlessly.

"My uncle would never show that much humanity and he would never trust Nathan again. His life is over. He chose wrong and the consequences are entirely his fault."

A loud noise broke the sleepy silence, someone's phone went and the girl who'd done most of the talking spoke excitedly, "they have them. It's time to go." As her and her friends walked out of the bathroom, I almost groaned allowed. My head was cleaving in two again as I saw the crowd around alternative us in Sligo. Nathan was being beaten and dragged away from me and I heard the crunching of bone and his cries of pain. He fought with everything to get back to me and I knew they would kill him.

My whole body wanted to break as I saw them drag him away from me, but I came back to myself and I splashed some cold water on my face as I breathed a sigh of relief. I stared into the mirror over the sink, when the door burst open and Nate ran in, grabbed my hand, and pulled me towards the kitchen of the pub. I didn't ask him what was going on. I just allowed him to pull me along with him. We ran out the back of the kitchen and he pulled me away towards a huge bin and pulled me behind it. It smelled so bad, of rotting food and rubbish that I felt like I would throw up.

I opened my mouth to ask him what was going on, but he turned towards me as I was about to speak and kissed me, pulling me towards him. I kissed him back, but then remembered after a second what had happened and pulled away, intending to say something, when voices on the other side of the bin stopped me.

"Are you sure it was him, Netty?" a hoarse male voice asked.

"Of course I am. I have known him since he was a baby," the other voice answered. They looked around and when they moved the bin, even though they looked right at us, they didn't see us. They then shoved the bin back and Nate stopped hugging me. I looked at him, wanting to ask how they had seen him, but I didn't know if it was safe.

We both knew we couldn't hide there forever and edged towards the end of the row. I got out first and Nate followed me. I walked forwards, to lead the way, when Nate grabbed my hand and told me to keep a hold of his; no demons would see or sense us if we stayed linked. I just nodded, again feeling like I was totally and utterly exhausted.

We walked out of the car park and up the hill to the big supermarket and shopping mall. We needed supplies to go into hiding with.

We walked through the doors of the shopping mall and went into the store nearest the exit. This brick-a-brack shop sold bits and pieces of everything. The walls were lined with dolls and trinkets, gifts, and tenting equipment. We bought a three-person tent, two sleeping bags, a gas cooker, a blow up bed, a torch with batteries, and a pump. We then went into the shop next door, and got two waterproof jackets, two backpacks, and some duct tape. I didn't ask what the duct tape was for and after we had paid for them, we had just over one hundred euro left.

We walked into the food store and got a trolley for the supplies we would need. We got tins of food — pears, canned meats, and potatoes, herbs, rosemary, thyme, sage, and basil, and bottles of water. When we had paid for all of our purchases, we had thirty euro left and we still needed clothes. I looked at Nathan and asked him silently if we were going to get clothes. He just nodded and when I asked him how he would pay for it, he smiled at me and walked over to the bank machine.

We then left the shop and walked down the hill, looking for some clothes shops. After about five minutes, we found one and after a quick sweep, we found that it was free of demons. As I was walking in, he took the bags I carried and gave me one hundred and fifty euro, telling me to get whatever I needed.

I looked at him and asked him why he wasn't coming in. He just told me he had something to do and would be back in half an hour. As he walked away, looking more like a packhorse than ever, I realised I was worried about him, but I didn't have space in my head for too much more. I needed to buy some clothes. I walked inside the shop, hearing a bell tinkle above me head. The shop assistant walked over to me and asked if I needed any help. I just shook my head, looking around the shop to see I needed anything.

I walked over to the denim part and picked up two pairs of black denims and two pairs of blue, checking the price tag as I went. Buy one; get one free, and twenty-five euro each. I then walked to the jumpers bit and picked up two black and one grey jumper, a large black cardigan, gloves, and a scarf that we're out of season, a pair of calf-high, flat, black boots, and a pair of trainers. I also picked up some underwear and a few pairs of thick woolly socks that were on sale.

By the time I had finished, I heard the bell tinkle again and I looked towards the door, in time to see Nate coming in. He walked over to me as I paid and asked if I had everything I needed. I just nodded at him, and watched him walk over to the men's section; pick up some jeans, jumpers, socks, t-shirts, and underwear. He paid for his items alongside mine and altogether we spent two hundred and twenty-three euro. As our purchases were being bagged, he smiled at me and said in a voice barely above a whisper, "I have a car."

I didn't know what to say and since he whispered it, I realised he didn't want anyone to hear. We left the shop, walked towards the car, and loaded our purchases. The car was parked just outside of the town, on one of the country roads leading away, in a small car park.

I almost collapsed onto the car. I felt weak with hunger and more tired than I had ever felt in my life. Nate looked at me and decided we should go and get something to eat before we left the town. He took my hand and half-pulled me into the centre of town, into a small, busy cafe, where no demons were present. We had a cooked meal for the first time in ages; he had fish and chips and I had a chicken burger. I was so hungry that after I had eaten, I felt a little sick, but I was full and content.

As we walked back towards the car, we passed this old-fashioned bookshop and I really wanted to look. Nate didn't think it was a good idea, but upon checking, we both agreed that the man inside was not a demon. We walked through the door and both looked around. The shop was panelled in pine-coloured wood, from floor to ceiling, and was small, but neat and tidy. The lighting was low coming from some chandeliers in the ceiling. The cash desk was up two wooden steps and had bookshelves running alongside it.

I looked around for books on potions and Nate walked over to a small table a little further in, and picked up a book on golfing. He laughed but I sensed that something wasn't right in this store. When I glanced around the shop, I noticed three other customers, looking at books, but I knew something was wrong. I walked over to Nathan and from the corner of my eye, caught one of the customers turning into an awful-looking creature, with red eyes, a brown grisly face contorted in anger, hands like claws, and much taller than myself or Nate. I spun around and the other two customers had changed into creatures that looked exactly the same.

I just stared, transfixed at them, watching them all come closer and closer. *Oh my God, we're done for.* I forgot all about my powers, forgot all about Nate. *We're going to die.* I could smell their putrid breath in the air and feel the heat from their bodies. I couldn't move; I was completely frozen in fear. I couldn't even turn my head to see if Nate was okay.

They came closer and one of them swiped a hand at me, throwing me across the room. I landed hard against a bookshelf and felt myself falling to the floor, surrounded by books. A few minutes passed and when I opened my eyes, I could see I was tied up in a corner of the floor and Nate was on the table he had been standing at. As I looked over, I saw the creatures peeling of a piece of his skin and heard Nate scream in agony. I saw him turn to look towards me and heard him tell me to get myself out of here before they started on me.

I looked at him, feeling tears fill my eyes and at that moment, I wanted it to be over. I wanted to die, but I knew things would not be that easy. As I thought this, one of the creatures spoke, in a horrible, raspy voice that made my skin crawl.

"When will they get here?"

"Not long now," his companion answered and with a look at me, he said, "We shall be handsomely rewarded for capturing these two."

At that moment, I felt the life drain away from my essence and I felt sick. Now they knew that we weren't really in Sligo. I wriggled about a little on the floor and managed to get my hand free. The creatures again became preoccupied with peeling Nate and hearing his scream of agony made my soul hurt.

I managed to get loose and untied my feet as they got another sliver of Nate's skin and his scream masked my shuffling around on the ground. They were all preoccupied with Nate so they didn't see my movements as I shuffled along the floor. Then as I stood I saw Nate's eyes widen in alarm, but he closed his eyes over, focusing on projecting his voice to me. He sounded weak, but he was trying to mask the agony he was in, "Jas. Get. Out. Of. Here. Now." Each word was painful and I shook my head to clear it as I made my way towards them.

Another creature had joined them. They didn't notice me and I realised, by looking at Nathan's face that he was trying to give me a chance to escape. He was using the last of his strength to cloak me from them. He was obviously more worried than he let on.

One of the creatures bit his arm, released, and bit again. "Nathan, oh cousin, you will stay awake for this," he said repeatedly, between bites.

I needed a weapon if I wanted to save Nate from these creatures, then I realised I was a weapon. I walked behind the creature, bit his arm, placed my hands on his neck and turned them. His neck broke with a loud crack that made me shudder, but I didn't stop. I couldn't. I had to save Nate so I crept around the table and twisted the neck of one of them on that side. The sound of his necks snapping was loud and I realised we were almost home free.

Mistakenly I laughed, as one of the creatures lunged for me, but I moved myself a fraction of a second before he would have hit me, and the creature flew right into the bookshelves, knocking himself out. Again, I looked at him and twisted my hands, heard his neck break, but at the same time, I heard a small groan as the one remaining creature, picked Nate up off the table and placed his hands around Nate's neck.

"Come out, come out, wherever you are. I will find you. Ask Nathan here how good I am at finding things."

He squeezed Nate's neck while doing this and I could see in Nathan's face that he was worried. I flickered in and out of view. I kept moving around for a few seconds. As Nate lost consciousness, the creature threw him to the side, and he bounced off a bookshelf and landed with a thud on the floor. I prayed that he was okay, but now I was visible to this creature. I knew it was a matter of life and death and that some of my powers wouldn't work on this thing.

The creature lunged at me and caught me on the chest, but I managed to stop him, sinking his claws into my body by breaking his hands. He yowled in pain and I struggled out from under him. When I got up, I saw him preparing to lunge at me again, from the reflection on the shop window and as he made a move, I twisted my hand and broke his neck.

After I had done this, I sank to the floor, exhaustion threatening to overtake me, but I knew that the demons would be here very soon. I needed to get Nathan and myself out of here before they arrived.

I crawled on my hands and knees over to Nate and gave him a small shake. He made no movement. I called out his name and got no response, but I could hear his raspy breathing. I sat up and looked around. The bookshop was covered in blood and bodies. I looked around me and saw a few books that would come in handy. I decided to take three of them, one for herbal healing, another on protecting home and dwellings from demons, and the last was baby delivery at home, which I thought would come in handy for Joe and Lisa.

I got up from the floor and walked over to the cash register. I placed thirty euro inside and picked up a brown paper bag to put my books in. I knew that his family would be here soon and it would be best if we were nowhere to be seen, or sensed, when they arrived. I walked over to Nate, pulled him up, and put his arm around my neck. I knew we weren't far from the car and I decided I would drag him along.

It was harder work than I expected, but I managed to get us outside the door. As I turned to look back into the shop, it disappeared. Clearly, it was only there to trap us and I fell for it. Now Nathan was hurt and guilt rose up in my stomach, choking me because it was me who wanted to go in there. I walked slowly, under pressure from Nathan and the books. The rain had started and the sky was black, but after ten minutes of toiling, we made it to the car. I fished around in Nate's pocket and got the keys out, before lowering him into the backseat and closing the door.

CHAPTER 24
HIDING OUT

I walked to the driver's seat and even though I had only had a few driving lessons, a few months ago, I somehow knew, or remembered what I was doing. I put the key in the ignition, put the car into first gear, and turned on the lights. I then moved forwards, paid the barrier, and drove out of the car park and onto the country road. I drove for over an hour, passing countryside and little villages, not that I could see any of it in the pouring rain, before as sense of anger crashed over me. The bookshop had been discovered.

I heard Mr Stevenson scream in fury at everyone around him and knew I would have to find a place to hide us soon. At this point, I drove along, hoping to find somewhere I could pull the car over and hide us for the night, when suddenly lights flashed in my rear-view mirror. "Damn it, it's the bloody Garda." They got out of the car and walked slowly towards us. I noticed that although one of them was human, the other was a demon.

I didn't know what to do, but I knew sitting here talking would mean that the demons would find us faster and then we'd be dead. Having an unconscious person in the back of your car raised an awful lot of questions. I mulled this over for about ten seconds and then I transported both men back into their car, on the road, making them forget all about us. This was dangerous; if any of the upper echelon of demons caught wind of that little bit of magic, they'd be on to us like sharks smelling blood. It would tell them exactly what they needed to know. Where we were, where we were going, and that we had a car. I could only hope that it went undetected, as I pulled out into the road again and drove.

I noticed woods coming up and turned the car into the pathway. I couldn't see much from the road and I put the lights on brighter to drive on the caretaker's road. The further into the woods I got, the darker it was, and the more tired I became.

After half an hour of driving in the woods, I saw a space between some trees just big enough for a small car, like this one to fit through. I drove towards it, just as it began getting dark and squeezed the car through the space. As I got through, I realised that the demons were on the hunt and were angrier than I had ever felt them, both at our lucky deception of them the day before, the hurting of those left behind in the shack, and the killing of the monsters in the bookshop.

I drove, twisting the car here and there, to avoid hitting branches and trees, and finally managed to hide the car behind a clump of bushes, making it invisible to anyone on the road. I then decided to move a tree there, which I just managed, not because my powers were weakening, if anything I was buzzed and full of energy, but because of the oppressive air in the woods.

I got out of the car and pulled my hand through the air, pulling some branches and leaves towards the car, and I walked around to the back, opened the trunk, and rummaged through the bags until I found the herbs we had purchased at the shops.

Looking around, I saw some conifer trees and I ran over to grab some leaves, before running back to the herbs that I had placed on the boot of the car. I mixed the herbs together and walked in a circle around us, creating a barrier between us and any evil. I could have used my blood to strengthen the mix, but I needed the energy I had left to help Nate.

I walked around to the back of the car, got out the sleeping bag we had purchased, walked around to the right-hand door, climbed in, and locked it behind me. I reached through to the front and turned off the headlights before locking all of the other doors. I put the inside lights on and moved the branches covering the car to make sure no one could see the lights. I knew this was only an interim measure to allow us to rest for the night. We would need to find somewhere safer to hide out for a while.

Nathan stirred as I ran my hand over the cuts, where his skin had been ripped off, on his arms, legs, and stomach, but they didn't heal completely. I ran my hands up his arm, trying to heal the bites, some right down to the bone, but I found after twenty minutes of trying, that I had no energy left. I was exhausted.

Nate then awoke, looked at me, and told me, "Don't worry, baby. I'm not in any pain."

He then fell asleep again, and I climbed over into the front seat to try to get some sleep, turning out the front light as I went. I lay there for a few minutes thinking about whether we were safe, when I heard some leaves and twigs rustling outside the car. I looked around and waved my hand in a very lazy way, creating a small space for me to see out.

As I looked out, I saw the faces of spirits, trying to get through the protection I had placed around the car. I could hear them moaning and groaning, alongside the sound of the wind. I waved my hand again, closing the gap, and tried to get to sleep. Just as I was about to drop off, I heard a voice that chilled me to the bone.

Jenny had arrived and was looking through the woods, not ten feet from where we were. I knew I had to find some magic and tap into it, because if I didn't, there was no way for us to escape now. I heard her walk into the space behind the bushes, but because the car was completely black, I knew she wouldn't see us, unless she had a torch. I placed my hand on the door of the car and tried with all of my might to make the car invisible, but my hand shook and my power waned.

I keep thinking how Nate was in the back, unconscious with cuts and bites, all over. I was so tired out from the last four or five days that I could sleep for a week and I knew that if his family caught us, we were dead.

But from somewhere, a little voice sounded inside my head, saying, "Come on now, lassie. You can do this."

Upon hearing this, I knew without a doubt that I could in fact keep us safe. I placed my hand on the car again and shifted us into another dimension, one that was parallel to our own, so I could still see and hear what was happening. Jenny walked into the space where the car was not ten seconds ago and wandered around looking for us, but all traces of us had been lifted and hidden.

After a few minutes, I heard a car on the road and a horn went off, shattering the silence like a gunshot, causing birds to fly squawking out of their trees. Jenny wasn't the only one there. Joe's younger brother walked into the clearing and grabbed Jenny's hand, pulling her away. I heard the car doors shut and listened as it drove away before my hands slumped down exhausted, and I finally fell asleep.

While I slept, I had the strangest dreams about faces pressing in, trying again and again to get through the protection and felt a level of malevolence that I usually only felt around Mr Stevenson and his family. But even after Jenny left, the feeling lingered and I was uneasy, although I was so exhausted that I had to sleep. There was no choice.

. I awakened suddenly at 4:20 a.m., hearing a wailing just outside. When I looked, I saw more spirits than ever before trying to break through the protection. I understood at that moment that this was their woods and we needed to go somewhere else. They didn't want us here. It was as if someone had said it, although no one had. I could feel it clear as day.

It finally lightened at around five thirty and the spirits disappeared, but not before warning me that we had better be gone before the day was over. I couldn't agree more. I just needed to find us a safer place to hide, where Nate could recover and I could rest. I checked on Nate before going out of the car. He seemed okay, still sleeping. I knew I had very little strength left for magic; the night before had drained me even more.

I walked out of the area and moved a clump of bushes, to cover it completely. Now the car was hidden, even from me. I picked my way through the woods, listening all the while for feet approaching, but for the best part of an hour, I heard nothing.

I kept walking, heading towards the sound of a river, or stream, hoping that there might be somewhere there that we could hide out for a while, when all of a sudden, I saw that I was in a clearing whose sole purpose was a witch catcher. I was more powerful than most witches, at least I thought I was, but not at this moment. I was too weak to fight and struggle to walk forwards, but I managed through sheer force of will and determination.

When I looked back, I could see markings on logs, on the ground, laid in a pentagram shape, supposed to drain a witch of power and give those powers to the person who set up the pentagram. I had no idea how I knew this, but I just did, which astonished me as much as it scared me.

I walked on, getting faster and faster; I could feel him following me. I didn't know who, or what he was, just that he was powerful and power hungry. I was something like a feast to him. All those latent powers, I had but hadn't gotten around to using yet. I also managed to escape his trap; his mouth watered and grasping that fact made me feel so angry that I just stopped and turned around to face this threat.

As I turned round, a small man walked into view and I recoiled, wanting to run again. The man was around five foot, with white hair, white eyes, and a huge nose. Once I had gotten past these things, his teeth were like stone. When I looked down, his hands were clawed, with his huge fingernails rounding at the top. He looked hideous.

Almost as if he knew what I was thinking, he smiled and the effect made him look more terrifying. "So, you're the one they are all talking about. Hmmm, you don't seem very powerful to me. Forgive me. I forgot my manners. Now I know who you are, but do you know who I am?"

I stared at him, transfixed, noticing as I did so that each time he spoke, he deliberately moved closer and closer to me. By the time he spoke again, he was directly in front of me, "I am Odoacer the Great." I must have looked my confusion, because he sighed and began again. "I am a sorcerer, the most powerful sorcerer, even more powerful than you, Jasmine. I have travelled far and wide before coming to rest in these here woods. Last night, I sent those ghosts to ward you off, but it didn't work, did it? Now here we are and I shall be quite sorry when I have to take you, but undoubtedly for you, it will be better than if the demons get you. For you shall live, but be completely mortal when I am through with you."

I saw him smile, as though he did me a kindness, and took one more step towards me. I realised that if I was going to act, now was the time. His power, at least some of it, I had managed to copy, giving me strength and power that I would certainly not have had otherwise.

I saw his clawed hands whip up towards my face in the seconds that I figured out about the powers and I put my hands up, placed them on his chest, and pushed him. I knew that I managed to push him through one dimension, but I wanted him as far away from me as possible. I stepped into the first dimension, a barren land full of fire and trees, but nothing else. It was one parallel to our own, and I shoved him through two more dimensions, thinking that it would keep him busy for a while.

I stepped back into my own dimension, and the sound of the forest came flooding back. I turned away and walked up a slope, which stood in front of me, hearing the sounds of animals as they started their early morning routines. As I got to the top of the slope, I noticed a waterfall and I walked towards it, noticing as I did so a small cave hidden beneath the flowing water.

That should be enough to hide us for a while.

CHAPTER 25
SAFEST PLACE TO HIDE

I walked into the clearing where the car was hidden and realised that it was now almost seven in the morning. I got into the car and decided that we should move to the sheltered cave and get some protection set up. Nate said nothing to me; he was conscious but still so weak. He grimaced when I placed my hands on the car, transporting it and us into the shelter I had picked out. I left Nate inside the car and went out to check around to make sure the cave was uninhabited.

It wasn't; there were a few small demons, but I shifted their dimensions without them even noticing. I looked down to the riverbed and saw some wild garlic, lavender, comfrey, ground ivy, and foxglove. Some of these plants would, if mixed together properly make this cave impenetrable to any evil creature, and help me to cure Nate's injuries. I also noticed an oak tree as I left the cave. Transporting myself down to the riverbed, I caught up a few of each of those ingredients.

Back in the cave, Nate sat in the car and looked around for me. When I got back, I could see he was panicking. I walked over to the car, my arms and bag laden with as many of the plants as I could carry. I placed a basic protection around the cave, and used some of my blood to strengthen it, running my blood from a slice on my finger across the entrance to the cave.

I made my way over to the car, ready to ask Nate about which potions to use and how to make them up, but when I opened the door and saw he was breaking, which surprised me. I had never seen him cry, not even when he stabbed me. Yet here he was... crying.

I put all of the plants onto the ground and climbed into the car, pulled him into my arms, and held him until the tears subsided. He looked at me and I could see the pain in his eyes. "I'm. In. So. Much. Pain." He gasped out, his eyes crunching as agony shot through him and his stomach rolled. I held tightly onto him, kissing his head and soothing his hair, trying my best to heal him as he lay in my arms. He closed his eyes and sucked in a breath, breathing a little easier, "Thank you, Jas. I know you are healing me." He drifted off to sleep and I made myself comfy in the back seat, falling asleep for a short time. After a few hours he kissed my arm and I jumped in fright.

"Jas, I'm sorry; it just keeps coming at us, all the time, from all sides. You ever think this relationship was doomed?"

"Sometimes, yeah, I really do. It's so hard just now, dealing with all of our issues, but we have to keep going. Otherwise we're dead."

He just nodded and said, "I'm sorry. I didn't sleep much last night."

We sat in the car, together for a few more seconds before I got out to prepare the protection spell. I crushed the garlic and some oak leaves, in one of the bowls we had bought at the supermarket, and mixed them together, before adding salt, sage, basil, and rosemary. I also added thyme and when I had enough, I walked over to the entranceway, scooped up a handful of water, and mixed that into the bowl with the rest of the ingredients.

I then picked up a few stones, poured the mixture in a line across the entrance, and placed a line of stones over it. I then walked in a full circle around the cave, placing the mixture on the walls and the floor, to make sure no evil creature could get in.

As I turned to go back to the car, I noticed that Nate couldn't be seen from outside the car and when I walked over, I saw a small demon, sitting on his chest. Without caring at all, I sent him into the next dimension, where I had sent all the other demons. As I approached the car, Nate lay there, spaced out. When I opened the door again to ask him if he was okay, I noticed his eyes were glazed and he seemed unconscious again. I ranted under my breath for a minute as I climbed into the car, mixture in hand and placed some of it onto Nathan's open skin, before running my hand down it to heal it.

The skin smoked and Nate yelled in pain; his eyes lost the glazed look, yet still terrified and in agony. Tears filled his eyes, but I kept running my hand over the cuts, using the power I had gained that morning to heal them.

Eventually, he stopped screaming and after an hour, his body healed. The combination of the powers that I had picked up from the sorcerer and the mixture worked, healing and cleaning out the wound.

When Nate was fully healed, he hugged me tightly for a few seconds and whispered a thank you in my ear.

"We need to unload, Jas and set up to stay here" I smiled at him and he leaned down to kiss me, but I turned my head away and he kissed my cheek. He sighed in frustration, but left his lips there for a moment longer.

As we got out of the car, he looked around and walked to the doorway, "How'd you know what to use for protection?" I smiled up at him, and winked. As he looked at me, he laughed and I was taken back to a simpler time, when we were in the shack. He looked at me like that then too, but I hadn't seen him look at me like that in the longest time. Now he looked at me as though I was more of burden to him, and I couldn't figure out my feelings about him anyway. I was so confused. While I stood next to the car thinking about all this, he walked back over to me, tilting my chin up with his finger so I looked into his eyes. His eyes looked more brown than green today and as he stared into my eyes, I shuddered right down to my soul.

"Jas, I know this is messed up and it's shit just now, but you need to know I love you. No matter what else you think, that has always been the case. I tried to love someone else, but it was you, always you."

He brought his lips to mine gently and kissed me softly on the lips as his arms circled my waist and he pulled me against his chest, speaking again, "I would choose this every time, not a moment has ever gone by when I've regretted my choices over you. The only thing I regret is how hard this is and how much I wish my family didn't exist." He kissed my forehead and let me go, leaving me stunned, bereft and annoyed.

He walked around the back and grabbed the tent, putting it up in about ten minutes before grabbing the bed and blowing that up too. He didn't let me help, and made me sit in a camping chair, kissing my head softly and running his fingers through my hair. "You've done enough, baby. Just relax okay and let me do something."

After the bed had been put up, he grabbed some supplies from the car and placed them inside the tent. His smile was dazzling as he moved towards me saying, "you're palace awaits my lady." He pulled me up by the hand and we moved as one to the car, sealing it by walked around it and placing some more of the mixtures around it. .

I made to walked towards the tent, but Nathan called me over to look at something and from the tone of his voice I was worried, very worried. I walked slowly over to him and he pointed to the riverbed, "Jas, look down there." His whole body shook and I took his hand, watching at his side as they walked up and down the riverbed. When they stopped and began gazing up at the waterfall, it made us nervous. We stood watching them for a while and we both sighed in relief as the word, "human," was muttered by us both at the same time. They were thankfully only humans exploring the area at the waterfall.

After the scare, we had tinned fruit to eat, and fell asleep. It was the first time in days that I had been relaxed during my sleep and the first time in months that Nate had gotten a proper night's sleep. The next day we didn't even leave the tent, eating a breakfast of tinned pears and strawberries, before falling asleep again. I awoke that night, and it was pitch black in the cave.

I had awakened to the sound of the wind howling and rain falling. I was stiff from sleeping so much. I decided to get up, but my movement woke Nate. He looked at me, smiled, and curled up deeper under the covers. I left him there, hoping he would fall back into a sleep, lifted the torch, unzipped the tent, and shone the torch around the cave. Water came in the back of the cave. I walked over to it and took a sip; it was clean and freezing cold. I stripped to my underwear, feeling a little self-conscious, and had a wash in the water.

I walked around the cave, thinking about the previous few days. How close we had come to getting caught. How Nate and I still had to talk about our relationship, if there even was one. I still had to figure out how I felt about Nate. I threw on some of my new clothes and continued to think about us. Yes, I knew that I loved him, but did I still want to be with him even after he had tried to kill me?

I hadn't been thinking or taking note of the time passing, but when I heard Nate whimpering in his sleep, I walked back into the tent. I heard Nate talking in his sleep.

"I don't know. I don't know. I don't know." He whimpered again and as I sat beside him, he awoke crying. "My dad was in my head asking where we were. I couldn't tell him anything. Thank goodness you drove us here."

He was really upset and worried, but he climbed out of the sleeping bag and crawled into my arms for a hug. He turned his head towards me and I looked into his eyes for a minute. He leaned in and kissed me properly, a kiss that tore at my inhibitions about us and our relationship.

He kissed me like a drowning man sucking down the last of his oxygen and I shuddered as I wondered what I should do. Damn, all these distractions were stopping me from making decisions. He shifted himself so he too sat up in the bed, and hesitantly he leaned in towards me. I looked at the floor, trying to figure out what I should be feeling at that moment, when he touched my chin, turning my head to him.

"I love you," he told me, "more than my own life and more than anything else in this world. I am so incredibly sorry for hurting you. I will do anything you ask if you will let me try to make it up to you."

I looked at him, tears brimming over my eyes, and watched as he leaned into me, lowering me backwards. The kissing became more intense and soon we were both panting for breath, gripping each other tighter. He whispered again that he loved me, as he stopped kissing me and pulled my jumper over my head. I helped him remove his jumper and we kissed again. We lay in the tent, lit only by the low setting on our torch, with his body draped over me. I never wanted this moment to end.

As soon as my head processed that thought, we heard a loud crash in the distance that made us both sit up so fast we banged our heads together. We fumbled about, pulling our jumpers back on and rushing out into the cave to see what the disturbance was this time.

As I ran to the entranceway, Nate stumbled and fell, but picked himself back up. We looked out, examining the river in the near total darkness. We didn't hear another sound, but we didn't need to. The moment had been ruined. We walked back to the tent slowly and zipped ourselves in, not a moment too soon.

Ten seconds after we had zipped the tent up, we lay in the darkness, having turned out the torch to save battery, when we heard voices. These weren't just any voices; it was the voice of Nick and Leanne, followed closely by Jenny and Gordon. We were in danger again. I felt myself groan internally and felt Nate stiffen beside me.

He told me silently that his dad was in his head again asking where we were. He blocked out the fact that his sister and brother were in the cave; if he had registered that thought, then Mr Stevenson would have realised where we were.

We heard them marauding through the caves, checking every nook and cranny, but they never came near our corner, or went near the car. The protection we placed did its job and hid the evidence of our location.

How did they get in here? I realised that the water from the rain must have washed some of the potion away. They wandered around the cave for over an hour, and passed by so close to us, I was sure one of them would hear us breathing.

The silence in the cave was shattered as a mobile phone went off. From the sound of it, it was Nick's. We heard him answer to a very loud but indistinct voice on the phone, saying, "Yes, Father... Over an hour... No sign of them... We will. See you in half an hour."

I prayed that they were leaving and, as if Nick heard my prayer, he told the rest of the group the plan. "We are going to cave this place in. Go back into the town and meet the family there before heading back to the UK. We think they might have headed there after nearly getting caught."

Jenny growled. "Why are we caving this in? If they have gone back home, why are we wasting time here?"

"Well, Jenny," answered Nick's voice, sounding as if he was speaking to a child, "in case they haven't gone home, we need to make sure this place is hidden. They could hide in here and protect it from us."

It went quiet again and then we heard footsteps heading towards the exit. Nate shuddered and gasped. I froze, hoping they hadn't heard him. They all turned around and searched the cave again, but found nothing. "It was just an animal. Never mind, it'll be trapped in here."

I had crawled to the entrance of the tent, when we heard the earth-shattering sound of the doorway caving in and the unmistakable sounds of laughter retreating further down the slope. I looked out into the darkness and couldn't see anything. Hesitantly, I turned around and searched with my hand, until I found the torch, but Nate's hand closed upon my wrist before I could turn it on.

'Don't,' he said, the fear in his voice unmistakable.

His hand shook. I turned around, crawled back towards him, and put my arms around him. The closer I was to him the more I could sense his terror. He told me, his father, upon realising that he would never turn me over, had told him that when he caught us, he would make him watch me being killed and had sent him a picture of this, which was why he had gasped and shuddered, almost giving us away.

We just lay there in the silence of the cave, listening for the sound of them approaching, but all the while praying that they had left. After a while, Nate fell asleep. This gave me the opportunity to get up and re-double the protection around us. I crawled towards the exit of the tent, picked up the torch, and went out into the cave, still feeling scared and worried that somehow they would find us. I walked over to the plants I had gathered and picked up a few sprigs of lavender, walked back into the tent, and placed them under Nathan to allow him to sleep free and unencumbered dreams.

Using the lowest setting of the torch, I cleaned out the bowl with the water from the cave. Mixing basil, garlic, rosemary, sage, thyme, oak leaves, and a tiny bit of water, I made the potion more concentrated than before. I walked over to the entrance and saw a sliver of light through it. There was a hole in the cave and as I looked through it, an eye looked right back at me.

CHAPTER 26
THE EYE

The eye was the single most menacing thing I had seen in a very long time and I jumped about ten feet into the air. The eye was twice the size of a normal eye and pitch black, almost all over, except for the slightest rimming of red around the iris. I poured my mixture over the stones, hoping and praying all the while that the creature hadn't seen me.

While I poured the potion, the creature cackled. The sound was terrifying; it made the hairs on my arms and my neck stand up. I was deathly afraid. I got to the end of the line and I heard the creature whispering through the cracks. "Jasmine, you can seal the cave up, but you can't keep us out forever. We will get into you and when we do, we will make what the Minotaur's did to you look like a parlour trick. Sleep well, for a while."

I walked away, not realising I shook like a leaf blowing in the wind, until I tried to zip the tent up after placing more potion around the tent. I couldn't believe we had another creature after us. I climbed into the tent, still shaking, and crawled into the bed beside Nate, wondering what could be worse than a Minotaur. Nate reached over and put his arm over me. Instantly I felt safer and comforted. Eventually I fell asleep.

I awoke the next morning to find the bed beside me empty, which made me jump. I was almost convinced the night before was a nightmare as I woke; finding Nate missing convinced me otherwise.

I looked around in the dark and saw him over in the corner, having a shower in the dripping water. I walked towards him and he shouted to me to stop. I didn't stop. I walked over to him, put my arms around him, and gave him a kiss on the mouth. The kiss went on and on, and all too soon, he pulled away. I felt so disappointed and rejected that I spun on my heel and walked back into the tent. He followed soon after, but seemed embarrassed by what had happened earlier.

I didn't look at him as he came in, preferring to concentrate on eating my cereal bar rather than look into his eyes. He sat for around ten minutes without speaking or moving, and then with a move like a cobra, he was beside me, pulling my chin up to look in my eyes. There were so many questions in his eyes, but they would have to wait. At that exact moment, there was an almighty roar from outside. We both jumped and then laughed, but the laughter soon died when we realised that the creature outside was trying to break apart the rocks and coverings to get into us.

I knew the only way to save us was to go outside and face this creature, but at that moment, I didn't want to. To delay some, I explained to Nate about the eye from the night before and he looked terrified, becoming a recurring theme with us.

He couldn't speak, just opened and closed his mouth a few times, but didn't say anything. We sat there for five minutes, listening to the constant roaring of that creature, but Nate just looked more and more scared.

He eventually found his voice and spoke to me in barely more than a whisper, "Jas, the thing outside is a Manticore, one of the most vicious and deadly assassins of my dad's people." He closed his eyes and couldn't look at me as he continued, "It will find a way in, they always do. That's why demons use them, because they can get in anywhere, but when it gets in here, we're both dead. I don't know how to defeat one." He ran his fingers up and down my cheek as I watched him and I knew that I had to go outside and face this thing head on, it was the only way.

"Nate, I need to go outside and fight this thing. It's the only way I can save you and us." His whole body shook and his eyes shot open in terror as he stared at me, "NO FUCKING WAY!" he bellowed at me, and I jumped back, moving away from him. He lifted his fingers to his head and rubbed between his eyes, before he swallowed and tried again, "Jas, there is no way. None, that I would ever let you go and fight this thing. It's a fucking monster and I'm supposed to protect you from monsters…"

I leaned in and kissed him, stopping his words and he pulled me tightly against him, kissing me hard. I moved back a little and whispered against his lips, "Nate, you have protected me for almost two years now, but I'm not a weak little girl anymore. You need to trust me. I can do this."

He nodded once and kissed me, "I know you're not weak, god you are the strongest person I have ever met, but please Jas. I'm begging you, please just stay here. Stay safe, in here with me."

I watched him, feeling his terror affect me, but I decided I would not sit in here like an animal ready for slaughter. Nate heard me resolutely decide this and looked at me in complete and utter horror. "You cannot be serious, Jasmine. This thing is more viscous and terrible than any other monster we have faced. Please, please stay with me and stay safe."

I looked at Nathan, knowing my mind was made up and told him I loved him, before transporting myself out of the cave, out onto the riverbed. I could tell Nathan was running around, trying to get out of the cave, but he was too weak.

I saw the creature look down at me, and felt it run towards me. There was power there that I never imagined. While the creature ran, I looked at it completely disgusted with what I saw. The body looked like that of a lion, but the fur was dark brown, with spikes coming out of the head, huge teeth, clawed feet, and an enormous black wingspan.

Terror washed over me and I froze as it moved closer to me, assessing me as Nathan's voice pleaded with me, to come back to the cave, but I ignored him. It was time I protected him. I wouldn't be the girl who always needed protection, not from anyone, anymore. If they wanted me, here I was and I would fight them for every single breath I would take for the rest of my life. I was sick of running, sick of hiding and it was time they all knew it.

As the creature drew level with me, it stood for a moment and looked at me. Before I knew what happened, spikes flew out of its hands towards me, but I flicked them away before they reached me. The creature lunged at me suddenly and I flew backwards, almost landing in the river, saved only by the root of a tree.

I hung onto this tree, trying to get my breath back, when the claws dropped over the side of the ledge and tried to scratch me, but I knew I couldn't let that happen. Nathan screamed at me, telling me that the claws of a Manticore held venom, from which there was no cure. I kept hold of the root and swung from side to side, as the Manticore tried again to get to me, worried about the freezing water below. I felt as if my life swung in the balance.

The creature then decided to cut the root to make me fall into the river and I knew I had one chance, and one chance only to make it safely onto the ledge. I waited until he loosened the root and, just before he cut it completely, I transported myself using all the power I had back up onto the ledge.

Standing just beside the creature and with one push, I threw him into the water. As soon as it made contact, the Manticore screamed in agony, or rage. I couldn't tell which. The creature floated down the river, glowering up at me. I was so weakened by having to shift myself that I sat down in the shade of the tree whose root saved me.

Nathan appeared beside me and transported us both back into the cave. I lay beside him, trying to heal him, as he looked pale and listless. His breathing came in short sharp gasps, and as I healed him as best I could, I could feel my powers ebbing away. I collapsed onto his chest and the sound of his heartbeat lulled me to sleep.

Waking up in the cave was terrifying; it was so dark, dank, and cold and I was worried that my eyes weren't properly opened since I couldn't even see my hand in front of my face. The wind howled, the rain battered on the stones covering the mouth of the cave, but something was missing. It took me a moment to realise that Nathan, the sound and smell of him was missing. Looking around the cave, I could barely see. I called out for him, sounding hoarse, and my voice thick with sleep.

"Nathan?" As it echoed around the cave, I realised I couldn't call out; doing so would risk us being discovered and wherever Nathan was, he would be in danger. The sound continued to bounce off the walls, until it became incomprehensible over the wind, but I was painfully aware that he was again in danger.

I sat in the dark for hours, going over different scenarios as to why he was missing. Where was he? What was he doing? Why would he risk exposure? What could be the purpose of his going? He was supposed to be with me; he wasn't supposed to leave. I couldn't think in the oppressive gloom of the cave. I was suffocating in the darkness. The cave smelled like dampness and terror, metal and cold on my skin.

Had he been captured? How would that have happened? Had he realised we'd been discovered and taken off to save me? Why wouldn't he have awakened me to tell me? Had he left me? We hadn't been right since that night on the beach, but I loved him with all my heart, surely he wouldn't just leave me. I began breathing quickly and feeling dizzy. Sitting with my head in between my legs, I forced myself to calm down. I was just panicking because I was in this cave, surrounded by nothing but darkness and fear.

I forced myself to think back to all of our moments together over the past fourteen months. How Nathan had risked his life again and again to save me. I thought about all our moments, kissing, hugging, and talking in the barn, the woods, and our other safe places. I knew for certain thinking back on this that the only reason he would leave me, was to either save me, or to protect me from his family.

On the thought of his family, I heard a noise, a dull shuffling and shifting of the stone floor. Holding my breath, I opened up a window, out into the cave, and saw Nick and Jenny looking around again.

"What are we doing here, Nick? Nate has been spotted in town and you know wherever he goes, she goes. We need to be the ones to catch him. I want to make him suffer for betraying us, for betraying our father. I will tear him limb from limb and make her watch, before I end her."

"Patience, Jenny. We will catch him and you can enact whatever torture you see fit, but she was seen around here. I just want to make sure that she is not here. I want to find her and make her wish she had never been born. Looks like no one is here. Let's go."

Waiting was awful. Unable to tell how much time had passed, I sat and chewed on my fingers, feeling tenser than ever. After a few hours, I grew impatient so I lit up my torch and saw a note from Nathan, on his side of the bed.

> Jas
>
> *I had to pop into town and get seen. We had to throw them off our scent. Plus I needed ingredients for my sleeping dust. I need to get nearer to a demon to enact this curse.*
>
> *I love you and I'll be back before you know it.*
>
> Nate

As I read the note, I wondered what ingredients he needed, or if he had planned to meet up with Joe and Lisa, as I was worried about them. We hadn't heard from them in days and had no idea if they were safe.

I was broken from my thoughts by the sound of the water cascading down over the cave, but over that I could hear footsteps and loose rocks, which worried me. Where was Nathan? What was he doing? Then I remembered the previous night, talking about how to enact the sleeping curse on them.

"I need to get close to a demon, Jas. Just one demon and then they will all fall asleep and we can escape."

At the time I hadn't worried about it, but now I was terrified. He was letting himself get caught. I realised that I needed to go to him. There had to be another way, when his voice sounded in my head, "Don't you dare. For this to work, I need them to catch me..." His voice in my head made me jump, but he sounded determined.

I muted the sound of the waterfall and heard Nick and Jenny. "He's on his way back here? You are sure?" I heard Nick say.

Jenny asked, "What's going on?"

"He's coming. Get ready."

Just then, I heard a shuffling at the mouth of the cave. As I began to move, Nathan said, "Don't move. They will catch you and then it's all over. I will come back to you. You have my heart so keep it safe. We will see each other soon."

I opened a window in the roof and watched as he walked up to his brother and sister. His brother conjured up ropes and wrapped them around him. Jenny punched him in the face and drew her nails down his face. His brother booted him in the stomach and he fell onto the window. Seeing his face scratched with blood coming from his lip and down his cheeks, I was full of rage, but he looked at me, whispering into my mind, "I love you. Be safe."

His brother stomped on his head and as his eyes closed, they dragged him away from me, back to his parents, and the world of demons. The only thing I knew was that I would do whatever it took to get him back to me. No matter the cost, I would pay it. I loved him more than my life.

The End

STALKING ME

I love hearing from readers and adore connecting with people. If you want to contact me, here are the best ways to do it.

Find me on FaceBook

https://www.facebook.com/authorstacymcwilliams/?ref=bookmarks

Twitter

https://twitter.com/stacemcw

Goodreads

https://www.goodreads.com/author/show/9796198.Stacy_McWilliam

s

Instagram

https://www.instagram.com/stacemcwilliams/?hl=en

Or Email me

authorstacemcwilliams@gmail.com

Can I ask that if you read the story, please leave me a review. Reviews are so important to authors and help us improve, make changes or let us know what readers think.

Thank you

Stacy

THANK YOU

This is much harder than I realised, trying to organise my thoughts to make sure I include everyone and thank everyone for their support. To start with, I would like to thank my amazing editor Susan Soares; she has taken my books on and made them better in so many ways and I am truly grateful. I can't wait to work with her on any future works, if she'll still have me.

I would like to thank my amazing friend, counsel, and girl Laura. You totally rock and you are incredible, always willing to listen to me when I have a wobble or freak out. I appreciate everything you have done, more than I can ever express and can't wait to go have wine with you.

Next up, I'd like to thank my street team. You are all incredible. Sophie, Katie, Danni, Jennifer, Sarah, Sarah, Lesley, Roz, Becky, and Cat, thank you for always being there and listening to me, giving me advise and reading first. Thank you for agreeing to be my beta's/ proof readers, especially Sarah, Sarah and Lesley. You all give me amazing feedback and are my first eyes on the story. I can't thank you enough for all of your support and sharing my stuff is appreciated. I have the most amazing team of loyal, willing girls and I wouldn't change a thing.

Danni, we've been friends for years and I always go to you for advice. Love you, honey. Thank you for being my rock and my girl. Thank you for always listening, making me laugh, and supporting me.

Katie, what can I say? You completely rock. Thank you for helping me, listening to me, and offering me advice. I really appreciate your advice and time, and I cannot wait to go to our signings and rock the place out. Love you, honey.

Next up, I want to thank my incredible writing girl Annie, you are an amazing author, incredible friend, and make me laugh with your wicked sense of humour. Thank you so, so much for the Ignition teaser and for always being there. Love ya chick.

To my amazing cover designer, Desiree, you seem to see into my head and pick out what my cover should look like. You are marvellous and I can't wait to see all the covers together.

To my incredible formatter, Leigh, you totally amaze me honey with how amazing my books look. I can't wait to work more with you over the next few years.

To my family, you drive me insane, push me, pull me, but I wouldn't be who I am today without the support of my amazing family. I love you all more than I can say. Mum, Dad, Jen, Shaz, and Morgan, you inspire me every day and I hope I make you proud. Gran and Boab, thank you for sharing your stories with me and helping me to see the bigger picture. Love you both. Marie, Richard, Alison, Mike, Russ, Maxine, and Arran, thank you all for your love and support. I am so lucky to have the most incredible in-laws and I love you all.

My girls Allie, Donna, Lynne, Tracey, Aimee, Lindsay, Katy, Suz, and Debbie. You are fantastic friends, there when I need to laugh, cry, or vent. I love you all and here's to many more years of friendship. To the boys, Blair and Steff, thanks for always being there and making me laugh with your stories. You guys rock.

To my incredible hubby, I love you more every day. When we got married, I thought I knew what love was but every day it grows and grows. Seeing you with the boys, watching you love them and raise them alongside me makes me love you in a completely different way. You are my world, hubby, and I love you more than you know.

To my gorgeous boys, I love you with all my heart and soul. You are everything to me and everything I do is for you. Every moment watching you grow is a blessing and I love being a mummy. You opened my eyes to the world and made me see it in a new way. I love you both as far as I can reach.

Also, I want to thank my favourite authors for bringing such amazing stories into the world and inspiring me with their tales. I would name them all but then we'd be here for years. So thank you to all authors for telling stories and helping to open people's eyes to the wonders of their imagination. Everyone has a story to tell and you make me believe that anything is possible.

Lastly, can I say a small thank you to someone else? YOU, the person who has bought this book. Thank you so much for making my dreams come true. Thank you for reading and I hope loving my characters. You are amazing.

Love to all

Stacy